The House Always Wins

Murder and spying in London and Berlin

Frank Daly

Published by:

FrankDaly.com

Dublin, Ireland

Copyright © 2016 by **Frank Daly**

All rights reserved. No part of this publication may be reproduced, distributed or transmitted in any form or by any means, without prior written permission.

**Frank Daly
Maretimo House,
Blackrock, Co. Dublin,
Ireland.
A94 EA37**

Frankdaly.com

Publisher's Note: This is a work of fiction. Names, characters, places, and incidents are a product of the author's imagination. Locales and public names are sometimes used for atmospheric purposes. Any resemblance to actual people, living or dead, or to businesses, companies, events, institutions, or locales is completely coincidental.

Book Layout © 2014 BookDesignTemplates.com

The House Always Wins / Frank Daly. -- 1st ed.
ISBN 978-0-9954506-0-8

For my mother, Eva Daly.

"Even if you are not doing anything wrong, you are being watched and recorded."

— EDWARD SNOWDEN

"We do not merely destroy our enemies; we change them."

— GEORGE ORWELL, *1984*

Acknowledgements

I'd like to thank Liza Costello, my copy-editor, whose advice and excellent work helped me hone this book into shape.

I'd also like to thank Piotr Lipski, Lin McBride, Berna Daly, Kieran Daly, Anne Marie Hayes, Brendan Phelan and Shannon Chance who helped by reading early drafts and providing feedback.

CONTENTS

The Funeral 11

Hacked 17

Day One 20

Theft on the Train 29

Fence and Fix 38

The Leak 43

The Killing 48

Scott Makes a Bid 56

The Crime Scene 64

Gambling 75

Grieving 86

The Investigation Begins 91

Press Conference 97

East Berlin 101

Birthday Surprise 108

An Impossible Journey 115

More Loans 122

Rachel 128

Trigger Point 143

Police Interviews 155

Reaching the Bottom 178

The Investigation Develops 189

Police Closing In	199
On The Run	215
Meeting Amy	235
Ethan Investigates	249
Going to Berlin	267
BND Information	287
Returning Home	309
Arrest	316
Prison	329
Evidence	338
Publication	340
Winning Bid	347
The New Frontier	350

CHAPTER ONE

The Funeral

28th July, 2015. Brompton Road, London.

It was the day that Ethan Harris had been dreading since the murder of his wife, Rachel, nearly a week earlier. The forensics team had finally finished their work and released the body for burial. He could not bear to think of her lying on that cold slab where the autopsy had been carried out.

He was so full of grief that he had not been able to make the arrangements and so his mother-in-law, Julia, had organised it all. She had also been taking care of Katy, his two-year-old daughter, as he was in no condition to mind her. He knew that Julia had never liked him, that she had always felt her daughter was too good for him. Now she was in control, looking after her granddaughter and making the final arrangements for her daughter's burial. Every time he looked at her, he felt the disgust in her eyes

– as though she had stepped in something nasty. He tried to ignore it, but all he could see in his mind was her tightly pursed lips and the cold stare of contempt.

Right now though, she could not make him feel any worse than he already did. He had been like a zombie over the previous few days, barely surviving them. Now he had to meet everyone and be sociable when all he felt like doing was to let everything slip by, crawl into some dark corner with a bottle of brandy and numb the pain.

It was to be a Christian funeral. He was not religious, but Rachel's family was, and he was okay just to go along with it. Julia had made the arrangements – contacting the vicar and a funeral director who had looked after everything.

On the evening before the funeral service, Rachel was laid out in an open coffin, in the funeral home. She had been embalmed and looked like a sleeping wax model of herself. Julia had wanted an open casket and so there it was. It disgusted him. But he had deferred all the decisions to Julia, so it was her call. He had just wanted to remember Rachel's smiling face from when she was alive, not a waxy death-mask, especially knowing that the mortician had had to work extremely hard to make it look like she had quietly passed away in her sleep.

A wave of sadness and emotion swept over him as he looked down at her lifeless body and his hand trembled as he touched her cheek and stroked her hair for the last time, knowing that he'd never hold her in his arms again or see her smiling face.

Some friends and family came to pay their respects that evening, but the majority waited until the next day for the funeral service and the burial. When he left the funeral home, it seemed like a darkness descended and enveloped him until the following day.

The next morning, Ethan was exhausted, as he had hardly slept at all, anticipating the funeral and haunted by memories and regrets. He walked alone from his house on Onslow Square, round by South Kensington Station, past the Victoria and Albert Museum, to Holy Trinity Church on Brompton Road, about ten minutes away. He was still in a daze from what had happened that week. As he entered the church he saw his father, Tom and his older brother, James, standing at the top, beside the altar. He stood with them for a while.

Tom hugged him and tried to comfort him, but to Ethan, he felt like a stranger. They had had little contact ever since Ethan left home to go to university. He had never returned home after that, and only called Tom on the phone once a year to see how he was getting on. The family had been irreversibly fractured after Ethan's mother had left when he was 12 years old; despite Tom's efforts, Ethan and his brother had had a difficult childhood. James had also left as soon as he could, but his life had taken a vastly different path to Ethan's. He had spent several years in prison during his early twenties, setting him on course for a life that was constantly on the borderline of drugs and crime. Ethan knew that James had been in prison a second time, much more recently, but there was so little contact between them that it did not feel right to bring it up.

So the three of them stood in awkward silence, broken by occasional failed attempts at conversation. Eventually, Ethan walked to the front door of the church to greet others who were arriving.

It was a small funeral with a scattering of people in the pews closest to the altar. The rest of the church was an empty, cavernous void, full of echoes and shadows mirroring the darkness he felt inside. He hardly knew anyone because most of them were Julia's old friends and neighbours who had travelled up from Kent to pay their last respects.

The casket was now closed and lying on a trolley at the top of the church, in front of the altar, surrounded by bouquets of flowers. Ethan turned away, briefly glimpsing David Powell as he slipped in quietly at the back of the church. David was Rachel's father, and his marriage had ended so badly that in a sense he was *persona non grata*, even if it was his own daughter's funeral. Especially since Rachel had seldom spoken to him since she was a teenager, as though she had divorced him as a father long before her mother had divorced him as a husband. Ethan had rarely heard Rachel talk about him, though she had once shown him some photos of the man. He had not even attended their wedding. It was almost as though he did not exist, except there he was, anonymously attending his daughter's funeral. As far as Ethan knew, Powell was a shadowy character who worked for GCHQ.

Bill Taylor, a colleague and one of Ethan's few friends, arrived. He shook his hand and then hugged him.

"I'm so sorry Ethan, we were all shocked at the bank. Harvey Waterman sends his condolences and his apologies that he couldn't attend."

"Thanks, Bill, I appreciate you coming and all your help in the last week."

Bill smiled and moved up into the church.

The service was mercifully fast and the vicar, who had no doubt been briefed by Julia, gave a short eulogy on Rachel's life.

A small crowd was gathered outside the church. Among them was Amy Knight, an investigative journalist unknown to Ethan or anyone in his family. Neither had she known Rachel. And, a little distance from the crowd, stood Detective Chief Inspector Scott and Detective Inspector Jones. They approached Ethan, shook his hand, offered their condolences, and then walked away.

The church bells were ringing mournfully as the funeral director slid the coffin into the hearse, placed the wreaths around it, and drove away, towards the cemetery, followed by two mourning cars – one for Ethan's family, the other for Rachel's family. Behind them, a small train of cars followed, to the final resting place in the graveyard about a mile away.

In the distance, David Powell slipped away, unknown to anyone there.

CHAPTER TWO

Hacked

4th July, 2015. Crystal Palace, London.

03:00

Dev Kumar, a professional hacker, finally succeeded in accessing MitaSimi Bank's computer systems in Canary Wharf, for the first time at 03:00 in the morning. He was working from his apartment at Crystal Palace but his digital location was well hidden as all his internet traffic was routed through the TOR anonymous network and browser. It wasn't a typical hacker's attack, which the bank's security staff were well used to fighting off using firewalls, long passwords and restrictions on access. No, he was in a different league completely and had gained access using an administrator's password.

In his earlier research he had discovered that only four people had administration privileges on the bank's servers. Two of them, he learned, played online poker on their home PCs. When a new version of the poker application was being installed, he hijacked it, replacing it with an alternative version which had 'Trojan Horse' software embedded in it. He had written this software specifically for this attack, so there was no way it would be picked up by anti-virus protection on the PC. Once it was installed, it activated a key-logger – a type of surveillance software that recorded everything typed on the keyboard, information that was then periodically sent back through anonymous servers in the dark web, to the hacker.

It was only a matter of time before the admin username and password for the bank's server was picked up by the key-logger and sent as an encrypted message to Dev.

Now he was all set. Armed with the administrator credentials, he was able to access the bank's servers without arousing any suspicion.

Once inside, his first job was to hide his tracks so no one would know he had been there. Tonight was the first night of a few week's work, and he would need to be able to come and go in the middle of the night, making some small, but crucial changes to the bank's clients' portfolios. If he went too fast and made significant changes in one go, then it would be spotted right away. But, by patiently making small updates, night after night, he would be able to slowly built up a significant change to the trading systems databases, one of the most crucial financial areas in the bank. Before he left each night, he would have to remove details about his access to the system, thus minimising the possibility of anyone knowing he had been there.

When Dev had finished his first session on the servers at MitaSimi Bank, that night, he moved on to his second target – Ethan Harris's home PC, where he had already installed the 'Trojan horse' software. He logged in and left a thinly disguised electronic trail from Ethan's PC to a number of websites, for others to eventually find. He then installed the TOR network and other software to make it look like Harris had been using the dark web. He also left a trail making it look like Ethan had accessed his wife's bank accounts, including her special savings account containing £500,000. From another one of her accounts, he transferred £10,000 to Ethan's account, which he subsequently transferred to a Swiss bank account.

CHAPTER THREE

Day One

23rd July, 2015. Onslow Square, Kensington.

00:01

It was midnight and Ethan had just finished yet another online poker session. He was sitting back in his comfortable leather chair in his home office on the first floor of his house on Onslow Square, Kensington, London. Once again, his gambling account was empty, but he was hopelessly addicted, having fallen off the wagon yet again. This was an early night for him; normally it would be well into the small hours of the morning before he was ready for bed, pretending to work late to his wife Rachel who had gone to bed two hours before him, exhausted by work and looking after Katy.

What prompted him to finish early was that while searching for a credit card, a new one that he had secretly ordered, he had come across a photo, in the drawer of his desk. It had been taken more than thirty years earlier, when Ethan was 12 years old. A small, old print with a crease across it, it brought him back to another place and time with a flood of memories.

"Measure twice, cut once." That was the mantra that Tom, Ethan's father, repeated as he worked on all the do-it-yourself jobs he did around the house where Ethan and his brother James grew up. Ethan hated that phrase because it reminded him of all the half-made furniture in nearly every room of the house.

It was a ramshackle, three-bedroom, semi-detached house in Norwood South London, full of bad DIY home projects, some half completed, some barely started, but all of them stamped with the characteristic signature of Tom Harris, an amateur do-it-yourself enthusiast and father of two boys.

The house was dirty; it had always been dirty as far as Ethan remembered, ever since he had been woken up by his brother James, telling him that his mother, Elizabeth, had left.

"What do you mean, left?" Ethan had asked innocently. "Left for work?"

"No, she's gone, she's left us, without a goodbye, or where she was going or anything," replied James, half in anger, half in shock. "And he's crying downstairs," he added.

"No, he never cries, he's our dad." Ethan choked on the words as the realisation began to dawn on him. He ran downstairs.

"Where's mum?"

Tom was in the living room and he did not reply. He did not even look at Ethan. He just blew his nose and walked into the kitchen.

Ethan ran back up to his parent's room, two steps at a time. The wardrobes were open and mostly empty, with a few crooked wire hangers dangling from the rail, moving in the breeze that came through the open window. All of the drawers in the tall-boy were open; papers were blowing everywhere. A small brown suitcase with a broken handle was sitting on the edge of the bed with the top flipped back. It looked empty, but Ethan reached inside the case and slid his hand under a flap on the side, checking to see if anything was there. He pulled out a small photo of his mum, James and himself and looked at it briefly trying to remember when his dad had taken it. He put it in his pocket and looked up.

James was at the bedroom door.

"What happened?" said Ethan, feeling isolated and terrified.

James shrugged his shoulders and looked at the wall and then out the window, as though he would rather look anywhere but at his little brother.

"Is she coming back? Perhaps it was just a big row?" Ethan said. He was trying to choke back tears that were starting to flow.

James said nothing. He put his arm around Ethan's shoulder.

Ethan shuddered back to the present. That was more than thirty years ago and still a painful and vivid memory, floating just below the surface, emerging every so often, accompanied by stabs of pain and regret. He did not know why he kept that photo; perhaps it was just to keep alive that vague hope that he might meet his mother again. He wondered where she was, and why she had left them. Was she still alive? She'd be older now, in her mid-sixties. After that day it had been as though a dark cloud had settled over his home. Nothing was ever the same. His childhood had ended, in one quick snip. All those earlier days of swings and friends and sweets and football were over forever. The shutters went down then and never came up again.

He looked in on Katy before he went to bed. She was fast asleep in her cot with her little hands stretched up. He adjusted the blanket and kissed her on the forehead. Then he crept into the darkened master bedroom without turning on the light, slipped into bed and curled into Rachel's back. She was sleeping so peacefully, with gentle little breaths. He moved his hand on her warm thigh and she murmured briefly, then continued those soft breaths. He drifted off beside her for a while.

06:00

At 06:00, as usual, Ethan woke without an alarm going off. He was just programmed to wake at this hour, even on a day off. Rachel was spooned into him like a warm limpet, her breath tickling the hairs on his shoulder and her arm around his thigh with her hand cupped under his stomach and the warmth of her body radiating into his back. He had been enjoying the comfort of this along with the ever so subtle fragrance of her hair when his phone rang.

As he reached over to get it, he knocked a glass half-filled with water onto the polished wooden floor of their bedroom. It made a resounding crash, followed by an almost instant cry from Katy in the next bedroom. Rachel recoiled immediately, pulling away from his back. The combination of the sudden draught of cold air, the crash of the glass and the baby's crying yanked him fully back from that place between sleep and wakefulness, into the land of the living.

"Answer it," whispered Rachel, as she slid out of bed to see to little Katy.

"Yes?" growled Ethan into his phone.

"Ethan, it's Bill." Bill Taylor was Ethan's friend from work. "We've got major problems here, and most systems are down."

Ethan closed his eyes, and took a deep breath, but said nothing.

"Ethan, can you hear me?"

"Yes, yes, I heard you. Can't you fix it?" he said snappily. "I'm on a day off today, and it's six am," he added in a lower voice, trying not to disturb Katy again.

"I know, and I'm sorry to call you today, and so early, but this is serious. Nothing's working and as you know, today is D-day for the new systems and those ultra-important board reports."

"Can't I ever take a day off?"

Bill said nothing.

Ethan leaned back in bed with anger building up inside. He clenched his left fist, thumping the bed lightly.

"It looks like hackers have attacked the bank's systems, but I don't know how," said Bill.

It was like a bolt of lightning. Ethan sat straight up in the bed and was fully awake now. Bill had pressed the panic button in his brain.

"Hacked? How do you know? What's happened?"

Bill took a deep breath, a large gulp of air like he was swallowing a bitter pill. "It's got all the signs of it. There was some unauthorised access to the system files on the central server, but there was nothing in the logs. I had the feeling that someone had changed something, but I couldn't put my finger on it until I started to look at the dates of certain critical files. Someone has changed the security permissions and then tried to hide it."

"But can you trace where they went on the server? And do you know what files they opened? Has anything been downloaded, uploaded, corrupted, or tampered with?"

"Hold on, this is overload, I've only just started to investigate, but nothing's sure yet."

"Okay, but we're going to need a bit of digital forensics here, and with your background in that, you should be able to find something left behind by these guys, even if they were trying to hide their activity."

They were both on the verge of panic now.

"I'm not entirely sure yet," continued Bill. "But I have done some initial work and uncovered the trail they left while accessing the database servers, where the most sensitive accounting and treasury information is held. I can see that data has been accessed and probably downloaded. But worse, a considerable number of updates were made over the last two weeks."

"So they've been in our systems for at least two weeks, changing stuff and watching what we do, and we had no idea of it until now," said Ethan. He was disgusted with himself that this could have happened.

"We're in for the chop," Bill replied.

"Who else knows this?"

"Just you and me so far, but as you know, those damn regulations say we should report this kind of event to board-level management right away."

"I know, I know, but we need to get a good handle on it before we say anything. I'm coming in right away."

"Okay."

"Don't say anything about this to anyone else until I get in, and we decide on a strategy. Continue tracking and checking and keep me up to date as you go. I'll be there in forty-five minutes," said Ethan.

"Fine, see you in a while, and I'll have investigated further by the time you get in."

Ethan put his iPhone down and stretched. "Fuck," he said under his breath. Rachel, who was back in bed having settled Katy, turned over to look at him.

"What's up? I hope you don't have to go in; you were working so late last night."

"The usual, they can't survive a day without me."

"But what about our trip?"

"This is serious, ultra dangerous for the bank and me."

Rachel sat up, rubbed her eyes and looked at him, with a worried look.

"How bad?"

His face felt hot. "It looks like the security at the bank has been compromised. We've been hacked, and I don't know how bad it is. Right now I've got to go in and stem the flow of information, and then assess the damage."

"Could you get fired?" Rachel cut to the chase.

"I don't know. External security is not my primary area, but everything inside the bank is. So I need to check the extent of the intrusion and exactly what's been accessed and changed. That will give me a good idea where the blame will land."

Rachel reached over, rubbed his shoulders and hugged him. He felt like a child being comforted by his mother. He knew she understood how serious this was, and now she was showing that she was behind him, giving him comfort and support. They kissed for a moment and then he pulled away.

"I'll try to get back as soon as possible. You have a lie in while you can, Katy is back asleep."

He groaned. Then he kissed her and rolled out of bed.

In the shower, the steaming water soon brought him back to life and ready for the trials ahead. Downstairs he looked around for his keys and wallet and stashed them with his iPhone and laptop in his backpack.

CHAPTER FOUR

Theft on the Train

23rd July, 2015. South Kensington Station.

06:40

Ethan walked out of his house and into the drizzling rain. On his way to the tube station, the rain grew heavier. He looked up at the dark, brooding clouds as the increasingly heavy deluge fell unrelentingly, turning the streets into rushing streams. As he walked, it seeped into his jacket, his shoes and his hair. It ran down his face and dripped off his chin. He pulled his collar up and quickened his pace.

Already the city was full of life; delivery vans were being unloaded outside shops, people were making their way to work, police sirens were going off and the smells of fresh bread and fried bacon came from the small shops and cafés he passed.

He was thoroughly soaked when he arrived at South Kensington station. Inside, he paused for a moment, to try and shake off some of the rain from his coat. It was busy in the station too – on the escalator he could hear an early morning busker playing a saxophone in the distance, barely audible over the hustle and bustle of people, and the arriving and departing subway trains, rumbling and screeching as they squeezed into the platforms, belching out their carriages of passengers before sucking up a new load and continuing their way.

He took the Piccadilly line to Green Park, then the Jubilee Line to Canary Wharf station. It usually took about thirty minutes, if everything was running on time, for him to reach MitaSimi Bank, where he was the IT director. MitaSimi was a small investment bank noted for punching well above its weight in the financial world. Like many other investment banks, it was also noted for exacting more than its pound of flesh from employees, piling on the pressure to achieve impossible targets.

It was electric at the office for 18 hours a day. Even in the quieter hours of the very early morning, some heavyweights and newbie ladder climbers had been spotted at all hours on the phone or working feverishly on some deal with global customers in a market that never sleeps. Since he and Rachel got married, Ethan had tried to reduce his regular twelve hour days back to ten hour days, but mostly with little success. They wanted him there, they needed him there. When he was not at the office, his voicemail and email box filled up, that is if they hadn't reached him on his iPhone. It was manic and in some ways he loved it. But he had started to hate the fact that it was squeezing every last ounce of life from him, leaving just a used-up, empty husk for everything else.

Rachel, he knew, hated this too. But he also knew that she enjoyed the financial benefits and the social climbing. Lately she had been fairly preoccupied with Katy and her job, and as her demands on Ethan's time had lessened, they had settled into a routine where each operated nearly independently of each other, except for the occasional day off when they tried to be a family for once.

So the prospect of losing one of those precious family days was a major annoyance to Ethan. However, he knew the seriousness of a hacking incident, and this mostly occupied his thoughts as he waited for the next train to arrive.

As he was changing train at Green Park, he noticed an old woman in front of him struggling to get onto the train on her own. No one paid any attention to her, or helped her, but she managed to get on the train despite her slowness and frailty, just as the doors were closing.

Ethan sat back and started to think about the problems that would face him at the office. How bad was it? What systems and who had been affected by the hackers? What would his damage limitation strategy be? Would it affect his bonus? Worse, would it affect his job? Rachel had thought of that almost instantly while he had been still trying to think about the impact on the bank. She had that knack of quickly finding what was paramount in any situation, and cutting to the chase.

At Bermondsey station, two stops before his destination, he was distracted again by the old woman. She struggled to get up while the train was still moving, so she would be ready to get off when it stopped, then tried to steady herself and get her two bags to the train door. He guessed she was in her mid-eighties and looked as though she felt every minute of it as she struggled to balance herself with the motion of the train until it was braking and she was pushed forward, so that she fell between her bags.

Instinctively Ethan jumped up to help her off the ground, leaving his backpack by the side of a seat, so that he could pick up her two bags. Once the train had stopped, he stepped through the open door and the glass platform doors and put them on the ground, then reached back to help her out.

The woman, who looked Indian, thanked him using broken English and by gesticulating with her hands. While she was doing that her purse slipped and fell on the platform, scattering a jumble of notes and mostly coins all around. Ethan bent down to help her pick everything up, but just as he did so the warning signal sounded and the doors began to close. He quickly pushed the handful of coins into her outstretched hands, and wildly grabbed for the door. But it was too late. Already they were firmly closed. The train started to move off.

He banged the glass platform door, but the train moved on. Through the glass partition he could see his backpack with all his valuable items, leaning against the seat in the train. Then he noticed someone else was looking at it too. The last thing he saw as the train moved off was a tall scrawny guy with long black hair, dirty jeans and a scuffed leather jacket bending down to look in his backpack.

"Stop, stop", said Ethan. He banged on the glass again, hoping to draw attention to his bag and the potential thief, but it was pointless; the only response he got was from a teenage kid, who pressed his face up against the glass door, so that it was squashed and hideous looking.

And then the train was gone, and it was suddenly silent on the platform, except for a dragging noise in the distance as the old woman made her way laboriously up the broken escalator steps with her bags to the exit. She was completely unaware of the disaster she had caused for him, and the whole series of dominos that would be triggered by that single helping hand he had offered her.

He sat down on the ground for a minute and clasped his head in his hands. What to do now? He still had his phone, but everything else was stashed in his backpack. Should he call the police? There was no signal, so that would have to wait. Another train would be along shortly. He would continue to the office and deal with it there.

At Canary Wharf station he realised that the Oyster Card was in the backpack as well as his wallet. He had to wait until there was a crowd of people pushing through the barriers, so he could tailgate one of them to get through.

07:55.

As the train sped away, Joe Morgan, the tall scrawny guy who had been sitting behind Ethan, smiled for a moment at his good luck. There was bound to be something valuable in that backpack, and it was his for the taking. He was so intent on stealing it that he failed to notice an old man sitting nearby who had seen everything: the old woman, the spilled purse, Ethan helping her, the backpack, and the interest taken in it by Joe.

At the next stop, Canada Water Station, when Joe slipped his hand down to scoop up the bag on his way towards the train door, the old man jumped up.

"Hey, stop thief! He's stealing that bag," he shouted, pointing at Joe.

Everyone in the carriage looked up, but no one reacted; most of them returned their gaze to their iPhone, iPad or newspaper. The doors closed, leaving Joe to walk freely to the station exit, as the train continued its journey, with the old man glaring at him through the train door window.

He smiled smugly at the old man as he made his way to the exit. Outside, he walked into a nearby café and opened the backpack. There were a few items of interest – a laptop, a wallet, a set of keys, some papers giving Ethan's home address, and his ID card for the bank where he worked.

08:10

When he got out at Canary Wharf station, Ethan walked through the wet streets, thinking about how he was going to handle the hacking at the bank. The buck stopped with him if it was an internal failure that had allowed it to happen. That could cost him his job and might even cause some difficulty in getting another one right away. If it had been outside his control, perhaps some senior manager losing a phone or a laptop that had led to it, then he would be partially off the hook. There would still be some price to pay, but a smaller one, perhaps the loss of a bonus.

There was a shopping mall, not far from Canary Wharf station, and relatively close to his office. It was still early, but he was hungry and thirsty, and he hadn't had breakfast, so he stopped into Pret-a-Manger to get a salt beef and gherkin sandwich and a can of ginger beer. This unlikely combination satisfied his hunger and was his favourite when he needed something tasty and fast.

He needed to compose himself so he did not look dishevelled arriving at the office. He always liked to display a particular image – a cool exterior, of a person always in control, regardless of what going on inside, like a duck, calm on the surface and paddling furiously underneath.

Ten minutes after his impromptu breakfast he was at the office. With no ID card, he had to call Bill.

"Bill, it's me."

"Are you coming in?"

"I'm outside, but I've lost my ID card, can you come down to security to sign me in?"

While he was waiting, he called home, but there was no answer; it went to voicemail.

"Rachel, I'm at the office now, I guess you fell back asleep. I lost my backpack and laptop on the train. I'll tell you about it later, and I won't be too long."

Bill arrived down to the reception, red-faced and stressed looking.

"My laptop and ID card were stolen on the tube. I don't want this to be yet another security incident for the bank, so I'll wait until later and call the Underground lost property, when they're open, to see if they have it, before I report it to the bank."

Bill nodded distractedly.

"So, how bad is it?" Ethan asked. He was barely managing to hide his rising sense of panic from seeing Bill in such a state.

"Let's say I'm glad you're here, Ethan," said Bill with a slight warble.

"Does anyone else know about it yet?" Ethan asked in the lift, as they made their way to the tenth floor.

"No, but there have been a few questions because some of the systems are down. I fobbed them off saying that there was some planned downtime for maintenance for a few hours this morning. But unless we get things running again soon that won't be enough to stop a more senior level enquiry into what's happening."

"I know, let's go into a conference room for a few minutes and map out the sequence of events, the impact and the plan to fix things. Then we can decide how we're going to reveal what's happened. I don't know the full extent of it myself yet, so you need to fill me in on the details."

They sat down in the small conference room, which, like all the other conference rooms in the building, was a glass box; walls and doors only offered audio privacy, so anyone could see that they were in there, and could come in to ask what was going on. For that very reason, Ethan decided not to use the whiteboard to map out the plan. Instead, he drew it out on a bunch of A4 sheets he had grabbed from the printer on his way.

"Let's start from the beginning."

CHAPTER FIVE

Fence and Fix

23rd July, 2015. Canada Water Station.

08:30

As he got off the Underground train, Joe called Rick to offload the stolen items.

"Hey Rick my man, did I get you out of bed?" he sneered. "Got any use for a new MacBook?"

"Maybe, but it's too early. Call me later."

"No, I need the cash now – three hundred and it's yours."

"No way, dude, two fifty is the max, 'cos you woke me up."

"Ok but I need cash this time – last time I had to wait and you know I can't wait when I need a hit."

"Okay, okay I've got cash to feed your little habit, but it better be new."

"It is new, man, brand new, and I've also got some access ID card for an office – that's gotta be worth something."

"Where?"

"It's a bank, Rick. In Canary Wharf. Interested? Could be worth a lot more than the laptop."

"Yeah right, like I'm a bank robber now."

"Okay, I'll just ditch it."

"No, no. I'll take it just in case one of my guys could be interested. That's included with the laptop, right?"

"No way man, it's an extra ton."

"Fifty."

"Okay, you got a deal. I'll drop by with the gear soon."

Thirty minutes later, Joe arrived at Rick's house, a tenement building covered in graffiti and barbed wire. He called Rick on the phone again.

"Hey man, I'm outside."

"When I said later, I didn't mean five minutes."

"But I'm outside now, man, and I really need a hit."

"Okay, I've opened the side gate."

Joe slipped in the door, through the archway, down some dark stairs, echoing with the sound of a baby crying and dogs barking in the further distance. Rick's door was protected with a sheet of steel, which was covered with what looked like imprints from something heavy and pock-marked with several small deep circular dents that looked like they had been made by bullets. There was a small caged slot about five foot up and a spy hole below it. Joe rapped on the door.

"Hey, Rick it's me."

Rick pulled back the caged door on the slot and looked at him.

"Let me in," said Joe.

"What have you got?"

"I told you, man. I don't want to get it out here, let me in."

The door opened about six inches. Joe pushed his way in. Rick was standing in the hallway with a baseball bat in his hand.

"It's me, Rick," said Joe. "What are you scared of?"

Rick hit the wall with a loud thud, and Joe jumped.

"I'm not scared of you. I need to take precautions."

"Okay, okay, sorry man, I just want to give you the gear and get my money." Joe was scratching now and twitching a bit. "It's been nearly two days and I gotta get something soon."

"Okay, let's see it."

"I told you on the phone. It's a super new MacBook and some guy's security pass." He took it out of the pack. Rick eyed it.

"Two fifty. That's what we agreed."

"No man, it's three hundred including the card. I need to get my shit man. You know me; don't rip me off." Joe was whining now, like a dog.

"Okay, okay." Rick pulled out a roll of dirty twenties and counted them out into Joe's hand.

Joe passed over the laptop and the ID card and then he disappeared in a flash, up the steps and out through the side door.

08:40

He walked back to the train station with a sense of relief. At the side of the station, he ducked down an alleyway, where a guy was crouched on the ground, coughing uncontrollably. Joe tapped him on the back.

"You okay, Nick?"

Nick stopped coughing for a moment and glared up at him. "What the fuck do you think?" he said, as he spat out a large knot of green mucus on the street.

"Alright man, I was just concerned you might die on me before you got me some shit."

"You got money? Cos you already owe me a ton."

"I know, and I've got it."

"What do you want then?"

"Smack. A major hit – it's been two days."

Nick stretched out his hand half-covered with a blood-soaked bandage. "Three hundred," he demanded, "including the ton you owe me."

"Whoa, hold on man, has the price gone up? Don't screw me over, you know I'm a regular customer." Joe was whining again.

"Okay, two hundred," said Nick, relenting.

Joe handed him a bundle of twenties, which Nick counted out before reaching into his pocket and pushing two plastic bags into Joe's hand.

"Thanks, man."

Joe's heart was pumping now in anticipation of the hit. He hurried to the nearby train station toilet, ignoring the suspicious gaze of the station staff who had seen him there before. Crouching down in a cubicle floor, he kicked the door closed and took out a spoon and a lighter and reached into his pocket for one of the plastic bags.

Less than a minute after he injected, it hit his brain like a mainline train, and he lay back on the floor and let it all rush over him.

An hour or so later, he looked around the squalid cubicle. Then he stood up and took a piss before grabbing the backpack. As he did so, a bunch of keys fell to the ground and as he bent down to get them an idea struck him. Surely there was more stuff to be had back at that guy's gaff. He reached into the bag and pulled out the other papers that were there and looked for an address. Then he got back on the train heading towards South Kensington, where he had started from.

CHAPTER SIX

The Leak

1st July, 2015. GCHQ Offices, Cheltenham.

10:00

David Powell was livid when he arrived at his meeting with colleagues in GCHQ. The project office was in a basement – a kind of bunker with no windows. It felt secure but isolated from everything else around it in GCHQ; as with the secret project itself, of which Powell was director, it was like a state within a state.

Three others were present: Turner the project leader, Smyth, an analyst who had been investigating a new leak of information and Randall, who had been seconded from MI6.

"From what I can see, there is a constant flow of information leaking from this project," said Powell. "We know from our MI6 agents in the field that some of the details are turning up in Germany, but it's not clear whether it came directly from the leak here or via some other route."

"I've had Smyth and his team track it," said Turner.

"Can you take us through it, Smyth?"

Smyth stood and drew a diagram on the whiteboard. As he spoke, he pointed to different areas, within GCHQ, the London area and Europe.

"This shows what information has been leaked and who has access to it. We've locked it down as much as possible, but there's still about twenty people here, including ourselves, who have access. So we still haven't been able to determine exactly who the mole is, although we have some suspects."

"Okay, let's look at it from the other side, outside GCHQ," said Powell. "Who is receiving the leaked data and where?"

"We know there is an agent operating in Aldgate, near Whitechapel in East London. Her cover is as a graphic designer," said Turner.

"Do we have any definite proof?"

"No. She appears to be receiving the leaked encrypted files and processing them, but there are no onwards links, so we can't track what happens to it from there. After she receives the data, it's like a dead end."

"Is the place tapped?"

"Yes, we've got her house and office bugged, and we're monitoring her as much as possible. But she's very careful, and we just don't have any proof. She seems to be working on the files at random times and in random locations. She also travels a lot abroad; it's harder to track her outside the country."

"Okay, for obvious reasons, I don't want to know names, but can you provide a bit more information about her? Is she married?"

"Yes, she lives near Kensington with her husband, an IT director for a bank in Canary Wharf, and they have a young child."

"What if there was some trouble at home? That would isolate her and make her more vulnerable," said Powell.

"Divide and conquer," observed Turner, smiling.

"Start with the bank where the husband works. Hack into it and leave a trail that causes him some problems at work. Then we take a look at his home PC."

"We could set him up," said Randall.

"First find if he has any weaknesses – women, men, booze, gambling or drugs, something we can work with. Once we split them up, she may drop her guard more easily. And when she does we'll be ready,' said Powell. He looked at Randall. 'You'll know what to do."

Randall understood. "We'll get on it right away," he said.

"I want this leak fixed as soon as possible, and I need you to take any action required to do it," was the last chilling directive from Powell.

"Do you want us to take her out?" said Randall.

Powell thought for a moment.

"No, not right now. Perhaps later. Without any hard proof that she's the one, it could get messy, and I don't want to cause any more problems than we already have. Let's see how you get on with the disruption first."

Powell left the room.

"I think Powell is just too cautious," said Turner. "Although we don't have proof that Rachel Harris is responsible, I believe we have enough circumstantial evidence."

"You mean that fact that some of the stolen files appear to have been transferred to her IP address?"

"Yes, although we don't know what she's doing with them. And she does have a profile as a privacy activist."

"But that's just a cover. It all points to her, and I think we should take her out," said Randall.

"I'm inclined to agree," said Turner. "Powell wants proof before we act, but we might never get that. Meanwhile, things are getting worse for us – apparently the Chinese or the Russians or some other foreign agency are getting everything we have."

"If we eliminate her without authorisation, then Powell will fire us, or at least take us off the project. We could even be charged if it got out to the public domain."

"That will never happen. The government will always protect themselves and us. Anyway, Powell can't afford to get rid of us. He's getting on. He must be over 65 now. And let's face it, you're his natural successor. He needs you to take over the reins of this project. After all, it's his legacy and if we don't keep it going, it might just fall out of favour – lose funding, get shut down. You're his champion to keep it going," said Randall.

Turner smiled. "Perhaps you're right."

"If we act and the leak is plugged, then Powell will be pleased. It's only an issue if the word gets out, which won't happen. How many cases have we kept quiet?"

"Hundreds."

"So why will this be any different? Powell's job is to do the right thing. Our job is to do what's necessary to get the job done. He knows that. In fact, I'd say he wants us to do our job, but he can't request it explicitly. It's better for him if he's disconnected from it. For God's sake, he doesn't even know her name or anything about her."

Turner thought it over for a while.

"Okay, let's do it," he said. "I'm sick of this waiting around for proof."

"I have an asset who's currently in Morocco. I'll ask him to fly to London for a day and take her out. It will be clean. There'll be no evidence," said Randall.

"So if Powell asks, we'll deny all knowledge of it. We can leave traces that show she was handling files belonging to other GCHQ programmes that could also be responsible."

"He'll investigate."

"Yes, but he won't have proof, and as we know, he never acts unless he has proof."

They laughed. "Okay, let's go for it."

CHAPTER SEVEN

The Killing

23rd July, 2015. South Kensington Station.

09:35

As the train moved off, Joe was looking again, for any possible target. He had £100 left in his pocket, but he knew that it would only last for another hit. He needed to eat and somewhere to sleep that night but he was banned from the shelters because of their no drugs policy. He had tried to stay clean but usually only lasted a week. Something always came up and he just needed a hit. He could always kip down in a doorway anywhere in cardboard city with all the other dossers. But Joe wanted to rise above all that. If he could steal some good kit, he could clean himself up and have himself some comfort for a few weeks in a hotel.

Perhaps he'd spot someone on the train or he'd get lucky in the gaff where he was headed. He was holding the bunch of keys in his hand in his pocket, thinking about his prospects.

When the train stopped at South Kensington station, the closest one to the address, he got off and checked the map on the subway wall to see exactly where the house was. In the reflection of the glass over the map, he saw two police officers, obviously eyeing him up as a possible suspect for some crime on their books. He was used to that. He had form, and they knew it just by looking at him. It was like having the words loser and thief tattooed on his forehead. Joe hated that. He had always hoped he would strike it lucky. Perhaps today would be the day.

The police moved closer and Joe moved off before he had fully figured out the way to Ethan's house. He had the general idea.

Five minutes later he was close to Onslow Square, where Ethan's house was. He was looking a little conspicuous as he checked the street signs. A woman wearing a blue raincoat stopped to ask if he needed help finding an address, but he just glared at her and kept moving. Finally, he found Onslow Square South, glancing over his shoulder as he made his way up the street. It was easy then to find the house. It looked like it was all clear; quiet, with closed windows and no lights on. He could see through the glass window in the door that the alarm had a green light showing, indicating that it was disarmed. Good, he thought. An easy job. Though it might mean there was someone else in there. He glanced around him again, noticed there was a single open window on the first floor, then quickly put his ear to the glass panel in the door. All was quiet. Quickly, he put the key in the lock, opened the door quietly and slipped inside.

Nice house, he thought to himself as he moved around downstairs. There must be some good stuff here. He saw an iPad on the table and slipped it into the backpack. There was also an expensive looking Sony camera, and he stashed that too.

09:40

Meanwhile, across the street, a small inconspicuous car – a black Toyota –pulled into an empty parking spot beside the park railings. Inside a man with a dark jacket and sunglasses and wearing a pair of surgical gloves reached under his seat, pulled out a small black box and opened it. Inside it lay a 9mm pistol, a cartridge clip, and a silencer, neatly packed in foam cut-out slots.

He took the gun out in a slow, measured fashion, as though he had done this a thousand times before. There was a sense of military precision about his movements, as though he was operating to a carefully planned sequence, perhaps under orders, as he loaded the cartridge clip, attached the silencer, all the time staring ahead, without looking down. He knew this drill well. He stopped a moment to watch a woman wearing a blue raincoat pass by. She did not notice him. The man finished assembling his gun, then waited a moment for the woman to move further down the street, before opening the car door and checking for security cameras on the street. At one end of the street, one pointed in the opposite direction, and the one at the other end was too far away to matter. He crossed the road and made his way to Ethan's house. The gun was in his inside jacket pocket, ready for action.

Inside the house, Joe was still working his way silently around the downstairs of the house. He took the backpack off his shoulders and left it on a counter in the kitchen. Suddenly a cat slinked by him and up the stairs. Joe jumped back in shock, knocking a picture frame to the floor with a small thump as he did so. Fortunately, it did not break. Fucking cat. He took a sharp intake of breath and listened carefully so he could hear if there was someone upstairs.

"Sapphire, are you knocking things over again?" Rachel's voice drifted down from upstairs.

A baby began to cry.

"Now you've woken Katy up," said Rachel.

"Fuck," whispered Joe to himself, and began creeping towards the front door, until he remembered the backpack. He turned to go back to the kitchen.

The man in the dark jacket, with a gun, came out of nowhere.

"What the hell?" Joe turned quickly to duck out of the line of fire, but not fast enough.

Pop. The silenced shot quietly found its target. Shot in the head, Joe fell forward with a light thud onto the carpet runner covering the polished wooden floor in the hallway. Thick dark blood oozed slowly from his head, ran down the side of his cheek onto the carpet and then out onto the wooden floor, drawing an outline of his head and shoulder.

The assassin looked down at the motionless body and was about to check his neck pulse with his gloved hand, carefully avoiding the blood, when he heard Rachel's voice.

"What on earth are you up to?" she shouted. But she sounded quite relaxed; presumably, thought the assassin, she was shouting at her cat.

He turned and moved quietly up the stairs, unbeknownst to him followed by the cat. With the sunlight streaming through the window behind him, he threw a dark shadow on the wall as he slowly and silently approached the bedroom.

Rachel had just got out of bed when the assassin saw his shadow fall across her face, as he came through the door with the gun outstretched. He fired twice in quick succession and she fell backwards onto the bed, wide-eyed, her mouth open in a frozen scream, silenced before it could escape.

Meticulously he checked her neck pulse to be sure. Then he turned to see the source of the strange squeal. The cat was just behind him; he turned and kicked her out of his way. She retaliated with a sharp scratch of his leg, darted down the stairs, jumped nimbly over the body in the hall and out through the front door, which was slightly ajar. She had stepped in the pool of blood on the wooden floor in the hall; as she fled she left a trail of bloody paw marks behind her.

The baby began to scream as the assassin walked down the stairs slowly. In the hallway, he glanced at the blood-covered body lying there, before slipping out the open door as deftly as the cat, although he managed to avoid the blood. He could still hear the baby crying uncontrollably through the open window as he walked across the street. He looked around to check no one had seen him then got back into his car, returned the gun to the black box, and drove off.

09:55

A few minutes later, the woman in the blue raincoat, walking back down the street, noticed that the door of the Harris's house was ajar. Then she heard the baby crying through the open window. She moved a little closer, straining on the wrought iron railings to check what was up. That was when she noticed the red paw marks on the ground in front of the house. Cautiously, she walked up the steps and looked through the open door, into the hall where Joe's body lay in its own blood.

She ran down the street.

"There's a dead body in the hall," she screamed. People came out of their houses to see what all the commotion was about.

"Someone has been killed," she screamed. "Call the police."

George Thornton, who lived two doors down, made the call. Within ten minutes a cacophony of police sirens could be heard in Onslow Square. Three cars pulled up outside the house, and a senior uniformed officer got out, wearing a bulletproof vest. He ran up the steps of the house and looked in the doorway at the body before turning and signalling to his colleagues. One got out and rolled police incident tape on the railing across the gate. The others ran in opposite directions to the ends of the street and spread more tape to stop any further traffic from driving there. The only other area that had to be secured was the gate into the park across the street; as the house was terraced there was no side entrance to the back.

The senior officer then called Control to report his actions and confirm that there was an apparently dead body lying in the hallway. Having done so, the police withdrew to the side of the street, mindful that there might still be a gunman in the house or the park.

A team of armed police wearing protective gear arrived shortly. They swept through the house and the park, soon confirming it was safe for the police to proceed.

A crowd had started to gather at the police lines at both ends of the street, straining to find out about all the commotion. A news reporter tried to push past the police line and walk up to the house, but a six-foot-three officer who looked like a rugby player in a police uniform stopped his progress by squarely blocking his path.

"Excuse me sir," he said.

"Out of my way officer, I'm a press reporter, let me through."

"I'm sorry sir, but this is a crime scene, and you could destroy vital evidence. I have to ask you to move back to the tape."

"But –"

"Sir, if you do not move back now I will arrest you."

Reluctantly the journalist moved back, grumbling about police harassment as he did so, before turning to face the police officer again.

"Officer, can you answer some questions?"

"I'm sorry sir, we don't have any information right now. There will be a press conference later when we've established all the facts."

At the other end of the street, a news crew had arrived, and were setting up a tripod, camera, and microphones. Beside them was a citizen reporter, recording the scene on her iPhone, and no doubt blogging it to Facebook or Twitter.

CHAPTER EIGHT

Scott Makes a Bid

23rd July, 2015. South Kensington.

10:15

Apart from his job, which he loved, DCI Scott's passion was for art and photography. Sometimes his job as a police inspector seemed to be even secondary to this passion. He was lucky that DI Kevin Jones knew this and often covered for him while he was out for a couple of hours at art auctions that ran during the working day. Scott referred to it as 'working on a background cold case for a few hours', which only Jones knew was code for an auction. He was particularly likely to get distracted in this way when a unique, limited edition art print or photograph by an artist he admired was coming up for auction, and the reserve price was within his budget. Since his wife Alice had died three years previously, this growing passion for collecting art had taken root in his life, filling a void that had emerged ever since she had passed away.

Scott also worked hard at his job. He had a lot of responsibility and sometimes that meant working long days, often into the night, as well as weekends. So he felt it was okay to take a little time off when he needed it. He just was not sure if Superintendent Foster would see it that way. Foster was a hardened workaholic, who was divorced from his wife; in a way he had sacrificed his family for the job and a chance at high office. This made him very one-dimensional and he thought everyone else should have the same level of dedication to the job as he had. Or, as others in the department put it, 'the same degree of obsession'. Fortunately, most of the others were not as fanatical.

As soon as Foster was informed of the murder by the duty desk sergeant, he called DCI Scott to assign him as the senior investigating officer on the case. There was no answer, so he left a voicemail, then sent him a text message, asking him to make contact immediately. When fifteen minutes had passed with still no reply from Scott, Foster started to lose patience.

"Where is he?" he grumbled to himself. "I need my staff to be contactable at all times." He called DI Jones.

"Jones, I'm looking for Scott," he said with a tone of impatience that Jones recognised as one step away from an outburst of anger.

"Will I come up to you, sir?" Jones said in his lilting Welsh accent.

"No, I'm coming down."

Foster was on the third floor; Jones and Scott's office was a section of the open planned first floor. When Foster appeared before Jones he was red in the face.

"Where is he? I can never reach him when I need him. The damn man never answers his phone or replies to a text."

"He's doing a few hours on a cold case while things are quiet. As you know, he likes to keep busy."

"Well I need to speak to him urgently, we've got another murder on our hands."

"I've just heard that sir, and I tried calling him too. But I think I've got some idea where he might be. I'll go and see if I can find him."

Jones put on his coat and Foster returned to his ivory tower. At Christie's, South Kensington auction rooms, which were not far away, the auction had already begun and Scott was waiting for his lot to come up.

"The next lot, 104, is a small print, part of an early limited edition by John Hopkins, a friend and fellow artist of David Hockney when he was working in California in the mid-sixties. It's dated around 1967; you can see the strong influence of Hockney's swimming pool paintings. Who will start me off at £1,400?"

A nod from the centre of the audience set the auction in motion.

"£1,500," the auctioneer invited.

A bid came from the edge of the room close to where Scott was leaning against the wall with a newspaper tucked under his arm, waiting for his opportunity.

"Any advance on £1,500 for this beautiful piece? £1,600?"

A lady in the centre nodded to bid.

"£1,700?"

Scott raised his rolled up newspaper.

"£1,800?" the auctioneer asked.

"£1,800, anyone?"

There was a short silence.

"Anyone? So £1,700 once. Twice –"

The woman in the centre nodded again.

"£1,800 from the lady in the centre. Do we have £1,900?"

Scott raised his paper again.

"We have £1,900 from the gentleman by the wall. Do we have £2,000?"

The lady bid again.

"£2,000. And do we have £2,100?"

Scott nodded. He recognised the woman bidding; she was a dealer. Already, he was beyond his limit.

"£2,200?"

She nodded, determined to win.

"£2,300? £2,300, anyone?" The auctioneer looked over at Scott, who did not meet his gaze.

"£2,200 it is then." The auctioneer's gavel hit the desk with a final rap. "Sold at £2,200 to the lady in the centre."

Scott left the auction, looking disappointed, passing the successful dealer who smiled at him as he passed. She was an attractive woman in her mid-forties, well dressed with perfect hair and makeup. Quite the opposite to DCI Scott, he was well aware, with his greying hair that needed a cut, yesterday's shirt not quite tucked in and its speck of brown sauce from last night's fish and chips. He had done battle with her at auctions several times before and each time she had been the winner. It was a pattern he wanted to break. He did not want a battle of wills; he just wanted to buy some art.

Later he went for coffee to reflect on his most recent loss. He was sitting at a table outside a café, smoking a cigarette and drinking a black and almost cold Americano, reading the Life and Arts section of the Financial Times. Several minutes passed before he glanced at his phone. Seven missed calls, read the screen. There was also a text message from Jones and one from Foster.

He called Jones.

"Scott, at last. Where are you? Foster is looking for you, and there's been a murder in Onslow Square."

"Jones, thanks, I was…"

"I know, your cold case work," Jones interrupted. "I'm nearly at Christies in South Kensington."

"I'm finished there. I'm close by, sitting outside, at Cafe Nero."

"Okay, I'll be there in a minute."

Jones arrived and he sat down opposite Scott.

"They'll kill you," he said looking at the cigarette burning in the ashtray with a long ash.

"Don't get on my case. I used to get that all the time from Alice. Now she's gone, and I'm still here," he said caustically.

"Did you get the call from Foster?"

"No, once I saw your call, I knew you'd be coming to give me the details."

"He said to ring him urgently."

"I know; he always says that."

Scott called Foster.

"It's Scott."

"Scott, I sent Jones out to get you as it looked like you were off the grid."

Scott knew that Jones would have covered for him.

He said nothing.

"I want you to handle the murder in Onslow Square," continued Foster.

"Okay, Jones is here now. We'll get onto it right away, sir."

"Good, I'll talk to you back in the office later."

Scott turned to Jones.

"We'll use my car, it's just around the corner. You can fill me in on the way."

In the car, Jones opened the window to let out the stench of stale cigarette smoke. "So," he began. "It looks like a double murder in Onslow Square – a man and woman. The murderer left a baby crying in the bedroom."

"A couple?"

"That's not confirmed yet. The man was young; he was found in the hallway downstairs. The woman was in her bedroom."

"Any sign of forced entry?

"I don't think so."

"And the baby?"

"Uninjured but distressed, a neighbour is looking after her for now."

"Any press?"

"Not when I was checking in a few minutes ago, but you know those guys, they'll be there by the time we are."

"Vampires. They love this kind of story – they'll be all over it. And they've been giving us such a hiding recently."

As they drove past Christie's, Scott glanced at the shop front.

"If the murder had been at the auction house," said Jones.

Scott smiled. "Ah, that would have been a crime of passion."

Jones laughed while checking Facebook on his iPhone.

"You're addicted."

"We all have our addictions" he replied, glancing at the full ashtray. "I see this story is already on my Facebook newsfeed. Listen to this. 'Double Murder in Onslow Square, London. Rumours that is was a drug-related revenge killing.'"

Scott glanced quickly at the screen of the phone Jones was holding up. "For Christ's sake. We don't know anything yet. That's one of the reasons I hate knee-jerk social media reporting. They mostly get it wrong and then everyone believes the first thing they read about the incident. I'll bet when we have the press conference the first question will be about drug gang killings."

"Well sometimes it can be useful to get visibility on a case, for witnesses to come forward. But I guess in this case it's complete disinformation."

"Why don't you use that thing for something useful? Call forensics and get Hamilton for me."

Jones made the call and handed Scott the phone when Hamilton had answered.

"No doubt you've heard about the murder in Onslow Square," said Scott.

"Yes, we're just getting a team ready to go there."

"Great, we'll be there soon too, who's the team lead?"

"Reinhardt."

Scott hung up, handed the phone back to Jones.

CHAPTER NINE

The Crime Scene

23rd July, 2015. Onslow Square, Kensington.

11:30

Scott and Jones had to edge their way slowly in the car through the crowd that had gathered at the barrier of the crime scene. Two officers lifted up the scene tape, and they drove under it and then up to the house. Outside, an elderly woman was holding a crying baby, surrounded by a group of sympathising neighbours. As Scott and Jones got out of the car the reporter who had been there earlier attempted to get a comment from them.

"Have you got a statement on the murder?"

"No comment," said Jones. "We'll let you know the situation when we have more information." Scott turned to the uniformed officer standing outside the door.

"You need to move everyone back behind the lines. I want this place clear when forensics arrive."

Then he brushed past the reporter, ducked under the second line of incident tape outside the door, and into the house with Jones following close behind.

*

12:30

In the offices of MitaSimi Bank, Ethan and Bill had agreed on a plan of action regarding the hacking. They had temporarily shut down the external network for thirty minutes while they locked down the hacked server systems and applied extra security policies and changed all passwords.

Then Bill's focus was to get the banking applications up and running again and send out an email notification to everyone in the office letting them know power outages had brought down most of the systems, but that this was now under control and everything would be back to normal soon.

While this was happening Ethan called security specialists for an emergency session to help with the hacking investigation. No one else knew what had happened, least of all Harvey Waterman, Ethan's boss. Ethan knew he would lose the plot if he heard, so he decided it was best not to tell him until everything had been solved. Only then would Ethan give him a report on the problems and the solution and future security recommendations, all at one time. Hopefully, everything would be fine.

Ethan's phone rang.

"Ethan Harris?"

"Yes, who's this?"

"It's Detective Chief Inspector Scott. I am calling you from your home."

The words that nobody ever wants to hear. A million possibilities ran through Ethan's head in a single moment.

"What's happened? Are Rachel and Katy okay?"

There was a pause.

"Can you put Rachel on?" said Ethan.

"There's been an incident, Mr Harris. Where are you?"

"Oh God, are they okay? I'm at work, in MitaSimi Bank, Canary Wharf. I'll come home right away. Are they okay? tell me what's happened."

"Stay where you are. I'll have a car pick you up straightaway."

By 13:15, the police had picked up Ethan and brought him back to his house, where a crowd was still gathered. Ethan jumped out and ran to the open front door, ducking under the police scene tape.

A uniformed officer stopped him before he got into the hallway. "I'm sorry sir, but you can't go in there. It's a crime scene."

"But it's my house. Where are Rachel and Katy?"

"I'm sorry, sir." The policeman held Ethan's arm.

"Let me go." Ethan pulled away.

From inside, Scott heard the commotion and came to the front door.

"Mr Harris?"

"Yes."

"I'm DCI Scott." He shook Ethan's hand. "We can talk in the car."

He led him down the steps to his car.

"Where's Rachel? What's happened?" said Ethan. He felt like he was in a dream now, strangely disconnected from the scene, like a nightmare. It did not feel real. They sat in the car.

"I'm sorry Mr Harris, but there has been an incident. Two people were found dead in your home this morning. Your baby is okay."

"Oh no, no, it can't be." Ethan was suddenly weak. He felt sick. A wave of emotion ran over him, and he began to shake and cry. DCI Scott put his arm on his shoulder to steady him. For a while, Ethan could not speak. When he could, he could not stop asking questions.

"How did it happen? Where? Who did it? And why? Where is she? I want to see her. And where's Katy?"

Then he got out of the car and tried to enter the house again.

"Let me in there, I've got to see them."

"I'm sorry, sir." Two officers restrained him from going into the house and sat him down on the steps. A female police officer sat down beside him.

"Your daughter is safe. We had her for a while but now your mother-in-law is here and she is looking after her."

Ethan followed the policewoman's gaze to see Julia, his mother-in-law, standing a short distance away, being comforted by two of his neighbours. She was holding Katy, rocking back and forth slowly to comfort the baby.

When she saw Ethan she walked towards him, crying. He put his arms around her.

"Rachel, my poor Rachel," she sobbed.

"Julia, what happened?"

"I don't know. All I know is that a neighbour of yours, whom I happen to know, rang me saying that your front door was open, and that she could hear the baby crying for a long time. She also rang the police. It was another of your neighbours who went inside and discovered the murder."

The word murder felt like a cold steel knife stuck into Ethan. It confirmed the awful reality of the situation. Rachel was dead. Murdered. In cold blood. She was lying up there on her own. She was never coming back, and he'd never see her alive again. He started to shake again.

"When I arrived, the police were there, and they wouldn't let me in. A police officer had Katy in her arms, and she gave her to me," continued Julia. "Then –" She broke down crying again. "Then they told me Rachel had been –" She choked on the word. "Killed."

They hugged each other again. Both of them were sobbing now.

He went to find DCI Scott again. "You said two people had been in the house apart from Katy. Who was the other person?"

"There was a man shot in the hallway. We assumed he was dead too, but I have just learned that he has survived. He is in a critical condition though – he's in a coma. Is he a member of your family?"

"No. There was no one else there except Rachel and Katy. Can you show me him or describe him?

Scott showed him a photo taken by one of the officers first at the scene. It showed a scrawny, long-haired young man lying on the hallway floor in a pool of dark blood. For a moment, something about him seemed vaguely familiar to Ethan. But that made no sense.

"I've never seen him before. Who is he? What was he doing in my home?"

11:45

A mid-sized converted black BMW van drew up outside the house. Three people got out and began putting on their protective white scene suits, masks and gloves. It was a crew of onsite forensics specialists: Evelyn Reinhardt, the team leader and ballistics expert; Tom Jenkins, the blood and bio-forensics specialist; and Nathan Jacobs, dealing with fingerprints, DNA and fibre analysis. They covered everything needed for gathering evidence at the crime scene. Jill Oxford, the forensic pathologist, and Zak Turner, the data analyst, were back at the forensic labs. Oxford would deal with the autopsy once the initial forensics were carried out. Turner had already started to acquire and analyse the phone records and CCTV footage, as he was working closely with DCI Clarke on Scott's team.

Reinhardt began by walking around the house, placing marker cards at key points and taking photographs from every corner of every room, so as to record everything exactly as it was, in case anything was disturbed as the work progressed. Although she had been doing this job for ten years, sometimes she had to detach herself from it, if the evidence of intense violence and the horror of a murder scene affected her. This house, which had been a family home only a day ago, was now an empty shell reeking of blood and death. In the bedroom, Rachel's body was covered up, but still lay where she had fallen, her back on the edge of the bed, with one arm stretched out against the headboard. The corner walls and some of the windows were blood splattered, and the bedcovers and sheets were soaked in her dark red-brown blood. Everything else in the room was untouched – a dresser, a small bookcase, an open wardrobe with clothes hanging in it and a teddy bear. It was a kind of surreal juxtaposition of life and death in one place. She shuddered for a second before regaining her composure and focus. She continued the walk-through.

Jenkins set up the circular camera to get 360-degree views of the crime scenes, in the hallway, living room and bedroom. These images would be used to recreate these scenes, which was sometimes required by court cases, and particularly useful in a murder case. It was like piecing together a three-dimensional puzzle that they had to put together frame by frame, thus reconstructing the incident and critical events as they happened.

After the walk-through, Jenkins and Reinhardt sat together for a while.

"We just need to focus on the hall, and the bedroom where the main events happened. Everywhere else is mostly untouched," said Reinhardt.

"There's no sign of any struggle in either location, so it seems that both victims were caught by surprise," Jenkins added.

"Yes. It possibly points to a professional killer. Can you focus on the bedroom first, Jenkins? I'll do the hall, and Jacobs can work on door, wall and floor surfaces for fingerprints and fibres."

Although three 9mm shell casings were found there was only one bullet embedded in a plaster wall in the hallway. The other two bullets were lodged in Rachel Harris's brain and would not be available until the autopsy had been completed. Reinhardt tried to visualise the scene and the movements of the killer and the victims. It appeared that the killer entered the front door and almost immediately fired a single shot that severely injured the unidentified male victim. He must have appeared dead to the killer; otherwise there would have been other shots. Also, the killer must have used a silencer or Rachel Harris would have been alerted by the sound and would have run for cover, possibly locking her bedroom door, or going to her daughter's bedroom to protect her.

The blood spattered on the bedroom wall was only on the wall below the window and on the window itself. This showed that the killer was standing above the victim when they shot her. Possibly she was sitting on the bed, where she now lay, the duvet soaked with her blood.

Back downstairs, Jenkins photographed the blood in the hallway, on the carpet runner and the polished wooden floor. From these details alone, he knew from experience that the victim had been standing when shot.

After taking samples and photographs, he determined where the shooting had occurred and how it may have impacted the head of the unidentified male victim, who had been removed from the scene earlier by the ambulance paramedics before forensics had arrived.

As expected, Jacobs found fingerprints throughout the house, which they would have to cross check against the fingerprints of the family members. But why had the male victim been wearing gloves? Was he somehow connected to the killer? It was a strange one, Jacobs pondered, but not for him to solve. Let the detectives figure it out. He was just there to record what had happened.

There was no break-in damage on the doors or windows, so it looked like the killer had keys or had been invited in. Either that or the door had been open. It also appeared that he had only been at the scene for a short time; it seemed that after shooting the victim in the hall, he went upstairs and killed the second victim with two shots, and left immediately. There was no other disturbance in the house. But Jacobs found some evidence that might prove useful: some cloth fibres caught on the edge of the front door and, later, while doing a painstaking floor search, a short blond hair, different to all the other hair samples in the house, and possibly a DNA source.

When the forensic examination of the bedroom was complete, Reinhardt called Oxford, back at the forensic lab.

"We're finished in the bedroom now, so we're ready to send you the body for autopsy."

"I'll send the van. What condition is it in?"

"Messy from the neck up, two shots to the head, otherwise clean."

By 23:30 that night all the onsite forensic work was complete. Evidence had been bagged and logged, and Jenkins went through the house checking every room and removing first the equipment and finally the markers that Reinhardt had laid down at the beginning. They were about to leave when Jenkins picked up a marker card in the bedroom and found a new blood stain under it, which had not been logged.

He called the others to come back up.

"The marker card was covering this blood stain," he said.

Reinhardt knelt down and examined it carefully.

"It looks like a paw mark in the blood. Jacobs, can you hand me the camera?"

She photographed the stain.

"It's a cat paw," said Jacobs, kneeling down to take a sample, "just like the cat paw marks at the hallway door. We know the cat stepped in the blood from the victim in the hall, but here there is no evidence of the cat stepping into Rachel's blood which is confined to the other side of the room. This is an entirely different sample."

"We'll put a special note about it in the report," said Reinhardt.

By 23:50 they had locked up and left.

Early the following morning, Reinhardt emailed the specialist cleaning company that they usually dealt with, asking them to clean the house and remove all traces of the horrific scene. The onsite work was complete, but it would be quite a while before the information gathered had been analysed and the autopsy completed. She had just sent the email when DCI Scott called her, at 07:30.

"Just wondering how the forensic work is going?"

"We finished in the house late last night, but as you know our work is only beginning in the lab and morgue."

"Thanks. Let me know when it's done."

CHAPTER TEN

Gambling

September, 2014. Casino, Canary Wharf.

It had started so easily for Ethan. He was incredibly busy at work; it felt like he was working day and night. But the bank just piled on more pressure as business expanded and with it, demand on the IT system grew. Then, one day, as a reward for reaching targets, his boss and a director on the board, Harvey Waterman, took the whole team out for a night at the casino. Strange as it might seem, Ethan had never been in a casino before and, apart from the gambling tables, he was struck by the amount of technology and cameras in the place. The bank sponsored a meal there, in a special dining room that the casino hired out to corporates. It was a fantastic meal, and afterwards, the bank gave each staff member a £100 voucher to try their luck in the casino. It seemed a bit unethical to Ethan as he had always viewed gambling as a bit shady and now here was the bank endorsing it – no, embracing it. Later, he compared it to the dealing rooms at the bank: it was also betting on the future values of stocks. Even the most complicated trades ultimately came down to a bet on whether the future value of the company stocks would go up or down.

He quite enjoyed the gambling night even though he eventually lost the £100 and he chose not to buy more chips with his own money. Instead, he just watched other colleagues lose their £100 in chips at the roulette tables or the card tables and then go on to lose a further £200 or £300 just to have a chance of winning more.

"Idiots," he thought, "It's a loser's game. Everyone knows that the house always wins."

But he understood that the possibility of winning a lot of money was only one of the reasons why all the people gathered around the tables in the gambling rooms. They were also here for the thrill, the sheer pleasure of all that money on the spin of a roulette wheel, which, if it landed on red, could either result in their winnings being doubled, or, in the more usual outcome, making them a lot poorer.

But soon he learnt the joy of gambling, the thrill of it, and how addictive it was – waiting for the ball or the cards to fall and not knowing if he had won a fortune or lost it, and not caring about that. The money didn't count really; it was just the feeling. Soon he was addicted, just small stakes at first, but addicted, never the less.

There was a casino close to his house, perhaps ten minutes away at Cromwell Road in South Kensington, so sometimes on the way home from work, he would get off the tube at South Kensington station and walk around to the casino instead of going home. They always had a great welcome for him. Why wouldn't they? And when he wanted a little variety, he had also found a host of underground, unlicensed casinos. Somehow the fact they were illegal added to the excitement.

He would text Rachel to say he was working late. How was she to know otherwise? Anyway, he had a standing arrangement with Bill, whereby if Rachel rang the office looking for him, he would say that Ethan had just stepped out for a few minutes and would be back soon. Then Bill would text Ethan, and he would call her at a suitable time. If Rachel rang his mobile, he just rejected the call and sent her a standard text to say he was in a meeting, and that he would call back when he could.

Back in the casino, Blackjack was his poison of choice. Three or four hours of it after a hard day at the office and then he would be ready for home. By the time he arrived home, Rachel would have gone to bed. When he started doing this first he made the mistake of coming home after two hours. Perhaps it was guilt. Rachel would still be up, very annoyed and ready for a fight. Soon he found that if she had gone to bed, and she needed to go to bed early because sometimes she had to get up in the middle of the night if Katy was crying, then no rows would happen. In the morning, it would be a sullen silence that he could handle much better than constant fighting. Also, often he had to get up so early the next morning he would not even have to deal with the sullen silence; she would be still asleep when he left. Sometimes this could happen for three or four days in a row. Then, exhausted from lack of sleep, he would just crash out on Saturday and Sunday morning.

Anyway, he knew Rachel hated the fighting as much as he did. And she thought the he was working late to advance his career, which would benefit her and Katy. She never noticed the amount of money coming in or mostly going out on gambling because they were relatively well off, and she rarely checked the accounts. After a while, Ethan opened up another bank account, a gambling bank account, not to hide his winnings (because that rarely happened), but to hide the constant transactions and also after a while the pretty scary amounts of money moving around the accounts. He diverted some of his pay checks into this account, so if Rachel ever looked at the statements, she would not spot the tell-tale signs of a gambling habit.

Soon, gambling became second nature to him. It was part of his routine, engrained in his everyday life, an almost normal part of it. He never really grasped how much money was dripping away, and how high his debt was growing. The casinos had their claws into him – he might as well have been a junky, dangling on a dealer's line, waiting for his next hit, distraught should anything get in his way. And things did occasionally get in his way. Sometimes he would give in to Rachel's request for a night out, get a babysitter and go for a meal. No matter how delicious the food was, or how scintillating the conversation, there was always that nagging feeling that he was somehow missing out. Soon it was the only thing that meant anything to him.

Then one day he discovered online gambling. The idea had never occurred to him before, even though he was constantly at the casino.

One evening after work, while Bill was showing him a new app on his iPhone, Ethan noticed some casino and betting apps alongside it. He did not ask Bill about them because he was ashamed about his gambling habit and certainly did not feel like sharing that information with his colleague even if he was a friend too.

Instead, he did a little research to find the best gambling apps. Many offered a free bonus to get started, knowing of course that they would get it back pretty soon.

It was an entirely new world to him. The actual casinos had offered a physical destination, a place to go after work where he could disappear and become a different person, live a different life. But the online casino apps were constantly there, 24/7, nudging him throughout the day to remind him of their pleasures. Not that he needed reminding; he had embraced them wholeheartedly. He had immersed himself or rather surrendered to them. Now it felt like every waking moment – a break from work, a trip to the loo, or lunchtime – was an opportunity for a gamble or two. And he could not wait to see the results of his previous bets.

He began to expand his repertoire. In the physical casinos, he played poker and roulette, but online he was betting on horses, football matches and other sporting events he knew nothing about – some he had not even heard of, but had somehow deemed himself an expert when betting on their outcomes.

It seemed incredible to him that he had spent all his working life in computer technology and yet had been unaware of this hidden subculture of online gambling. It was a source of joy and pain, a hitherto undiscovered life, exciting because it was ever present when he wanted it to be: the promise of riches or ruin.

It was a glorious time, the best of times, the worst of times, and he was entirely consumed.

December 2014

At the real casinos, Ethan was always conscious of his losses; every time he looked at his bank account or withdrew cash to pay for chips, he was reminded of the money he was spending. But when he began gambling online, mostly on his phone and sometimes on his PC, at home or work, all the money was handled virtually. He became disconnected from his losses to a degree. He could certainly see his account balances going down, but it felt much less relevant. Debt built up without his realising it.

Then one day, after a hard week of losses, he looked at all his bank statements and found himself terrified: he had lost £35,000 over a period of about six months. How could that be? He thought for a while but then his focus changed to the matter of hiding that loss from Rachel. More importantly, how was he going to get more money so he could continue? There was no thought of stopping. He needed gambling. He had to do it, at all costs. How else would he be able to live his life from day to day? It would just be too unbearable without the comforting thoughts of the thrill of betting to look forward to every evening. He deserved it. He worked hard, and he was entitled to spend his hard earned money as he pleased.

He just had to find a way to get some extra cash. Just until this losing streak was over. Then he could pay it all back.

As the gambling obsession grew, the weeks blurred into months, and nothing else mattered – not work, Rachel, Katy, or home life in general. Nothing mattered, except the thought of the next hit and the high of a bet placed. This he craved with every fibre of his being, and he became blind to everything else.

At work, his dedication and former attention to detail fell, and it showed. Harvey Waterman, his boss, knew there was something wrong, but he could not put his finger on it. "Perhaps it's just a temporary lull in his work," he thought. But he was annoyed that the IT director was not in control of his department and that things were slipping. Things slipping meant downtime and downtime meant less money – the bottom line and all that Waterman cared about.

Bill had noticed it too. The problem was hard to define. But Ethan's determination to succeed seemed to have waned. He was deferring and delegating more work, in itself not a bad thing, but he appeared to be doing nothing with the extra time created by this. Perhaps he had some personal problems. Bill had his suspicions of what the problem might be, but he did not want to interfere, and anyway he did not mind as such; after all, he had learned an awful lot from Ethan. He reported directly to him while managing the team. However, as time went by, Ethan was becoming less crucial to the department. While once he had been its central pivot, there to solve any problems that may arise, now it seemed that Bill was taking over the reins to a certain degree.

When Bill decided to sell his car to raise money to put a deposit on an apartment he wanted to buy, Ethan saw an opportunity. He had often chatted about selling it with Ethan, and shortly after he sold it for £15,000, they went for drinks after work. When they had had a few, Ethan broached the subject.

"Bill, I've run into a little cash-flow problem this month. It's not a big issue, but I've had a lot of unexpected expenses recently. My health insurance didn't cover all of Katy's treatment when she was in hospital last year, and now a big £10,000 invoice has come in."

Bill nodded and listened, guessing where this was going.

"I have 5k readily available, but I need to find another 5k in the next week, just for a few weeks."

"I could lend you the 5k if you like. But you'd have to pay me back by the end of the month."

"You're a life saver". Ethan patted him on the shoulder. "That would be great. I just need it for a couple of weeks. You'll have it back by the end of the month."

"Okay, no problem, I'll transfer it to you tomorrow."

"Now it's my round, what are you having?"

The money was transferred the next day. Ethan knew that would keep him going for a few weeks, maybe longer if he could just beat this losing streak.

That evening he splurged on the betting. He did his usual online bets, and then he planned a big night at the casino. He'd have enough to bluff better now, so he would be bound to come out on top tonight and once the losing sequence had been broken he could repay Bill and all would be well.

He made a mental note to consider all the other people who he could borrow from, just in case he needed it in the future.

The day came when Ethan had used up all the loans he could get from friends. At that stage, his credit cards were no longer working, having been maxed out well before then. The only conversation he had with the credit card company now was a regular weekly call from them to pressurise him to start repaying the debt.

He did not want to get money from a loan shark as he knew their reputation when repayments were delayed. But he was desperate for a bet. He convinced himself that it would only be for a short time, and as soon as he won he would pay them back and then he would be okay.

It started with a visit to a pub in Lewisham. The barman gave him a number to call and he arranged to meet the guy around the corner in a café on a side street. Modern day loan sharks had moved on with new technology. The person he met was not at all what he expected – a twenty-something young woman with hard features who, though not exactly menacing herself, gave the impression that she had associates who would have little or no hesitation in inflicting the most severe pain on him should he fall behind on repayments. She took a small laptop out of her bag and got some details from him, including his phone number and a photo of his driving licence.

He was looking for £10,000 for two weeks.

"That will cost you 15k to repay the loan," she said.

He was stunned at the interest rate being charged.

"And if there is any delay in repaying, there are penalties," she continued.

As she looked up at him, her hair fell back from her face. It was then he noticed a long hairline scar from the side of her nose, passing the edge of her mouth, down to her chin. She did not have to elaborate on the penalties involved.

"So are you taking the loan?"

He looked at her for a moment. "You'll get it back on time," he said.

She said nothing, just reached into her bag and took out a bubble-wrapped padded envelope, the type used to send delicate items through the post. She put it on the table in from of him.

"It's all there, but don't count it here." She looked at him intensely again. "This place, two weeks' time, full repayment, okay? Call me when you're here and I'll come and get it. Don't make me come looking for you."

And that was it. She put the laptop back in her bag and walked off, leaving him sitting with his coffee and an envelope containing £10,000. His heart was beating fast, from the encounter but also because he was now back in the game. Before he left, he looked inside the bag. It was stuffed with wads of used £20 and £50 notes.

Back in the pub, he went straight to the bathroom, sat down in a stall and counted it out, note by note. It was all there. He was all set for his next hit.

CHAPTER ELEVEN

Grieving

Friday, 24th July 2015. Wandsworth, London.

08:30

Ethan lay in bed, staring at the ceiling. Ben's ceiling – a friend of his who lived close to Putney Bridge in Wandsworth, who had insisted he stay with him the night after the murder because Ethan's house was locked down as a crime scene. He had tossed and turned all that night, only managing to get to sleep just before dawn and now here he was awake again already. He was exhausted and shell-shocked. Just when things were going reasonably well for him, to suddenly have his world ripped apart, leaving him with nothing to live for. Well, maybe not nothing. He still had Katy. His little girl. But that was all he had left of Rachel.

His phone on the bedside locker vibrated suddenly. He picked up.

"Hello?"

"Mr Harris, it's DCI Scott here."

"Yeah."

"Are you okay?"

"Eh – yeah."

"Just letting you know that our forensic officers have finished at your house, and it's clear to go home, whenever suits you."

"Right. Thanks."

"We'll need to talk to you of course. Possibly several times over the next few days."

"Okay."

"We'll be in touch."

Ethan hung up, set the phone to 'do not disturb' and tried to go back to sleep. But how would he ever sleep again? His life had been hacked in two. There was nothing left for him, at least nothing that had any meaning. Unable to sleep, he stared at the ceiling again while another wave of emotion came over him. He pulled the duvet over himself as he began to shake and cry.

Eventually, he fell back asleep, for perhaps another hour, before waking to hear movement in another part of the house. Ben was getting up. Ethan listened to these noises until, at about 09:00 Ben slowly opened the door of the bedroom and put his head around the door.

"You're awake. We're going out now, but you stay in bed as long as you like. We'll be back later."

Ethan glanced at him. "Okay, thanks."

Later, struggling to get out of bed he noticed there were nine missed calls on his phone. Everyone was looking for him, but he just wanted to curl up and disappear.

A shower helped. But he was still in a kind of a daze, operating in auto mode, not thinking, just doing. The longer he could avoid thinking, the better.

On the radio, someone was describing the murder. He turned it off. He did not want to hear gory details no doubt exaggerated by the press just to make a good story. His life was not a show. It occurred to him that he might be accosted by the paparazzi and have to give an interview. The thought filled him with dread.

Then the questions started. Why did it happen? How did it happen? Who did it? They piled up thick and fast in his mind. He took up a blank page from the printer in the corner and started to write furiously as if the paper was at fault. He just had to get the thoughts onto paper to free his mind.

After a few minutes he stopped. Little Katy. Ignoring the list of missed calls, he phoned Julia. He had never really liked her, or rather she had never really liked him. On the surface, she was okay and pleasant to him, but he had always detected an undercurrent of distrust from her. He suspected she did not think he was good enough for her daughter; she never said that to him, not in so many words, but the message had been well and truly received.

The call rang out, and it went to her voicemail.

"Julia," he said. "It's Ethan here. How is Katy today? Give me a call when you get a moment, thanks."

Only then did he start looking through the missed calls. His boss, Harvey Waterman, had rung twice.

"Ethan, it's Harvey here, we're so sorry to hear of the tragedy; you have our deepest sympathy. Let me know if I can help with anything."

And then a few minutes later: "Ethan, Harvey here again, sorry about this but Bill is missing some vital information. When you get a moment could you ring him? Thanks."

The second message was more like the Waterman he knew: cold, unemotional, direct. The first one had been so out of character; it sounded false. He was the guy who did not care about anyone or anything except the precious bank. Why would he care about anything in Ethan's life? It was only a show for the open plan office, so they could hear him express his condolences. The second call was clearly made from Waterman's office. The man did not give a shit about him; he just wanted to make sure everything was running smoothly at the bank.

Then there was a message from DCI Scott:

"Ethan, we're going to need a lot more information and soon. Sorry about this. I know you are grieving the loss of your wife. But it's crucial to get vital information early on, to help the investigation. Call me when you can and we can arrange a time a place to discuss it. Once again, I'm so sorry for your loss."

Julia had called, sobbing into the phone as she spoke: "Hi Ethan, we're devastated as I know you are. Katy is missing her mum so much, she is just crying all the time.

We're going down to the house in Kent. We're taking her with us. Talk later." She and her ex-husband David had bought a second house in Brighton-Hove about fifty miles south of London when they were still married. When they divorced, she got that house as part of the settlement.

Three reporters had called. One left this message: "Mr Harris, my name is John Shepard, a freelance crime reporter, I'm so sorry to hear about your wife. I'd like to have a chat with you about the murder. I know this is a difficult time for you. Perhaps I could come by at a suitable time for just a ten-minute chat?"

Then there had been two anonymous callers. How did they get his number? The first one left no message. There was just someone breathing heavily followed by silence. The second one did leave a message: "Harris, you bastard, I'll bet you did it, I'll see you at the funeral."

"Who the hell was that?" wondered Ethan. He did not recognise the voice.

The funeral. He had not given it a moment's thought, but from then on it fully occupied his mind.

CHAPTER TWELVE

The Investigation Begins

24th July, 2015. Kensington Police Station.

14:30

DCI Scott grabbed a coffee from the canteen and brought it back to his desk. He needed to prepare for the murder investigation team meeting, which he had arranged for 15:30. An hour later he gathered his papers and walked over to the temporary incident room, which had been set up in a small office, off the main open-plan area. Jones had put up some boards and posted some of the critical information that they had gathered so far: a map of the area, photos of the deceased and seriously injured person, a rough timeline of events and photos of the possible suspects.

Detective Alan Coulson, a tall, thin 39-year-old who had a background in forensics came in holding his coffee and a bundle of papers in his hand as he had compiled a summary of the progress made by the back-office forensics team. He was followed by Superintendent Foster and then Detective Lucy Clark, a small, plump woman, 35 years old.

With the team assembled, DCI Scott started the meeting. They sat around a large desk that was being used as table and Scott stood up.

"Okay, here's what we've got so far on the Onslow Square murder: two victims, one dead and one in a coma in intensive care. We need someone on duty at the hospital. Both victims were shot in the head at close range."

"Do we know what the weapon was?" asked Detective Lucy Clarke.

"It seems to have been a small calibre pistol with a silencer," said Scott. "No direct witnesses so far, but next door neighbours did not hear any gunshots. And, as far as we can determine, there were three shots. It looks like a professional killing from what we can see, but the forensic reports should help us confirm that."

He turned to Detective Alan Coulson.

"Do we have any update from forensics?"

Coulson opened the paper file he had brought with him. "I contacted them this morning. They're working on this case, but with two other murders in north London, they're flat out. They said that fingerprint evidence so far had turned up nothing – the unidentified victim was wearing gloves and apparently so was the killer who shot him and Rachel Harris. The fingerprints they took from the injured victim have been run through the system with no match, but they noticed a Celtic design tattoo on his arm, so, in case he's Irish, they've contacted the Irish police force for possible identification. Also, they're looking at biometrics and social media facial recognition."

"Anything else?"

"Forensics have identified three bullets. Two are lodged in Rachel Harris's head, so they'll only be recovered at the autopsy. The other one was found in the hallway, having passed through the unidentified victim. The initial ballistic report on that bullet says it was fired from a 9mm pistol, but they're continuing work on that. They also need to confirm if all three shots were fired by the same gun. Finally, three blood samples have been identified – one from each of the victims and a third, unidentified one. This may have come from someone living in the house, though it was a fresh sample. It was found in an animal paw print both upstairs and in the hallway. Probably the prints were caused by a family cat."

"Thanks Coulson. Keep in contact with forensics and let me know when there are any further updates."

Coulson nodded.

"We need the updates on DNA and fibres," continued Scott. "It would be helpful if they could supply us with copies of some of the photographs they've taken at the scene. We also need to start looking at phone records and security camera recordings. Clarke, can you check those?"

"Yes I thought you'd be needing that, so I've already got some details on the cameras. There are two cameras on the street – one at either end of Onslow Square South. There's another one just around the corner on the other side of the road at St Paul's church. Even God needs security these days". She grinned. That raised a laugh.

"There are recordings available from all three cameras for the time when the murder occurred, but I haven't had a chance to look at them yet," continued Clarke. "I talked to Zak Turner, the data analyst in forensics; we're coordinating our activities on this case."

"Good work Clarke, we'll need phone records too, but we'll come to that in a minute."

Superintendent Foster stood up. "Guys, I just came in here to get a handle on how this case is progressing. It seems like it's moving ahead well. I have had some enquiries from press contacts about a press conference."

DCI Scott looked at him. He hated press conferences and always put them off for as long as possible. Foster knew that. Clearly he thought a little encouragement was necessary.

"I'll be arranging a press conference shortly," said Scott.

Foster smiled at him as he left the room to return to his ivory tower on the third floor.

"So, moving on, the witness and suspects," continued Scott. "There are no known witnesses so far, except perhaps the unidentified victim in a coma. A few neighbours saw what happened before and afterwards. Jones and I have already interviewed some of them."

Jones reached for his iPhone and notebook.

"We don't need that information just yet, Jones. When you've compiled it and interviewed anyone else who was close to the scene, we'll look at it all then." Jones nodded.

"So that brings us to the suspects. Our prime suspect is an unknown professional killer. Assuming that this is correct then we need to find out who hired this killer and why. As usual, the surviving partner is a possible suspect. I have interviewed him, and although he appears entirely innocent, Jones and I both got the feeling that he was lying in some areas. So we're treating him as a possible suspect for now. We need his phone and financial records and his email accounts."

"Should we get a warrant to seize computers and phones from the house and his office?" asked Jones.

"Yes, we need to get on that right away, before anything is covered up."

"Right. I'll talk to Foster and the DA and arrange it later this morning. This guy has some secrets, and we need to find them."

DCI Scott stood.

"Okay, that's it for now. You know what you need to do. Contact me immediately if anything unusual turns up. Otherwise, we'll have another meeting in a day or two. I'm going to call a press conference for later today."

He turned back to Jones. "Can you help with the press conference organisation and I'll write the statement? To keep them off our backs."

"Sure".

"Okay, thanks everyone. Oh wait just a second. One last thing. Clarke, can you ask Sergeant Carter to arrange a 24-hour watch on the 'John Doe' who is still in a coma at the hospital?"

"I'll get on that. As far as I know there's an officer there now, but a 24-hour watch hasn't been set up yet."

"Thanks. We also need a camera surveillance to be set up on the house in Onslow Square. If anyone approaches the house, I want to know about it."

CHAPTER THIRTEEN

Press Conference

24th July, 2015. Kensington Police Station.

17:30

When DCI Scott and DI Jones arrived in the conference room, it was about half full – 15 or 20 people, most of them news reporters, a couple of two-man TV crews and some radio reporters. DCI Scott stood, cleared his throat. The hum of conversation ceased, and the room went quiet.

"A murder and a near-fatal shooting took place in a private house on Onslow Square, SW7, between eight and ten am yesterday morning, 23rd July 2015. It was not a domestic disagreement, and it appears that the victims were not related. However, there is no sign of forced entry, so the perpetrator either had a key or was let in by one of the two victims. Nothing seems to have been stolen from the property. Rachel Harris, a 45-year-old Caucasian woman who appears to have been a native of London, was shot dead on the scene. She is survived by her husband Ethan and two-year-old baby daughter Katy. He was not home at the time of the murder. The autopsy will be completed soon, and this may reveal further information pertinent to the case."

He paused for a moment, then continued.

"We are currently investigating the murder and are following a number of leads. However, no one has been arrested yet. The victim of the near-fatal shooting is a man, Caucasian, mid-twenties. He is currently unidentified; however, we are following some definite lines of enquiry on this and expect to have his identity shortly. He has been in a coma since the incident."

Scott sat down.

"We can now take a limited number of questions," said DI Jones.

First up was the news reporter who had tried to enter the house the previous day.

"John Shepard, freelance journalist. DCI Scott, there are rumours that this was a drug-related killing. Can you confirm or deny it?"

DCI Scott's mouth curled upwards as he glanced at DI Jones. "So far in our investigation we have had no indication that this was a drug-related killing, despite all your Facebook or other social media-based fabricated sources," he answered.

Shepard blushed and sat down and another journalist spoke up.

"Alex Trent, Independent TV News. What lines of enquiry are you following concerning this murder? Do you have any suspects yet?"

"Although the forensics team have finished at the house, they are still processing the information gathered. The results from this will inform this investigation and how we proceed."

"So you have no suspects yet."

"No," lied Scott. He did not want to reveal that Ethan was a possible suspect as he might destroy some evidence before the full search warrant had been issued to seize all computers, phones and related equipment at the house.

"What is the age, ethnicity and general description of the unidentified victim?" continued the journalist.

Scott turned to Jones, who held up two large photographs of the victims.

"We've included these photos and other related information in the press kit."

The conference continued for another ten minutes; then DCI Scott wrapped things up. On his way back to his office, he passed Foster.

"Nice work, Scott, especially debunking that social media rumour."

Scott smiled.

"Thanks. Lucky I have eagle-eyed Jones to cover my back. He spotted it on Facebook earlier." He nodded at Jones who was just coming up the stairs behind them.

"All the same," continued Foster, "a deeper trawl through social media sites might be beneficial in discovering other background information, especially if this Ethan Harris guy was active there."

"Certainly. We'll include that in the investigation," replied Scott, not mentioning that it would be low down on his list of areas. He preferred the more traditional approach; let Jones deal with the technology.

CHAPTER FOURTEEN

East Berlin

1986

Petra Meyer was sixteen in 1986 and living in East Berlin with her mother Zoe and her father Gerhard in what was considered to be relative luxury – a large two-bedroom apartment on the fourth floor of a building on a street off FrederichStrasse. The building was modern and had all the latest luxuries, like a lift that worked most of the time and soundproofed walls, which kept out a lot of their neighbours' noise. It also had a beautiful view over rooftops to the park. Petra's father was a member of the Communist party. He was also a scientist. At that time, he was working on a secret project jointly funded by the HVA and the Stasi (the foreign and internal intelligence services). Her mother worked for the state-run television service.

They had a comfortable life. They could use the exclusive shops reserved for the elite. These special shops, although poorly stocked in comparison to the shops in West Berlin, had a variety of goods, and the shelves were always half-full, in stark contrast to the regular stores used by the majority of comrades living in nearby neighbourhoods.

Petra was aware of how privileged she was, especially as one of her best friends, Nadine Richter, lived or rather endured a much more frugal lifestyle. They had been friends ever since they met in school. However, when Petra's father took up his new Stasi position and the family had moved to a new apartment, she had had to move to a new, closer school. It was also a more exclusive one. But Petra longed for the company of her friends at her old school, particularly Nadine.

She and Nadine were both radicals. At that typical age of rebellion – adolescence – together they rejected everything about the Communist party and the lifestyle that went with it in East Berlin. They longed to be in the West where they imagined they would be free to think and do as they pleased and have a better lifestyle. Their conversation often turned to people who had managed to escape over the wall and into the freedom of the West. They listened to western music; they aped Western fashions and ignored the disapproval of their parents who, they believed, probably secretly felt the same as they did, but were afraid not to tow the party line. This was more the case for Petra than Nadine, whose parents worked in a printing company; after all, Petra's father was working for the Stasi. In fact, Nadine's father had often spoken out against the surveillance of the Stasi when Petra was at their house. But every time, Nadine's mother would shush him and tell him to mind what he was saying in case any of their neighbours were listening and might report him. He did not care. He said what he believed in and gained a lot of respect from the rebellious girls for doing so.

Then one day the Richters simply disappeared. Petra called to see Nadine, and there was no answer at her apartment. She stayed a while, assuming that they had gone out to buy whatever was available on the shelves of the local shops and that they would return soon. But they never did. After waiting around for an hour or so, she was about to leave when a neighbour opened her door and asked if she could help. When she said she was looking for Nadine, the neighbour's expression turned to one of fear. She beckoned Petra to come with her, out into the street. Even when they were there, she kept looking around checking that no one was looking or could hear them. Then she whispered to her that Nadine's father and mother had been taken into custody by the Stasi. Someone had reported that they were spreading anti-Communist ideas, and they had been arrested and brought to the Stasi prison for interrogation and undoubtedly a long stay. Nadine had been sent to a foster home, to a family who were loyal to the party and the state.

"Where?" asked Nadine.

The old woman shook her head. "I don't know," she said.

And that was it. Petra never saw Nadine again. She tried to contact her through Nadine's old school, but they just said she had moved and that they had no further information.

That was when Petra made up her mind that as soon as she finished school she was going to leave East Germany and make a break for the West over the wall. She was fearful when she heard of so many people having been either killed or captured and sent to one of the Stasi prisons when trying to cross it. From what she had heard about those prisons, she was not sure which would be the worse fate.

To her parents' dismay, their once top-of-the-class girl lost all interest in school. She fought with her parents, particularly her father, who she blamed for working for an evil regime. Desperately her parents tried to calm her and to keep her quiet, in case anyone else might hear her say such things. Even though they were living as a privileged family and Gerhard was working for the Stasi, they feared that they too could have a fate similar to the Richter family, just by having an out of control daughter.

Then in 1987, Gerhard announced that he would be attending a conference hosted by a university in London and that he had managed to get a special visa to allow the whole family to travel to London for a week. Petra was ecstatic. She could not believe she was managing to get out of East Germany, even if it was only for a week. Her mother was more apprehensive about the trip as she knew her daughter could plan to "go missing" in London and that they might never see her again. When she raised this with Gerhard, he brushed her fears aside – there would be no problem, he said. He would make sure she was kept under a watchful eye. Anyway, where would she go? They knew no one outside East Germany, and she had no money to go anywhere. They began planning for the trip, which was about a month away.

That month passed quickly; soon the family found themselves travelling by bus through Checkpoint Charlie into West Berlin, en route to the airport where they would fly to London. Once they were through the checkpoint, Petra was amazed by how different things were in the FDR (Federal Democratic Republic of Germany). It felt like going from winter to spring, from black and white to colour. They had time for a quick walk around the streets of West Berlin – it was like entering another world, a richer, brighter one. The shops were full of products she had never seen before. Even though she knew the shelves in the shops would be full, it was still a surprise to see them. And the shops seemed so bright.

But what surprised her the most was the amount of advertising. The posters seemed to everywhere – on billboards, bus shelters. The sheer volume and impact of them left a lasting impression on her that day and in many ways influenced her choice to become a graphic designer later on.

Then they were back on the bus and off to the airport. Her amazement only increased when, hours later they arrived at Heathrow airport. There was so much to see and buy though, of course, she had no money to buy anything. Her father had exchanged some currency for English pounds at the airport, and he was surprised how expensive everything was. He wondered if he would have enough money for the trip, even though the flight and hotel costs were being paid for by work.

That night, Petra lay on her bed, listening to the low, inaudible mumble of her parents talking to each other in their room. She was thinking how wonderful it was to be in London, if only for a short time.

The next day, while her father was at the conference, she and Zoe went on a tour of the city – an art gallery, the Tower of London, some restaurants and shopping. She was both enthralled and scared. Back home was safe, secure and predictable. Here it was noisy, colourful, exciting, random and possibly dangerous, and she loved it.

The following night came and again, she found herself listening to the sound of her parents talking in their room. This time though, something seemed different. There was a change in how they were speaking. The mumbling came more frequently. It was louder. She got a glass from the bathroom and pressed it against the wall, but even with her ear right up to it, she could not make out anything they were saying. Twice the phone rang and her father spoke to someone. Then she heard the door of her parent's room click shut.

Out in the corridor, she followed her father at a safe distance down to the lobby. She watched as he walked up to a group of men in suits and began to speak to them.

Petra ran back to her mother.

"Who is dad talking to downstairs?"

"No one. Just some people from the conference. What were you doing down there anyway? You should be in bed asleep."

Lying in bed, Petra listened for the sound of her father returning until she drifted off to sleep. When she woke, her mother was shaking her shoulder, telling her to wake, that they were going on a trip. She should pack everything, her mother was saying. They would not be returning to the hotel.

"A trip? Where?"

She got no reply.

CHAPTER FIFTEEN

Birthday Surprise

January, 2015. Onslow Square, Kensington.

The two weeks following Ethan's meeting with the loan shark went by faster than he thought they would. It had not taken long for all the money to be spent. He had placed a big bet, on the basis of a tip on a 'sure thing' at a horse race, with odds of ten to one. But the horse fell at the last fence, and with him fell £5,000. After that, Ethan had used the rest more sparingly, betting on online poker games and also at the casino card tables. But although he made an early win of £2,000, that was quickly swallowed up, along with another £4,000 over the next few days. It was all happening so fast, almost in a blur. It was scary to see that amount of money disappear almost as quickly as it had appeared, but that was also part of the thrill – a ride into the unknown with the possibility of winning or losing.

Finally, he was down to £1,000, which he used very sparingly, so it lasted a little longer. Inevitably though, he lost that too.

Then he moved to what was previously unthinkable – the savings account he and Rachel had set up for Katy's future. They had started it out with £5,000, and it now stood at £12,000. He knew Rachel would not be checking this and, as always, he hoped only to have to borrow a little for a short while. He withdrew £5,000 and with it, soon made another £6,000. He was on a roll now – should he put the borrowed £5,000 back and just use the £6,000 winnings? Of course not, it was a roll. He wanted – no, he needed – to make a big killing.

But it never happened.

That was how he found himself three days before the repayment was due with all the money gone – the loan shark money and the savings account money. He had three days to come up with £15,000 or else face a lot of pain. The image of that girl's hard face with the scar from her nose to her chin was what kept him awake for the next few nights. He stayed away from the gambling for a little while. He knew he needed a hit but now it also sickened him. He was so conflicted; he craved it, and yet he despised it. What to do?

He and Rachel did have other savings accounts. The problem was, raiding them would mean Rachel would find out about his little habit. Could he sell something? A watch maybe or perhaps a piece of Rachel's jewellery, a piece that she didn't wear very often? Maybe. The time was getting closer; it was less than 24 hours to make that repayment. He was growing more agitated and desperate by the hour. It felt worse than needing a betting hit. The fear of the pain drove him on in the search for the money he needed.

He could not work that afternoon; it was just too stressful. He told Bill that he had a doctor's appointment in the afternoon, and that he would work the rest of the day from home. After all, Bill was well used to Ethan taking time off. As he walked out of the offices at Canary Wharf in a bit of a daze, Ethan looked at his watch. It was three hours to go. His blood pressure was up. His heart had been beating fast all day. Would they accept a part payment? Maybe the pain would be less. No, they would get their pound of flesh if they did not get the money. And his pockets were empty. He sat down on a street bench to think.

There was no way he could raise the money now, and he was so fearful of being beaten up or worse that he decided his best action was to not turn up. The meeting time came and went without any contact, and he breathed a sigh of relief. He deluded himself by thinking that perhaps they were giving him a little extra time.

His heart was still pounding. Although nothing had happened yet, the waiting was just as bad. He could not place a bet because he had no money and anyway he was sick with worry. He decided to go home early for once and surprise Rachel.

When he arrived back at the house, Rachel was talking to a tall, well-built man at the door. She was laughing and smiling. That relieved him a bit, but when he went in and asked her about the guy, her answer sent a wave of fear through his body.

"You know who it was," she answered. "He told me about the surprise you were planning for my birthday."

Damn, he thought. He had forgotten it was her birthday. But who was this guy and how did he know it was her birthday? He smiled, trying to cover up both the fact he had forgotten her birthday and that he did not know anything about any surprise.

"Go on," she smiled, "You've arranged for a limousine to pick us up tonight and bring us out for my birthday dinner. That guy, Jack, such a nice guy, needed to check some details so, as he was passing, he called in. He was so sorry to have ruined the birthday surprise."

Ethan hugged her.

"So where are you bringing me?"

"Well the limousine surprise might be blown, but the dinner location is still a surprise."

"Well, just a little hint then?"

"No, you'll have to wait until eight."

"He said seven-thirty."

"You're right. I was going to arrange it for eight, but then I changed my mind and set it for seven-thirty, so we'd have more time. I just need to make one or two calls before I get ready."

She kissed him before he went into his home office, his quiet haven located on the first floor of the house.

"Don't get sucked into work now," she called after him.

"I won't. In fact, I came home early just to celebrate your birthday."

"You're such a sweetheart sometimes. I wish it was like this all the time. Like it was when we met first."

He walked upstairs to the office and closed the door behind him, before collapsing onto the seat in a cold sweat of terror. Where were they going tonight? Was this the end? Should he just tell Rachel and then plan their escape, leaving everything behind? He needed a drink. He reached into the second drawer in the filing cabinet, took out a half-empty bottle of cognac, poured himself a large glass and gulped it down. The warm tingling glow calmed him a little and allowed him to think. At least, he thought, if they were going to kill us, then they would have done it already.

He went into the bedroom and got ready. At seven-thirty, the limousine arrived and they got in. They sat in silence as the car drove through the streets until it pulled outside the Dorchester Hotel in Piccadilly.

"Your table at the Alain Ducasse restaurant is ready, sir," said the driver.

Rachel was delighted. "Ethan, how wonderful," she said, hugging him. "You're such a dark horse, I never dreamed you'd be bringing me for dinner here, it's one of the best restaurants in London."

Ethan was relieved, even though he knew that dinner for two at this famous three-star Michelin restaurant would cost more than £500. It was a superb meal and for a while he forgot his concerns and just enjoyed the food, the wine, the ambience and the pleasure of relaxing with Rachel, who was in such good form. However, on the last course his fears and worries returned when the maître d' walked over to their table.

"Mrs Harris, there is a phone call for you," he said, handing her a cordless phone.

Rachel looked at Ethan, who shrugged his shoulders. He had no idea what was happening. Rachel took the phone, turning up the volume so Ethan could hear the conversation.

"Mrs Harris?"

"Yes, who is this?"

"You have my deepest sympathy."

"What do you mean by that? Who is this?"

But the caller had hung up. Rachel put the phone down. Ethan began to panic and was starting to sweat.

"I've no idea what's going on. Ethan what is this about?"

He shrugged again and loosened his tie. "I've no idea either. Who was the call from and what did they want?".

"You heard him. It was like you were dead and he was sympathising with me."

"What can it mean? What trouble are you in?"

"I've no idea what it's about," Ethan lied.

They decided to leave. When Ethan called for the bill, the maître d' came over again.

"That's okay sir, it's already been paid," he said.

Rachel looked at Ethan.

"What's going on, Ethan? Now I'm really worried."

He shook his head, and they walked out in total confusion.

The limousine was waiting for them when they got outside. On the way home, they argued, but Ethan insisted he had no idea what was going on.

At home, after Rachel had gone to bed, Ethan got a text from a number he did not recognise.

"Ethan," it read, "I hope you enjoyed your evening. I've added the cost of the night onto your account, which, along with the interest for late payment, is now £25,000. I expect full payment at the same place next week or the next limousine calling will be from the funeral directors."

He felt weak at the knees, then panic. He staggered over to the kitchen sink and began to get sick – violently sick.

CHAPTER SIXTEEN

An Impossible Journey

1987. London.

Outside a hotel, a minibus was waiting for them. Gerhard was sitting at the front with the driver. Petra and Zoe got into in the back.

"So are you going to tell me where we're going?" Petra demanded.

"Petra," said Zoe, "there's something I need to tell you. As you know, your father works on a top secret project for the Stasi, and it was only because of his hard work and dedication that he managed to get us all to go on this trip together."

"Yes, it's such an adventure, it's nothing like I expected. It's even better."

"What if I was to tell you that there was a possibility of staying longer than the week?"

"How long?"

"Permanently."

"How would that be arranged? We're only allowed to be here for one week." Then it dawned on her. "He's defecting, isn't he? I knew there was something up with all those meetings and phone calls over the last few days."

"Yes, we thought about it and talked it out and decided that it was the best thing for all of us."

Petra's heart was thumping now with excitement.

"Won't they want to get him?'

"Who?"

"The Stasi or the HVA. Won't they want to send some of their agents to kill him? Maybe all of us." The idea had only struck her.

"They'll protect us," said her mother.

"But how?"

"You'll see."

"Are we going into hiding?"

"Not really, more like they are going to disguise us, give us new identities."

"New names and passports?"

"Yes, and a lot more." She paused. "It's like we have to actually become our new identities. No one can ever know our real past."

Although Petra was excited by what lay ahead, the thought crossed her mind that taking on new identities and leaving all their past behind was a bit like what she had read about some German Nazis after the Second World War was over. They had just changed their identities and left all the crimes of their former lives behind. She hated that analogy, but she could not get the thought out of her mind. Perhaps her father was leaving some crimes behind?

"So how come you didn't include me in the decision to defect?"

"We had to decide for you, we know what is best."

"But I'm an adult too, and I make my own decisions. You should have consulted me."

Zoe put her hand on Petra's hand to try and calm her, but she pulled it away. Regardless of what country they were going to live in, Zoe knew she was losing her. Later they talked again.

"Will we see more of dad, now that he's no longer working on that Stasi secret project?"

"I don't know," said Zoe. "Perhaps."

The mini bus arrived at a compound. It was a low profile, single storey bunker-style building. And all they could see were soldiers in stone-coloured camouflage uniforms, the kind worn at barracks. That was when she realised that this was a kind of barracks.

Inside the building, it was Spartan and drab, reminding Petra of the some of the places back home. They were brought into a small conference room with two tables, office chairs and some easy chairs. After a few minutes, two men in uniform came in.

"Hello, Mr and Mrs Meyer and Petra. Welcome to Hanson – that's what we call this compound. It's a kind of induction centre where you'll be spending the next few weeks."

Weeks, thought Petra. What will we be doing during that time?

"I know you probably have lots of questions and are wondering what exactly will be happening to you during the next period," he continued. "Hopefully, I can answer most of your questions."

Hours later, the conversation was over. By then Petra felt shell-shocked at the amount of change that they were facing, and she could sense her parents did too. It was much more intense than any of them had imagined. Even for the next three months, every day of their lives would be carefully planned.

First were the debriefing sessions. This was mostly for Gerhard; they hardly saw him during that period. But Petra and Zoe were also debriefed, every little part of their lives discussed, analysed and documented. It was draining and in some ways, it also felt like an interrogation, like they were the enemy who had been captured and were now being forced to give up their secrets. Not that they never thought of them as secrets; It was just their way of life. A life with good and bad but which, for the most part, had been blighted by the insidious and ongoing surveillance. Soon they would be free of all that forever.

By the end of the first few weeks, they moved from talking about their past lives to being told about their future lives – their new identities. It started with their names. Gerhard Meyer was now David Powell. Zoe Meyer was now Julia Powell. Petra Meyer was now Rachel Powell.

They were issued with new passports and David and Julia got new drivers' licences. They would have to learn to drive on the left-hand side of the road. How strange to be driving on the wrong side of the road.

But the most difficult part of it all was forgetting the details of her past life – growing up, her friends, family photos, holidays taken – and replacing them with the fabricated details of her new life. And then there was British popular culture to learn, the language, ways of dressing, what was on TV, pop stars, football teams, other sports and cultural references. There were also elocution lessons every day – listening to the sounds of words, practising them, different pronunciations, different emphases, difference sentence structure. It felt like they were being brainwashed, their old memories erased and replaced with new false memories, a new culture, and new ways of interacting.

It was scary to become someone new. Petra knew they all felt it. Losing your identity, something so fundamental to yourself, and becoming someone new was like a roller coaster ride, something that did not exist in East Germany – it was exciting and scary. They were travelling at high speed, with no control, through a new landscape, with dips and turns and drops; it felt like an impossible journey and yet, somehow, it ended. It had been a mammoth task to get through, but somehow they managed it.

They were moved to their new home in Islington, where they settled in very nicely. Rachel started attending a new school. By then she had an English accent. Her false memories and background were both deeply ingrained. It was like she had always lived there and East Germany was in the distant past. It was a bit more difficult for Julia; she had many more memories to forget than Rachel, and it seemed to take her longer to learn things. She was not allowed to work in television, as she had done in East Germany, because of the risk of someone recognising her; instead, she got a job selling property for an estate agent.

David was given a post at GCHQ, which was based in Cheltenham in south-west England. He travelled there every Monday morning and returned home on Friday evening. Rachel and her mother were already used to not seeing very much of him anyway so this new arrangement worked well. Although Rachel had secretly hoped she would see more of her father in England, she realised that no matter where they were, East Germany or England, he was not really there for either herself or her mother. It suited him to have a family but he was really focused on his job; nothing else seemed to matter.

Each of them had their own life to lead. Six months later, it felt like this was how it had always been, even if, at the back of her mind, Petra had to always remember that she could never discuss their past, or even think of it. If any of them let their guard down, even for a minute, their cover could be blown and their lives would be under threat, no doubt about that.

It was an exciting time for Rachel. She was leading the life she had dreamed of, and often fantasised with Nadine in the past. But Nadine was gone now, and she had long accepted that she would never see her again.

As time passed, she grew more and more distant from her father. He had never had any time for her growing up and now as a young adult, she would never have any time for him. When they were living in East Germany, she always hated that he worked for the Stasi, the oppressors of the common people. Now he was working for GCHQ; that too was a shadowy sort of organisation that she knew little about. Over time, she began to hate the secrecy of it. In fact, that was all she had ever known – her father had replaced once secret organisation in Germany with an equally secret organisation in England.

By the time she was in university, he was completely out of her life. He might as well have been dead because she never saw him, talked to him or even thought of him. And as time passed, her relationship with her mother also began to deteriorate, especially when she moved into an apartment with her friends.

Finally, she was living the life she always wanted to live. But she never forgave her parents for denying her a normal family life. And although the years passed, a desire for revenge never quite went away.

CHAPTER SEVENTEEN

More Loans

February, 2015. Kensington High Street.

Ethan arranged a meeting with his bank manager to get a loan. He used the pretext of some room conversions and the creation of a granny flat. He was looking for £100,000. That would let him pay off the loan shark debt but leave enough to gamble at ease and even take part in larger poker games with the possibility of winning larger amounts. The small fish would be kept out; he would be in with the big boys. It was pro time.

The bank reckoned he posed a low risk (how little they knew) even with his maxed-out credit cards; he had a lot of equity in the house and a good job. They just needed Rachel's signature. That was not a problem – he had already forged her signature without detection for another withdrawal from a joint account. Why would this be any different?

Within two days the money was transferred into his gambling account, and he was ready to rock and roll. But first he had to pay back the loan shark her £25,000. The meeting was not for another three days, enough time to withdraw the cash from the bank without arousing suspicion. Using three different banks, he made five withdrawals of £5,000 each. When he had all the cash, he put it into the same envelope that the original loan came in. It barely fit. That was when it hit home – he had only borrowed £10,000 two and a half weeks previously, and now here he was packing in £25,000 to repay that loan. The bastards. If he could have defaulted on that loan, he would have, but he feared for his life and also for Rachel and Katy.

When the day arrived to pay back the loan, he was not as sick with worry as he had been the first time. This time, he had the money. But he was still feeling nervous – he was carrying around £25,000 in cash after all and they had really scared him the previous week. He wanted out of it – to pay it off and be done with it.

He waited at a terrace table outside the same café. The arranged time came and went with no sign of the loan shark. He looked at his watch. He looked around nervously. The street was empty.

Suddenly there was a strong arm around his neck, and he was thrown to the ground and kicked. He curled up, trying to protect his head with his hands. More kicks to the back and head followed. He felt blood trickle down his neck. All he could hear was the thug breathing heavily from the exertion of working him over. Then the kicking stopped, and he looked up. A huge guy, perhaps six foot six, was towering over him. Beside him, the little hard-faced woman stared down at Ethan, dwarfed by her companion. She had the envelope in her hands.

The big guy opened his trouser zip and pissed all over him.

"I told you not to make me come looking for you," she said. Then she spat on him. The saliva dripped down his face and mingled with the blood already pumping out of a cut on his cheek.

He was wet and sore, but he was afraid to get up in case the beating started again.

"It, it, it's all there," he stammered.

"It better be. We know who you are, where you live, your little family and your lovely house."

He regretted ever having borrowed the money – opening this Pandora's box.

The thug kicked him one last time, this time between the legs. Ethan groaned in agony and rolled over on his side.

A minute or two later he turned back again. They were gone. He dragged himself up onto the chair and looked around. The laneway was empty. He limped into the pub around the corner to clean himself up in the toilet. The barman smiled at the sight of him. No doubt he had seen it so many times before.

Ethan looked in the mirror over the grubby wash-hand basin and saw that he had two cuts on his face and bruising under one eye. His ribs felt sore too and when he pulled up his shirt to investigate he could see that his back and right side were swollen, red and tender, like raw meat.

Back home, Rachel was out. He had managed to clean the wounds and change his clothes before she came back.

"Ethan, are you okay? Oh my God, what happened?"

"I was mugged in a laneway. Two guys jumped on me, beat me and kicked me, looking for my wallet and phone."

She put her arms around him and held him gently. It had been quite some time since he had felt that gentleness. He savoured the moment.

Then she pulled back. She looked at him.

"What is going on? First that incident last week after the meal on my birthday and now this. Are you in some kind of trouble?"

"No, there's no connection. These guys were probably looking for money to buy drugs."

"Where did it happen? Did you go to the police?"

"No, what's the point? There were no witnesses, and it was over in a minute or two."

"But you'll need the police report for the insurance on your phone."

"They didn't get my wallet or my phone. I held on to them and took the beating."

"You could have been seriously injured, or killed."

"I know; it was just an instinctive reaction."

He rested up for a few days before going back to work. By then his face had healed, although while the swelling on his back and side had eased it was still covered in black bruising. The cravings had returned. He needed to get out to bet on something, anything. There was also that big poker competition coming up. It was a pro game and had a £20,000 entry fee with the possibility of winning £500,000.

He opened a premium gambling account at the casino and transferred £50,000 into it. Then he put up the £20,000 for the tournament that was starting the following night. It would run very late, possibly all night. He primed Rachel by letting her know that they were doing a big IT systems upgrade at the bank, and it might be an all-night job. He was so excited that he left work early that evening to prepare.

In the casino, about thirty or forty people had shown up for the tournament, most of them men. He took his place at the table and the game began. Three hours later he had got through the first round. There were only ten players left. He was buzzing from the action. The £500,000 prize was all he could think of. When he won, he could stop gambling for a while, pay off his debts, pay back the £100,000 loan from the bank and still have £250,000 for betting.

That savoured thought was short-lived as the real poker pros – those hardened guys who had paid their dues by years of dedication to the game in endless days and nights of poker – began showing their true form. They sorted him out in less than an hour. He was out, gone, and so was the money – the £20,000 and the dreams of the £500,000.

It was raining heavily now, and the black dog of depression returned to hound him as he made his way home, beaten down with bitterness and shame.

CHAPTER EIGHTEEN

Rachel

New Years' Eve, 1999. Paris.

Ethan was working as a software team leader on a "Year 2000 Bug" project. As December 1999 approached the project was running behind, and there was a lot of pressure to work day and night and weekends to finish on time. He was single and so working over the Christmas period was not that much of a problem; anyhow, they were paying treble the daily rate for doing so. He was based in Paris for the last part of the project and with a tremendous effort by him and his team, they managed to get the project finished, tested and installed by the morning of 31st December 1999, having worked 14 hour days for one whole month and overnight for the last two nights. Exhausted, he went back to the hotel where he was staying to sleep for a few hours and then hopefully go out to join the celebrations later that night.

He arranged to meet his team in a bar close to the Eiffel Tower at 21:00 that evening. After a meal and a few drinks, they planned to watch the spectacular fireworks show promised for the new millennium's arrival. He got into bed at 11:00, setting his alarm for 19:00, to give himself time to get ready and to travel to meet them. He was staying in a different hotel to everyone else, on the other side of the city, as every room had been booked up over the Christmas period.

When his alarm went off, he was so tired that he slept right through it, eventually waking at 22:00. He looked at his Nokia mobile phone: five missed calls and the battery down to about 10%. While he quickly dressed, he tried calling his colleagues but to no avail. By 23:00 he was at the Metro station with his camera and tripod stashed in his backpack. But by the time he reached the bar it was too late – they had come and gone, and had given up waiting for him and trying to reach him. That was how he found himself alone in Paris on New Year's Eve, surrounded by thousands of people enjoying themselves.

He made his way to the Eiffel Tower, hoping to find them there, but there were tens of thousands of people crowded into the area surrounding the Tower. His phone battery was now dead so calling them was not an option. He decided to find a good spot where he could view the firework show and perhaps even set up his tripod so he could take some decent photographs.

At 23:50 he was ready, and so were the crowd of about fifty thousand around him, drinking, singing, shouting and dancing. As the countdown started, there was a stunning fireworks show that seemed to go on for perhaps twenty or thirty minutes. He got some great shots. Then suddenly the crush of the crowd pushed in on top of him. There was panic, as people were being shoved against their will, closer and closer to the barriers. He grabbed his equipment just before he was carried forward on a sea of moving bodies, moving relentlessly towards the barriers. He could hear the cries of those who were being crushed. There was no security, no police support, nothing to stop the motion or help those who had fallen and were being trampled underfoot.

Then he saw her. She looked German or Scandinavian: long blonde hair, slim body and a beautiful face. She had fallen on the ground and people were walking over her. She was calling for help – there was a real possibility of her being seriously injured. He pushed against the crowd, ignoring the protests of those around him, who were being pulled forward. Standing his ground, he helped her to her feet. She had hurt her leg and needed some assistance. Together, they pushed through the crowd, holding on to each other for support. Eventually, about twenty minutes later, they were safe, away from the crowd. They found somewhere to sit down.

Her name was Rachel Powell, he learned. She was on holiday for a few days in Paris. Her home was in Islington, London. She had lost her friends, and so had he, but they had each other for a while. There was an instant attraction between them. They walked back through the streets, laughing and joking, mingling with crowds celebrating with music and beer. It seemed like everywhere was one giant street party. They would have joined in but with her injured leg, she needed to get back to her hotel, which they reached eventually, her leaning on him for support. She was only able to limp slowly. Outside the hotel, she wrote her phone number on a piece of paper, which she gave to him. As he was going home the next day, they arranged to chat on the phone when they were back in London. Then she kissed him, before going inside.

But the phone call never happened because Ethan lost the slip of paper with her number. He searched everywhere in the hotel room, but had to reluctantly conclude that it fell out of his pocket on the way back to his hotel. He rang lots of numbers that were similar to the one wrote down (he remembered half of it) but none was correct. Eventually he had to give up devastated that he had found and lost perhaps the love of his life. He often thought of her after that and made several trips to Islington, where he walked around for hours, hoping he would see her. But he never did.

By chance he had met her in Paris and by chance he had lost her contact details, perhaps forever. Then one day he remembered she was a graphic designer. That set him off on a new search but again to no avail. It just was not to be. Eventually he had to move on, but he always hoped he would meet her again someday.

London, August 2011.

Late on Monday 8th August, 2011, London was burning. It felt like a total social collapse in many areas across the city. The Metropolitan police were overwhelmed with all the rioting and looting in Tottenham, Peckham, Clapham, Croydon; it seemed like it was everywhere.

Young looters, both male and female, in hoodies, tracksuit bottoms and covered faces, were out on the streets after dark (and sometimes before), driven by an urge to steal and destroy. They swept over vast areas of the city like a plague of locusts, destroying everything in their path. Long-established shops, some of which had even survived the London blitz seventy years before, were targeted, looted and burnt out in a trail of fury and destruction. The Met were stretched to breaking point and David Cameron, the prime minister, had been forced to cut short his holiday, and return to deal with the emergency.

Everywhere there were copycat lootings and burnings. It emerged that the apparently random riots were being orchestrated via Blackberry mobile phones. The looters had used Blackberry's encrypted messaging service to communicate without surveillance by the police.

London reeled with a third night of violence. For the ordinary people, it seemed impossible that this was happening in London. Maybe it used to happen in Belfast on a nearly yearly basis around the 12th July 'celebrations', but that was Belfast, and its unfortunate citizens had had to tolerate decades of violence; even in the relatively recent calm, they still expected a rough ride in July. But this was London, centre of the civilised world, a melting pot of cultures.

Yet the disinherited youth, abandoned by the mostly Conservative government to unemployment and boredom, bereft of social justice and morals, driven by anonymous electronic herders, assembled night after night. The locations were decided by a chosen few, to wreak havoc, to vent their fury and fill their pockets and cars with stolen luxury items, destroying livelihoods where they went and leaving behind a trail of broken glass, smoking buildings and ruined lives. A seemingly unstoppable plague had landed on the city.

Raj Patel was restocking the shelves of his off-license wine and beer corner store in Hackney when he heard shouting and glass being smashed outside his shop. Given what had been happening in London over the previous few nights, he knew instantly what was going on. Glancing out the window, he could see a huge crowd of teenagers smashing cars and throwing anything they could get their hands on. He quickly turned off the lights and started to close the metal shutters at the front of the shop.

But he was not fast enough. A shout went up from the crowd and half a dozen guys wearing hoodies and scarves or balaclavas, and carrying clubs and sticks and rocks in their hands ran shouting and roaring towards the shop. He ran inside and locked the door as a hail of stones hit the windows that were only partially covered by the metal shutter. But they jammed wooden sticks in the shutter rails, which stopped it from closing further and then they began to pound the door, roaring for him to open it.

Raj was petrified, as were his friends and neighbours in shops and houses on either side and across the street. Many of them rang the police and eventually some police vans and about ten police in riot gear were dispatched from the nearest station. But by then they were smashing the windows and jeering at Raj, who was still hiding inside.

Something that was not a stone was thrown through the broken window. It took Raj a moment to realise it was a homemade petrol bomb. Almost immediately, a fire started at the front of the store, close to where the bottles of spirits were stacked. Suddenly there was a blast as the bottles of whiskey and vodka shattered. The crowd outside gave a cheer. They broke down the door and piled into the store to steal trays of beer and other bottles of spirits before they were destroyed by the fire.

Though Raj was now bleeding, he stayed at the back of the store hoping they would take what they wanted and spare him. But they quickly found him. He was dragged outside by one of the leaders of the mob who had a cricket bat in his hand. He began to beat Raj. When he collapsed onto the ground the other thugs started to attack him, kicking and beating him senseless on the pathway outside his shop. Only the sirens of the approaching police vans prevented him from being killed. By then, the fire was in full fury in the shop. The looters scattered through the billowing smoke down the street carrying their loot with no police in pursuit. The police had wisely decided to secure the area first before attempting to engage the mob. The fifty or sixty youths fuelled by alcohol and drugs and the high of the rampage and the beating, were best left to themselves for now, until reinforcements arrived. In any case, the only reinforcements were DCI Scott and DI Jones in an unmarked police car, severely damaged from the previous night's riots; all others had been diverted to another riot and looting case in Mile End.

The mob taunted the police for a while, shouting and throwing rocks. Eventually they began to disperse, though not before they had rained down a hail of rocks on the ambulance as it approached. As the medics attended to Raj Patel, DCI Scott and DI Jones began to interview the witnesses and take their statements.

The fire brigade arrived and began to hose down the shop. But it was just a smouldering empty shell.

Rachel Powell's apartment was over a shop next door to Raj Patel's shop. She had moved there after her parents had divorced and had been living there for ten years. After the divorce, her mother Julia had grown dependent on her for emotional support and, as time went on, Rachel had begun to feel increasingly trapped; hence the move. As a graphic designer, she spent a good deal of time working from home.

She also had a secret life, operating as part of a spying operation, handling files that had been stolen from

GCHQ, processing and passing them on to other agents located in Berlin. She was not doing this for the money, although it paid well. Something her father had said a long time ago made her suspect that he had had some involvement with the Stasi arrest of her best friend Nadine and the rest of the Richter family. He worked for the Stasi at that time, although he was in their research area. But during an argument with Rachel he had said that the Richters had confessed after they were arrested. Then, realising what he had said, he had tried to deny it. But from then on, Rachel knew in her heart that he was the enemy and began to plan her revenge.

She needed a cover for this work as she often accessed part of the dark net, which most people would not normally use. So just in case this clandestine work was discovered, she also maintained an online presence as an activist, campaigning for digital privacy. She used anonymous systems like TOR to hide her identity when she published articles and often commented on Google and Facebook's invasion of personal privacy. Her primary focus as an activist, however, was exposing the secret gathering of personal information and surveillance by government intelligence agencies.

Some of her spy-related files were on her MacBook, as well as some data regarding her activism, which was possibly illegal and which she did not want it discovered. So she was seriously concerned about the fire in the shop next door. She had also captured all of the assault and robbery on a security camera outside her apartment. The irony of invading her neighbour's privacy by recording their movements on the streets with her private security video, while still advocating personal internet privacy, was not lost on her, but she justified it to herself that it was there for her protection. The last thing she needed was for the police to be poking around her computers, looking at that video and possibly seeing other stuff she would prefer them not to see. So she gathered her equipment and some essential clothes into a suitcase, and quickly left the apartment by the back door.

As she was leaving she noticed a man standing across the street, in the shadow of a doorway, observing her and the police and the crowd in the distance. He did not look like a reporter or a policeman. So who was he? When she glanced over he quickly withdrew into the shadow. Still feeling as though she was being watched, she walked across the street to confront him, but he set off at a fast pace in the opposite direction.

"Who are you? What are you doing?" she shouted. He did not reply. She decided not to pursue him as the police were just down the street; the last thing she wanted was to involve them. No, she would spend the night in a hotel and figure out what to do later.

DCI Scott was calling at houses, trying to gather evidence from witnesses. He had noted the external camera over Rachel's apartment window and hoped it might have recorded some evidence. But when he called, she was already gone. In any case, soon afterwards he was watching the fire spread to her apartment. Before long, the combination of fire damage and subsequent water damage from the fire brigade's efforts to put out the fire left the flat completely uninhabitable.

Eventually, he and Jones decided to call it a night. It was 01:00 and they had collected as much evidence and as many statements as they could. As Scott surveyed the destroyed shop, a message came through on the police radio that the shop owners at Mile End were joining forces to protect their properties – fighting off the looters. London was fighting back. Too late for this unfortunate shop owner in Hackney though. The last Scott had heard was that he was fighting for his life in hospital.

The case was hopeless, he decided. Even with the countless security cameras that were dotted around the area, the youths had kept their faces carefully covered up and most were unidentifiable. Unless something turned up in the evidence collected that might be of use. Maybe there would be enough to convict just one of these thugs. The thought brought a grim comfort to Scott as he made his way home to his house in Ealing, an area that had been thankfully spared that night.

As he climbed into bed at 02:00, he hoped that he might get at least a few hours of sleep before the madness continued. He glanced up a painting on his wall over the bed – a rare art auction win – that depicted a haven of peace and calm, threatened by an approaching storm. Then he turned out the light and almost instantly fell into a deep sleep.

When Rachel returned to her flat the next day, she was only able to rescue a few of her items. Then she had no choice but to return to the hotel and start a search for a new apartment.

London, September 2011
A month after the riots, Ethan met Rachel again. So much had happened in the meantime that he had long forgotten that chance meeting on the night of the Millennium New Year celebrations. He was working for MitaSimi Bank in Canary Wharf. On his way home one evening, he stopped at a Chinese restaurant near Sloan Square. While he was sitting alone at a table by the window, she walked by outside. He recognised her immediately; she had hardly changed at all, except for a slightly shorter haircut. He stood and waved until she looked back, at first clearly frightened. But then her face changed – she began to laugh. She came inside.

They hugged. The memory of that brief encounter eleven years earlier was instantly unlocked for him by her scent – that same delicate smell he had enjoyed the first time he had kissed her. She was on her way to join some friends, she said. She could only stay a moment. Hours later, they were still talking. They hardly noticed the food.

Not long afterwards, she had moved into his house on Onslow Square.

London, June 2013

Rachel was due to give birth in late May 2013. Both she and Ethan were eagerly awaiting the baby's arrival. But the end of May came and went without anything happening. They were both worried although the doctor assured them that all was well and that it was quite normal for a first birth. But that was exactly it – for a first birth everything was new. It was a journey into the unknown. Ethan continued to go to work early every morning after checking that Rachel was not in labour. There were a number of false starts.

On 5th June 2013, Rachel was as big as a house and ready to pop at any time. The morning papers and all the news reports were full of the Edward Snowden story. He was a former contractor for the NSA and had released a huge cache of files showing that the NSA in the USA and GCHQ in the UK had been spying on everyone, listening in to phone calls, reading emails, viewing everything online. The story fascinated Rachel; Ethan was not as interested, but he was glad it took her mind off the birth.

The next day – 6th June, 2013 – after checking that Rachel was okay, Ethan left for work as usual. At lunchtime she called to say that the baby was well on the way. He left work immediately; by the time he arrived forty minutes later she was packed and ready for the maternity hospital. As they drove through the busy streets, he put some music on to calm her down: Handel's Water Music interrupted only by the occasional moan from Rachel as the contractions increased in frequency. By 13:30

they were at the hospital and by 15:30 Katy was born. A lovely, perfect baby, seven pounds, and cute as a little peach.

Exhausted, Rachel fell fast asleep for a few hours and it was only later that evening that the doctor called back to the ward to discuss something urgent with them. Although baby Katy seemed to be in perfect health they had noticed something unusual in her blood tests and initial indications were that it might be a small cancerous growth. Rachel and Ethan were devastated. First the high of the birth and now the low of the unknown illness. Rachel cried, while Ethan held her close and comforted her. She was physically exhausted from the birth and now mentally exhausted from the diagnosis and the fear of the unknown for their daughter. She fell back into a deep but restless sleep.

It was a hellish few days before they had more information after a series of tests were run by the hospital. By then Rachel was back home, but Katy was still in the hospital, sleeping mostly. The medical team discussed the options with them before recommending they wait a month or so until she was stronger and bigger before they could consider surgery. Until then, they would be keeping a watchful eye on her, waiting for the opportune moment to operate. Her care was transferred to the Royal Marsden Hospital, which was so close to Onslow Square that they could walk between home and hospital, and they took it in turns to keep a vigil beside her. Finally, when she was two months old they were ready to operate.

It was Katy's birth and illness that brought them closer together. Somehow other things began to matter less. Finally, they had a good perspective on what was important to them. And little Katy eventually pulled through the operations. The day she came home with them was one of the happiest days in both of their lives. The family had arrived, finally, at Onslow Square and they were happy, for a while.

For a few months, Katy became the centre of everything. But as time passed, Ethan began to spend the occasional ten hour day at work. Soon, every day was a ten hour day. Rachel was wholly preoccupied with Katy, while Ethan fell away to a distant horizon.

Gradually the old habits crept back in and became the norm again. What had seemed to bring them closer together was now driving them apart.

CHAPTER NINETEEN

Trigger Point

18th July, 2015. Cheltenham.

In GCHQ offices in Cheltenham, Powell and Turner met to discuss progress on the information leak. Turner knew Powell would expect some progress to have been made. But he could not learn about the decision to take out Rachel Harris.

"We've made some progress, Powell. An asset was tasked to hack the bank where the husband works two weeks ago, to cause pressure for the target's husband at work. However, the bank hasn't discovered it yet," said Turner.

"I can't believe that. Incompetent idiots. Do we need to leave something more obvious there?" said Powell.

"I was surprised too – I thought they'd discover it within a few days. But apparently, the target's husband, who is the IT director, is too consumed with his gambling problem to focus on his work."

"So you've found his weakness?"

"He has a major gambling problem and a lot of debt – that's taking all his bandwidth, from both work and his family."

"So we don't need to help it along?"

"No, he's sabotaging his family quite well by himself. We'll keep an eye on it, just in case things change."

"It's ironic, his involvement in gambling. It has a lot of parallels with our business."

"I'm not sure I understand," said Turner.

"Gambling is all about, risk, random chance, control, money, and an undermined result. In many ways that's like our business, although with much greater stakes."

Turner nodded. "Though there's one small difference," he said. "He's a punter, but we're the House."

Powell smiled. "Yes and we control the show, no matter how much the punter thinks he can win."

"We also had his home PC hacked, just to set up a few clues the police can find if we have to take the target out."

"Good, because we may just have to do that."

"Randall has discussed it with some of his MI6 colleagues," said Turner. "He has lined up an external asset who is in north Africa at the moment, but if necessary, he can be tasked to fly in to do the job at short notice. It just needs your authorisation."

"I'm still considering it. Our plan – break up the target's family and hope that her resulting vulnerability leads to her dropping her veil for a moment – may just be too slow. It's also a long shot," said Powell. "Taking her out is cleaner and quicker. The problem is we still have no proof it's her."

"Do we need it?" asked Turner.

"Yes, if this thing unravels."

"If that happens we're all going down."

"Not necessarily. We always have our 'get out of jail free' card, which can be played if we're caught."

"You mean, 'in the interests of national security'?"

"Yes, the Home Office will always protect us; they're just protecting themselves."

"It never fails when something fucks up."

"So, why don't we just go for it then?"

"No, only if there's another leak. I need definite proof before we act."

Powell walked towards the door. Then he turned back to Turner before he left.

"But we need this sorted out as soon as possible."

"I understand," said Turner.

*

Aldgate, London. 18th July 2015.

Rachel was working at her office near Aldgate in East London. She had called her regular child-minder for Katy that morning. It was good to get out of the house and work from her office for a change of environment. But the main reason was that she had received a secret signal online via a small yellow logo on a webpage of an online news site that she read every day. It meant they had work for her in encrypting leaked files from GCHQ and passing them on to her German intelligence agency contacts in Berlin.

Her work as a freelance digital media artist was an excellent screen for her undercover work. She ran a blog to support her business and maintain contact with her hundreds of customers across Europe and the US. She travelled on a regular basis to visit customers, albeit a lot less frequently since Katy was born.

The first thing she had to do was to find the files to be processed. This was a complicated process, involving various locations on the dark web, where she operated anonymously. It was like walking in the countryside at night-time; she could not see much, but once she knew where she was going and did not stray off the path, she was okay, even though there was a lot of dark and scary stuff around her.

Once she had uploaded the files, she divided their contents into smaller files, which she encrypted before embedding them in ordinary images whose appearance remained the same despite their hidden content. Then she posted those images in a number of locations across the net.

She was not one hundred percent sure what was in the files; all she knew was that it was top secret information that came from GCHQ and which was going to the BND in Berlin. When she was finished, she wrote a blog entry, as she normally did. It was about graphic design but had a small blue logo attached. This was the signal to her contacts in Berlin that the files had been processed and were waiting to be picked up.

In that way, she had no contact with those who provided the leaked data or those who downloaded her processed images. She was operating as a disconnected, independent cell. She was well paid for the work, but that was not her motivation, although the money would be useful to ensure Katy had the best education and opportunities in the future.

Sometimes a desire for revenge never goes away.

*

Berlin, 2010
Rachel had not been in Berlin since her family had defected from the Communist party in 1987. Years later, as a fortieth birthday present to herself, she had booked a flight to Berlin Schönefeld Airport. She planned to stay in Berlin for a week. Her memories of her childhood there often felt more like dreams than an actual past. No doubt the three-month induction course following their defection had not helped there. How would it feel to confront her real past? To break open those memories of Petra Meyer? She did not even know if that was possible.

Of course, all had changed in East Berlin since reunification. Rachel tried to get her head around the fact that the place had long been completely westernised. Her past had not only been papered over mentally; as a physical reality it had also become less visible.

She had heard about a few old East Berliners with an 'Ostalgie', or nostalgia, for life there before the wall came down. That was not her motivation. It was turning forty that triggered this desire in her. Something to do with time passing, and a need to revisit her past life.

She booked a hotel near Friedrichstrasse, which had been transformed into an upmarket area, close to the apartment where she and her parents had formerly lived. Initially, when she arrived, she felt like it could be any modern German city. But after walking around for a while she started to see that some of those old communist style apartment blocks were still there, although modernised to a certain degree. What was most surprising to her was that fact that the Wall, once the symbol of oppression in everyone's life in East Germany, was now a national monument, a major tourist attraction; some parts of it were a mile-long open air art gallery. It had all happened within three years of her leaving and now it was a part of cultural history, just like remnants from the Second World War.

Walking those streets, she began to wonder about her best friend from those days – Nadine Richter, whose family had just disappeared one day; her parents were sent to a Stasi prison and Nadine was fostered somewhere.

Back at the hotel, she began to search for her online. It was not as though Nadine would ever have been able to find her, after all, with her changed identity and life in the

UK. As she trawled through social media sites, she began to hope that she could find Nadine easily, while she was still on her trip to Berlin. Then they could meet and talk about old times. If only she had thought of looking her up before the trip and had the meeting already arranged.

And then she did find her, after searching hundreds of profiles on LinkedIn. It was an old photo – Nadine looked about thirty in it, when in fact she would be in her mid-forties. Her job title was hard to understand, some sort of administrator; there wasn't much explanation about it. Nadine's face was more serious now than Rachel's memory of it, but there was something in that slight smile that reminded Rachel of her cheeky grin when she was a teenager. She longed to know more about what had happened all those years since they parted.

They arranged to meet on the second last day of her trip, in a café near Prenzlauer Berg. It was 24 years since she had seen her. She wondered if she would recognise her, even though she'd seen the LinkedIn photo. But it wasn't a problem; as soon as they set eyes on each other, they both smiled. Nadine was heavier and her hair was short and dyed blonde. When they hugged, they both cried for the lost life and friendship. It was their reunification.

"So good to finally meet you again, Nadine."

"And you too, Petra, I wondered if we'd ever meet again. I know you had your name changed to Rachel."

"Yes. All our names were changed when we defected to the West."

"You're still Petra to me."

"I'm okay with that. So, your whole family suddenly disappeared. What happened?"

"You probably guessed that the Stasi took us."

"It seemed like that."

"That morning I can still remember it. They broke down the door at 06:00 and four of them ripped our apartment to pieces, searching for evidence. They found nothing but they still took us all away, initially treating me as an adult although I was only 16. Eventually, both my parents were charged on the evidence of neighbours who reported us. They had often heard my father complaining about the abuses of the Stasi. He must have annoyed one of them. They got their retaliation."

"What about your mother?"

"They interrogated both her and my father. Later I learned that they had used sleep deprivation on them for a week or two, until they confessed. They would have said anything just to get some sleep at that stage."

"So they were charged?"

"Yes. They were sent to the Stasi prison at Hohenschonhausen and were still there when the Wall fell, two and a half years later. The prison is now a memorial to the past."

"And did you get to see them then?"

"No, I was placed with a family loyal to the party, who kept everything from me. I didn't see or hear anything from them for about four years. But everything had changed by then. I was twenty and in a relationship and my parents had changed and were utterly different, particularly my father. He had become quiet and hardly said anything. I guess they tortured him and kept him in solitary confinement for a long while. My mother too was just a shell of her former self. She never recovered from the ordeal. She died a few years later, when she was only 49. Cancer. I guess that's what stress does to you."

"I'm so sorry to hear that; they were so brutal."

"You were so lucky to escape it all."

"Yes, I know I was but you know it made no difference to my dad."

"But he was the reason your whole family were able to defect."

"Yes, but he was just the same in England. We never saw him in East Germany because of that secret project he was working on, for the Stasi. But in England, it was just the same. He went to work for GCHQ, the British intelligence agency, and he was always gone. I still feel angry about it. Sometimes I even feel a desire for revenge."

Rachel felt surprised at herself. It was the first time she had verbalised this, although the feeling had been with her for a long time.

"Vengeance," said Nadine. "But he's practically an old man now, probably in his mid-sixties."

"Yes he is, but that still doesn't change anything. He's still working for GCHQ. All that mattered to him was his work. My mum and I meant absolutely nothing. And then in an argument with him once he let it slip about knowing that your parents had confessed after their arrest. When he realised what he'd said, he denied it, but he could not take it back."

Nadine was shocked.

"Bastard. How could he have been involved when he knew we were such close friends."

"He didn't care for anything except his precious work and when we moved to England, his work with GCHQ was the same. Nothing else mattered. I've often felt that if I could have sabotaged his work maybe he would feel the pain we did."

"Perhaps you could."

"What do you mean?"

"Well, I haven't told you yet – ironically, I now work for BND, the German intelligence agency. I'm not spying or anything like that, but I am involved in projects that, let's say, gather information from the public."

"You mean like the Stasi?" Rachel was shocked.

"No, it's not like that now. There aren't neighbours spying on each other or anything like that. But we do gather information on businesses and people, especially those who have a lot of contacts abroad."

"And how would that have any connection with what I said about my dad?"

"Let's say we have agents embedded in other countries' intelligence agencies, including GCHQ, leveraging information about what they are up to. You could help by handling that information and passing it on. You'd be getting back at him, and making some money too. A lot of money."

"It's not about money. Is it risky? What if I got caught?"

"That's a small possibility, a risk you'd have to take. But you'd be getting back at your dad, getting that revenge, by destroying everything he's worked for."

Rachel thought for a while. It was not what she had expected from Nadine, and certainly it had never had occurred to her. But she might be okay with this idea.

"I'd have to think about it."

"I know you're going home tomorrow. You don't have to decide before then. Think about it and if you want to do it then let me know. But you'll have to use a private channel, secure email or perhaps the dark web."

Rachel had never heard of the dark web before. Nadine filled her in.

Over the next week, Rachel thought of nothing else. She felt excited as well as scared. She knew she would be crossing a line that she could never go back on. But the fact that her desire for revenge could be satisfied also made her feel empowered. The more she thought about it, the more she wanted it. She needed it. It was the least she deserved, after everything he had done.

Using the contact methods Nadine had given her, she soon received instructions from her. Within a short period of time, it was all set up. Every few weeks she felt that pleasure, which came from a sense of empowerment over getting payback. He would never know it was her who was working to tear down that secret empire he had been building.

CHAPTER TWENTY

Police Interviews

24th July, 2015. Wandsworth, London.

11:30

As Ethan left Ben's house he called DCI Scott but it went immediately to Scott's voicemail. He hated playing phone tag but left a brief message.

"DCI Scott, this is Ethan Harris. You left a message for me earlier saying you wanted to talk to me. I'm going back to my house soon and I'll be there for a while. Perhaps we can talk there at around 12 noon."

He opened the door and walked out into the street. There was a cold wind blowing along the Thames as he headed over the bridge towards Putney Bridge tube station. As he approached he could hear a train arriving on the platform overhead. But he did not run to catch it. Somehow he was operating in a different time zone now. Instead, he decided to walk home. It would take about forty or fifty minutes along the Fulham Road and it would give him time to clear his head.

As he walked, he thought back over the last 24 hours and how his life had changed forever. Two days ago he had been busy at work and perhaps not as focused on his family as he might have been. But he had been happy, with no worries. Well, almost no worries. There was the gambling, but it had felt as though that was under control. Then suddenly out of the blue his life was like a car crash. Why?

Back at his house, the scene tape lines were still outside. He noticed two different neighbours glancing down at him from their upstairs windows as he walked along the street. They ducked back behind their curtains when he looked up at them. At that moment, he become intensely aware of a spotlight on his life that illuminated him from all angles. It was as if his normal anonymous life had been stripped bare and he was in the public view now: the man whose wife had been murdered.

Inside it was freezing, colder than ever before. Somehow it now felt alien to him. No longer part of his life. It was a crime scene, a murder scene. How could he be part of that? He sat on the couch like he was in a waiting room for the dentist. He was nearly afraid to go upstairs. There was a semi-translucent plastic sheet covering part of the floor in the hall. Through it, he could see dark red-brown stains below. Then he noticed the blood splatter on the wall. He shuddered and nearly walked back out into the street. He felt sick.

He heard his alarm clock buzzing upstairs. Dimly, he realised it had been buzzing ever since he had arrived. Stepping gingerly over the plastic sheet, as though worried about disturbing evidence, he made his way upstairs. But why had they not cleaned the place up? Would he have to do that? He felt a sense of foreboding. His heart was beating fast. What would he find there? But as he got to the top of the stairs the doorbell rang shrilly, making him jump. Relieved, he returned down the stairs immediately to open the door for DCI Scott.

In the living room, Scott and Jones sat at the table opposite him. It was beginning to feel like a TV crime interrogation, yet not a single word had been spoken.

DCI Scott began.

"We're so sorry about this awful event, Mr Harris."

"Call me Ethan."

Scott nodded. "But we need some crucial information to progress the case."

"Okay. Just ask what you need to know."

Jones took out a small recorder and placed it on the table. "Is it okay if I record this? It will be more precise than my sloppy handwriting," he said.

"No problem."

Scott smiled as he took out a notebook. "Jones is the high-tech guy, I like the more traditionalist pen and paper." Then he continued, "Some of these questions may be painful for you but we need to know the circumstances around this incident."

Ethan thought it was strange he was calling it an incident. It was murder, bloody murder.

"So who is, or rather was, living in this house?"

"Just Rachel and me and our baby daughter, Katy."

"Was anyone else staying temporarily?"

"No, I know you found someone else dead in the hallway, but I've no idea who that was."

"We'll come to that later. For now, I just need to get the basic information about you and Rachel."

"Okay."

Scott cleared his throat. "A possible explanation for this incident may be that you were the intended target."

It was like a slap in the face. Ethan gulped as a wave of sheer terror ran through him. He had not even considered that.

"Is there any reason someone would want to kill you or your wife?" continued Scott.

"No, I have absolutely no idea why this happened. We were a normal family with work and everyday problems and friends and absolutely no one who we could call an enemy."

"Just think for a moment. Maybe it could be connected to your job?"

Ethan smiled slightly nervously. "They might want to kill me if the IT systems were down, but I can't see them hiring a hit-man."

Scott gazed sternly at his notes.

"No," continued Ethan, more seriously. "There's no issue at work that would ever result in this."

"What about outside work, anything?"

Suddenly, Ethan thought of the money issues and he blushed. "No, nothing outside work either," he said, faltering a little.

Scott looked at him. "Okay, so how about Rachel? What did she work at?"

"She was a freelance graphic designer and web designer. She did a bit of commercial art sometimes."

"And where did she work?"

"Mostly from home but occasionally she travelled."

"Where to?"

"Mostly to Europe – she had some clients in a few different countries and occasionally she had to visit them to understand their requirements for work. It was only a few times a year."

"And so she worked from home the rest of the time?"

"Yes, but she also had an office in the city that she used occasionally."

"Where was that office?"

"In Aldgate; she had some clients close to there and the office space was much cheaper than around here. It also got her out of the house."

"So who minded Katy while she was there and you were at the office?"

"We have a part-time child-minder who lives locally."

"I'll need her details too."

"Sometimes Rachel's mother looked after Katy."

Scott noticed a slight frown on Ethan's face as he mentioned his mother-in-law. He was drawing a mind-map on his notepad, a kind of spider diagram, which he used to build up a picture of Ethan's life and relationships.

"Let's talk about your relationship with Rachel. Was everything okay between the both of you?"

While Scott was talking to Ethan, Jones was observing his reactions, sizing him up to get the measure of him and to see if he showed any signs of involvement in the incident.

"Yes, everything was perfect, Rachel and me and little Katy." Ethan felt an emotional twinge just mentioning her name.

"So there were no rows then?"

"No, nothing more than the usual little tiffs."

"And what were they about?"

"Just everyday things. It's a part of living together, you know."

"So you had a happy family life?"

"Yes."

"How about money? Any financial problems? This lovely house must have cost a pretty penny."

"I've got a good job at an investment bank in Canary Wharf."

"So no debts then?"

"No." Ethan could feel a certain panic building up inside him. His blood pressure was rising and his face felt hot. He knew they would be noticing this. Maybe they would suspect that he was lying, which he was, a little. Things had not been so great between him and Rachel. But he had been trying to improve them. And yes, there had been money problems in recent times but that was none of their business. This was a murder they were talking about and they should be out there trying to catch who had done it, not interrogate him, the victim's husband. He felt frustrated and angry, but he tried not to show it.

"Let's go back to the previous day," said Scott. "Did anything unusual happen on that day?"

"No, it was an average busy day, extra busy in fact as I was trying to get things done; I was due a day's leave the next day and we were planning a family trip."

"So you'd planned to go somewhere together on the morning of the incident? But you were at work when I called you."

"Yes, I had to cancel the day off as there were some problems at work."

"Some problems?"

"Just work related, nothing serious." Ethan realised he was starting to lie again. But the hacking incident at the bank wasn't any of their business. In fact, the bank would most likely not want the police involved as it would reflect poorly on their security and that would cause lots of other issues. No, they would just want to investigate the hacking quietly, and then cover it up in some internal report.

"But severe enough to make you cancel your plans. Were there not other people at the bank who could have dealt with it, and leave you in peace on your day off?"

"No, that's not how it works there. I had to go in and deal with it and now it's fixed." He was lying yet again.

It was not fixed, not yet. In fact, when he left work the whole thing was still wide open. Bill, poor bloody Bill, was dealing with it. Things could only be getting worse there, hour by hour.

He looked up. Scott and Jones were watching him closely. Ethan nervously looked at his watch.

"Do you have to be somewhere?" Scott asked.

"No, it can wait."

"So, as you know there was another person in the house when we arrived."

"Yes, when I got here yesterday they told me that someone else was dead in the hallway. And I saw the blood stains on the floor and splattered on the wall when I came in here earlier today."

"I'm so sorry you saw that. It should have been cleaned up after the forensics guys were finished. I'll arrange to have it cleaned after we leave. And yes there was another person, but he was not killed, although it looked like that. He's in hospital in a coma, though he might never come around. He was shot in the head at close range. It looks like he moved just as it happened."

Ethan wished it had been Rachel who had survived the shooting. "I've no idea who that guy was."

"Maybe a client of Rachel's?"

"No, she never brought customers to our home."

"I'm sorry I have to ask this but, could she have been having an affair?"

Ethan was stunned. He had not thought of that. But no. Surely he would have noticed if she had been playing around?

"No. I don't think so."

"He had no ID on him so we're still trying to find out who he is."

"Can you give me any info about him? If she was having an affair with him, then I need to know."

"Well it's not really our business if she was having an affair or not, if it is unconnected with the incident. But if she was having an affair, then her death and his attempted murder here could implicate you in this case. But it's early days yet. We're still gathering information."

Ethan felt traumatised. He knew he was innocent but moment by moment, his life was being further ripped apart. First the hacking at the bank, then the theft on the train, then Rachel's murder, then a possible affair, and now a possible murder charge. Could it get any worse?

"Let's leave it there for now," said Scott. "We'll pick up a little later. It will give you time to do the things you need to do."

"So you've more questions?"

"As things progress we'll need to talk to you perhaps several times. Is that okay?"

"Sure, but I've told you everything I can think of."

"Thanks, but sometimes other questions come up. Additional information might also occur to you as you think things over."

Scott looked at Jones, who reached over and turned off the digital recorder.

"Thanks very much, Mr Harris, for your time," said Jones. "We'll let ourselves out."

"Oh, one last thing," said Scott. "We'll need access to the phones and computers you have here. I'll contact you about it later."

Ethan said nothing.

As the two detectives stood to leave, Scott turned handed Ethan his card.

"This is my card. My mobile is on it so you can contact me at any time, day or night, if other things occur to you."

"Thanks."

"Oh and we'll need you to give a formal identification of Rachel's body at the morgue."

Just hearing the words "Rachel's body" brought home to Ethan the finality of it. It had not occurred to him that he would have to do an identification. The thought of it filled him with dread. He did not want his last image of Rachel to be of her lying cold and lifeless in the morgue. With a gunshot wound.

"When will that be arranged?" he said.

"Later this afternoon if that suits you?"

"Fine, I guess." His voice was quivering now.

"Why don't you go out for a few hours? The clean-up will be done by the time you get back. Then I'll call you about the identification."

Ethan stood. The two men shook his hand and then left. He watched them as they got into Scott's black Saab, which was parked right outside, and drove off.

Although DCI Scott and DI Jones had been reasonably friendly and very courteous to him, he felt a certain uneasiness about the interview. Who was being investigated? He put his coat on to go for a walk, and straight away his mind was flooded with fears. He hated the house. He wanted to close that door behind him and never go back, just leave all his misery behind him.

12:30

DCI Scott drove slowly from Onslow Square around onto Old Brompton Road past the Royal Marsden Hospital.

"What did you think of him?" he asked.

Jones thought a moment. "He's not giving us all the information is he? He's hiding something I think."

"Exactly what I was thinking. We need to do a bit more digging before we talk to him again. You talk to the neighbours and I'll talk to the bank."

"Okay, drop me off here and I'll walk back to Onslow to dig around."

Later, alone in the car, Scott took out his notebook and flicked through it. He called Detective Alan Coulson back in the office.

"Can you find out for me the name of Ethan Harris's boss at MitaSimi Bank in Canary Wharf?"

"Sure, sir, I'll call you right back."

One minute later his phone rang.

"It's Harvey Waterman and his number is 555-6049."

DCI Scott dialled the number. It rang through.

"Hello?"

"Harvey Waterman?"

"Yes, who is this?"

"It's DCI Scott from the Serious Crimes Investigation Unit. I'm the senior investigating officer on the Rachel Harris murder case."

There was a sharp intake of breath. "And how can I help you, Inspector?"

"I need to talk to you about Ethan Harris."

"Dreadful business about his wife."

"Yes, awful, we're just getting the full picture for the investigation and I've already spoken to Mr Harris. Could we meet and discuss it later today?"

"No problem, but I'm not sure how I can help you. Harris reports to me but he's a very private guy. I know nothing about his personal life."

"I understand but sometimes the tiniest thing that you may not think relevant can help us with the investigation."

"Okay, I'm happy to talk if it helps. Would two-thirty suit?"

"Great, see you then."

Harvey Waterman put the phone down. He was extremely annoyed. It was irritating, how that Harris guy's wife gets murdered and he goes and involves the bank. Not to mention Harvey himself. If he's had any connection with it, then that's it, he decided. He's out of here.

12:45

Ethan walked down by St Paul's Church on Onslow Square. The door was open so he went in, just for the quietness and calmness of the place. He was not religious; he had never even been there before, even though it was just around the corner from his house. But somehow it felt like the right place to be. It felt safe. Or safer anyway.

He sat down, gazed at the sunlight streaming through a stained glass window. What was that interview about? Was he a suspect? Surely they did not think he was involved? Well, he had answered everything they had asked and quite willingly too. Maybe he had been a bit short on the truth in replying to some questions. Had they noticed that? His relationship with Rachel had been a bit rocky and there were money worries, but that was none of their business. Or was it?

Comforting himself with the thought that if they had suspected his involvement in Rachel's murder, they would have arrested him, he walked back out into the street. This time he walked back around to the Fulham Road. As he passed his house, he noticed a black van parked outside it. The clean-up unit.

As he passed the Royal Marsden Children's Hospital, he remembered the awful time Katy stayed there for treatment when she was ill. She had only been two months old. The memories of Rachel sleeping in a bed beside her flooded back and a rush of emotion swept over him. Shaking, he sat on a bench at a bus stop to try to calm down.

His phone, which was on silent, buzzed constantly with missed calls and messages. He turned it off.

The 211 bus stopped. When the door opened, Ethan got onto the bus without thinking, tapped his Oyster card and sat down, with no idea where he was going. He had to think now. There was so much to do. There would be an autopsy, an inquiry, the funeral arrangements, organising his life with Rachel gone, looking after Katy, the hacking issues at the bank, the money issues that he did not want to think about. Then there were all the people trying to contact him.

He tried to blank it all out as he looked out the window at the passing traffic.

Eventually, he got off the bus at Victoria Coach Station, with tourists and travellers swarming around him. But he felt alone, utterly alone. After walking around aimlessly, be began to head back towards his house. It was a mile or two away so it would take perhaps forty minutes. It was unseasonably cold and stormy. He pulled his coat collar up and headed into the wind.

15:00

The van that had been outside his house was gone by the time Ethan arrived back at Onslow Square. His mind had cleared a little but as he grew closer to his house, he began to feel apprehensive about going inside. Somehow it did not feel like his home anymore. It was someone else's home, someone else's life. He simply was not ready to accept what had happened.

When he opened the door, the fresh smell of cleaning products and polish wafted around him. The blood stains were gone and the hall was clean. The plastic on the floor was also gone. The blood spattered wall had been cleaned and the paintwork touched up. It was just as if nothing had happened. As if it had all been erased.

As he walked up the stairs, it occurred to him that he had been lucky not to have seen the awful, bloody bedroom scene, where Rachel had been killed. That would have been hard to forget. Instead, the bedroom was clean and tidy, just as usual, except the house was now an empty shell. With Rachel gone and Katy not there, he felt as though he was just visiting. It was no longer his home. How could it ever be his home again?

Back downstairs, he walked into the kitchen. That was when he saw his stolen backpack on the counter. It was immediately clear: the unknown victim in the hallway was the guy who had taken his backpack on the train. He remembered DCI Scott showing him the photo of the guy. Of course. It was the same person. He must have used his keys and was burgling the house when someone else entered the house and had shot him. What a strange kind of justice that was. But how weird was that? Someone else arrived at the same time, shot him and then killed Rachel too?

There must have been some plan behind it all.

The forensics guys who checked the house must have just thought the backpack was part of the house contents;

apparently they had not touched it. They must have focused on the crime scenes in the hall and bedroom; probably they had little interest in the rest of the house.

Ethan sat down and opened his backpack. His laptop was gone and there was other stuff in there that was not his. The guy's wallet was in there. No wonder the police had not been able to identify him – when he stole the backpack, he must have put his wallet and other items in there along with the stolen stuff.

He stopped for a moment. This was evidence, after all. Was he destroying evidence? But then he remembered how the two detectives had seemed to be suspecting him. He kept looking.

There was £100 in cash in the wallet, an Oyster card, two slips of paper with what looked like phone numbers on them and an old tattered driver's licence with a photo of the guy. Joe Morgan, aged 35 years, with an address in Brixton.

Ethan's credit card was still there but his Bank ID was missing. He took out his phone and photographed the scraps of paper and the driver's licence. Then he put it all back into the wallet. He had still not decided whether or not he should call DCI Scott about it.

Then he noticed all the missed calls, messages and emails on his phone. That damn phone, it never gave him a moment's peace.

14:00

Scott decided that it would take too long to drive over to MitaSimi Bank in Canary Wharf, so he parked off Pelham Street and walked around to South Kensington station. There he took the tube, first to Green Street and then to Canary Wharf. On the train, it occurred to him that this must be the route that Ethan took to work every morning. Perhaps there was some useful information to be observed in following that journey.

When DCI Scott arrived at the offices, he was ushered into a small conference room where Waterman was waiting.

"Good afternoon, Mr Waterman. Thanks for taking the time to meet me."

Waterman smiled, thinly. "Good afternoon Inspector, now how can I help you?"

Scott sat down at the table. "As you know, Ethan Harris's wife, Rachel, was murdered yesterday. As part of the investigation I need to get background information on him."

"I'm happy to help, Inspector," replied Waterman disingenuously. "But as I said on the phone earlier, Mr Harris is a very private man and we know scarcely anything about his personal life."

"So what is he like as an employee?"

"He's the IT director. He manages all our technology operations at the bank. MitaSimi is a small specialist investment bank and we leverage our expertise in financial trading and other financial instruments to help our clients to be profitable. Technology is at the core of our business and without it, we are nothing. So Harris plays a significant role in the bank and has a lot of responsibility and pressure on him constantly."

"So he's always stressed?"

"Yes."

"Does he work long hours?"

"Everybody does in this industry, late nights and weekends too, sometimes."

"Harris was married with a young child. How was he managing all that work alongside his family life?"

"With difficulty, I'd say – he was constantly stressed. It had been taking its toll because the IT department's performance has been declining recently, most notably with a significant outage yesterday."

"What time did that happen?"

"We're still investigating but it was about four am. But how does this have any connection to your murder investigation?"

Waterman was clearly getting impatient. Scott glanced up from taking notes. "We gather all the information about the event," he said. "Even apparently unrelated information. Then we try to piece together a picture and timeline of what happened. So, do you know if he had any money problems?"

"I'm not sure I can discuss his finances with you, without some authorisation."

"We're not looking at forensic accounting on his accounts." Scott paused a moment for effect. "At least, not yet. But I could request a warrant. I'm sure that would be very disruptive for the bank, though, so I'd prefer if we could proceed in a more informal manner."

"I suppose we could provide you with some information on his accounts," said Waterman grudgingly. "But this is an investment bank. It's highly unlikely he would have an account here. He'd be using retail banking for that. However, we'll have a look and let you know. It will have to be tomorrow."

"And phone calls too."

"Okay."

"Thanks. That will do for now, Mr Waterman. I appreciate your cooperation."

As Scott got up to go and shook hands with Waterman, he added, "We may need to talk to some of his close colleagues later."

"No problem Inspector, we'll email you the information you requested and call me personally if you need any more." He handed Scott his card. "I hope you understand that this bank relies wholly on trust, and that police investigations can erode that, especially if it becomes public."

Scott nodded. He shook Waterman's outstretched hand and left.

13:00

After he had got out of the car, Jones walked back to Onslow Square and knocked on a few doors close to the Harris household, to see if he could get some information from the neighbours.

The first person he talked to was George Thornton, a neighbour two doors down from the Harris's house. George had called the police and ambulance after he had heard another neighbour screaming.

"Thanks, Mr Thornton, for taking the time to talk to me about the incident. We are trying to build up a picture from all sources. Can you tell me what happened before you rang the police?"

George thought for a moment. "I was having breakfast, a late one – it was just after ten am. I heard some people in the street shouting, right outside my front door. As it's normally very quiet here, I opened the door and I saw two people at the railings close to the Harris's. Then one went up to the door, which I could see was partially open."

Jones was taking notes as the man spoke.

"A moment later she came flying down the street screaming about a murder."

"So did you go into the house?"

"No, I just walked into the street to look at the house from the outside. Then I took out my phone and called the emergency number."

"Did you notice anyone running away or driving off in a hurry?"

"No, but my security camera might have caught it."

Jones had not noticed the small hidden camera set into the wall above the window over George's front door. It was positioned to capture images of people calling to the house, but it could also have recorded the killer in the distance arriving and getting out of their car.

"Could we have the recordings from that camera?"

"Sure, I can put it on a memory stick for you in a few minutes."

"That would be really helpful. Just one more question. Was there anything unusual about the Harris family?"

"Ethan Harris seems a nice chap but I've only talked to him a few times. He keeps very odd hours, sometimes going out very early, at about five-thirty am and often not arriving back until late. Also, sometimes I walk the dog in the middle of the night – I'm an insomniac and now so is the dog."

Jones smiled.

"Anyway," continued the man. "It could be three in the morning and I'd see a light in one of the rooms upstairs at the front, which I think he uses as an office. It would be often enough. As if he was still working away on his computer. Seems like he never sleeps."

"And his wife, did you noticed anything about her?"

George smiled faintly. "She was a beautiful woman. I heard the news reports say than she was in her forties but I would have thought she was ten years younger. She was in the house a lot after the baby was born and I rarely saw her. Their child was very ill in the first few months – Ethan told me one day when I met him coming out of the house when they were bringing her for cancer treatment to the Royal Marsden Hospital. I was so sorry for them and their lovely little kid."

"Who was the woman who found the body in the hall?"

"Oh, that was Eleanor Ryan, our resident news gatherer." He smiled again. "It was only fitting that she should find it, she's always out there searching for news and gossip."

He pointed to a house further down the street.

"She lives there."

"What does she look like? Just in case she's not home."

"I'd say she's in her early sixties, grey hair, plump, about five foot two."

"Thank you very much. I will take that copy of your CCTV footage, if it's not too much trouble."

Five minutes later, Jones was at Eleanor Ryan's house. There was no answer when he rang the bell, so after ringing it a couple of times, he walked down the street and into the park opposite. It was a private garden for all the residents of the square, but the gate was open and he walked around the pathway that was sheltered by trees and, on the other side, spotted someone who fitted her description.

He walked up to her. "By any chance might you be Eleanor Ryan?"

"Yes."

He sat down beside her, introduced himself and explained his mission.

"I'd only be delighted to help,' she said. "It was awful. A man lying there in the hallway, covered in blood. I thought it was Ethan Harris at first but then I saw he had long dark hair, I couldn't see his face but I knew it was someone else."

"So tell me about earlier, before you found the body at the Harris's house."

"I was doing my usual walk around the street and the park."

"What time was that?"

"Around 09:30 or so. On my way back up the street I saw a man looking at the street signs as if he was lost. I offered some help but he just ignored me."

"What did he look like?"

"He had scruffy jeans and was tall and thin with long dark hair and a backpack." She paused, staring at Jones. "Could that have been him? The guy who was killed in the Harris's hallway?"

"Perhaps," said Jones. "Did you see any cars drive up the street?"

"No, I just walked around the park twice and then headed back to my house. That was then I found the dead body."

Jones thanked her and left. He had enough information for now and was anxious to get back to the office and have a look at George's CCTV footage.

CHAPTER TWENTY-ONE

Reaching the Bottom

March, 2015. London.

And so, a certain depression came creeping into Ethan's life. Now he mostly saw the dark side of things. He was feeling the pressure from everyone around him – Waterman, Bill, Rachel, the casinos and the online betting apps. They all needed a piece of him, no, they all wanted all of him and he could not give that. Waking up early in the mornings, before his 06:00 alarm, he found himself not wanting to get up and face the day. He wanted to curl up and sleep; even with the shafts of sunlight beckoning him and Rachel encouraging him, it was still a struggle, more so every day. It was drudgery and a treadmill and he had to get off it.

Then he would think about what he could bet on that day; that was what motivated him. Going for a shower, he brought his phone into the en-suite bathroom and closed the door so he could check the details in privacy. He knew Rachel had noticed this change; before the gambling had started, all doors had always been left open and they used to chat as he got ready – even when he was on the loo. Now all that had changed. He was quieter, more introspective, more distant, like he was in a different world. He knew that was what Rachel thought and she was right – he was in a different world. Although it was stormy there, it was inviting too. It always lured him with the promise of excitement.

But recently a kind of helplessness had crept into his life. He felt isolated. He could not talk about it to anyone, but there was a certain feeling of impending doom. He dreamed about it and when he was awake, he felt it, tangible and real. He was out of control and although he knew it, he felt powerless to do anything about it. He also felt frustration and anger inside. He wanted to hit out at anything, vent his frustration, but why was he frustrated? He did not know. He could just feel that darkness and that anger welling up inside the void that was his core.

And then one morning, he did lash out, at Rachel, stunning her into silence. He had never been like that before. All she had ever known of him was a gentle, kind man who loved her and their daughter Katy, and now he had pushed back. No, he had thrown her back on the bed angrily, for absolutely no reason, and stormed out of the house. It made her recall all those tiny changes that she had been noticing over the past few months. Something was wrong, really wrong and she had to do something about it.

She went online to find some insight into what the trouble might be and some advice. She found lots of advice and a number of potential causes. Perhaps he was depressed; there were definite signs of that, but what was causing the depression? Was it their relationship, which had been on a downward slide for some time? Was it the relentless pressure at work? Or perhaps it was money issues, although she had never seen any signs of this being the case. Maybe it was a health concern that was bothering him. Whatever it was she decided she needed to make time for them to discuss it and somehow try to get him and their relationship back on the right track.

That evening she made a special effort. She tidied the place up, putting all the baby stuff for Katy, and her toys, neatly away. She then prepared a delicious meal before texting Ethan.

"Hi Ethan, I hope work is going well for you today. Can you try and get home this evening by 7pm? I've cooked a tasty meal – your favourite. And we need to talk."

She knew his favourite meal was roast stuffed pork steak with apple sauce and roast potatoes, followed by a bread and butter pudding with jam, meringue and custard on the side. It was a childhood memory for him, a meal his mother used to make on a special day or perhaps an occasional Sunday. His whole family had loved it. That was before she left them.

Rachel knew it was a risk making that meal; it might remind him of his mother and when she left and drive him into an even darker mood. But she felt that the smell and taste would just bring back the happy memories and that he would be in a good place to talk.

Almost as soon as she had sent the message came the reply.

"Hi Rachel, I'm so sorry about this morning, it was totally out of character for me. Thanks for making the effort. I'll be home by 7 and we can talk later."

Rachel was delighted.

Ethan fully intended to come home, eat dinner with her and discuss or hint at what was getting him down. But when he walked out of South Kensington station, he turned right rather than left, by force of habit. He paused, and thought about it. It would be like climbing a mountain, telling her about everything. And the outcome of that was so uncertain. Unlike the welcome he would certainly receive at the casino and the pure pleasure, no, exhilaration, of the gambling. There was no competition. He continued on his way to the casino.

Hours later, after he had lost even more than he expected, he arrived back at the house. It was dark. He had ignored all her calls and messages by turning off his phone. There in the dark he turned it on. The rush of messages hit him like a smack across the face. He felt so ashamed he even considered not going in and finding a nearby hotel for the night. But that would only make things worse, if that was possible. It would also bring up the spectre of infidelity, which, for all his shortcomings, was not his style.

In the kitchen, the dinner was still laid out for both of them, with a solitary candle in the middle of the table. He sat down in the dark, with what felt like an unbelievable weight on his mind and considered what to do.

The light came on. She was at the door. When he looked up, he could see that she had been crying, perhaps for the whole evening. She said nothing, just looked at him with her sad eyes. A tear rolled down her cheek.

"Ethan, I was so worried something had happened to you."

"It has." He felt like crying now as a huge wave of emotion flowed over him.

She came over to him and put her arms around him. She held him close. "Whatever it is, we can deal with it together," she said softly in his ear, caressing the back of his head slightly with her hand.

That evening marked his first breakthrough. Bit by bit he told her how he had slipped into the deep, deep hole he was in. She said nothing, letting him talk, getting it all out. The only part of it he did not share was the financial mess he had created along the way. Then when he was spent and was ready to listen, she spoke.

"I will find an addiction counsellor and we'll face this issue together," she said. He nodded, relieved at her acceptance and resolve.

She suggested that it should be an evening appointment as the gambling could not be mentioned at work. If the bank heard about it, he would be out of a job and they would have even more problems to worry about. She would make the appointment as soon as possible and in the meantime, he would have to give her his credit cards and delete the apps on his phone. She would give him some pocket money each day for food, but that was it and he would have to come home every evening by 19:00. If he did not agree to these terms, then it was over between them. He was out. She would get legal advice to secure the house for her and Katy.

Reluctantly he agreed. He knew that this was the best thing for them, but already he was dreading the thought of missing his precious gambling.

Rachel found a counsellor and made an appointment for the following week. By then, Ethan was desperate to place a bet. He had even considered not eating at lunchtime and going to a betting shop on his way home as there were none he knew of at Canary Wharf. But he forced himself to spend the money on food and then he had no way to bet on the way home so he just could not do it.

That did not stop his cravings and in fact, they got worse every day. He did nothing at work – he had no concentration, he was nearly shaking from the withdrawal. But somehow he made it through to Tuesday evening, when they had the appointment with the counsellor.

That night, Julia, Rachel's mother came to look after Katy. Ethan heard Rachel lie about where they were going; she knew as well as he did her mother's opinion of him. The last thing she would want was to give her proof.

When Ethan and Rachel arrived at the counsellor's office they sat silently together in the waiting room, looking around them vaguely, waiting to be called in.

"Ethan, Rachel, welcome. I'm Dr Erika Muller." She shook hands with both of them, before leading them into her counselling room. She was an attractive woman in her late thirties. Ethan was immediately impressed at the softness of her hands and the warmth of her personality. He felt at ease. Rachel, however, he sensed, was feeling more cautious, perhaps unconsciously a little threatened by this strong, attractive younger woman who was going to be seeing her husband on a regular basis.

"You can just call me Erika," she said as they sat down in the comfortable armchairs beside her desk.

"So, Ethan, tell me how it all began, I know it will take some time to fully understand the underlying problems, but first I need to know how you reached this point."

Ethan nodded and Rachel held his hand gently as he began to describe the feeling and pressures that started him on that downward spiral. Dr Muller made some notes as he talked and after about twenty minutes she interrupted him.

"Okay Ethan, that's a good start, perhaps we can pause now for a moment. I'm going to outline what I think is the best approach to dealing with this problem. We'll start with a counselling session twice a week and Ethan, you will need to go to an addiction support group every day, for the first while."

She handed him a sheet listing more than one hundred support groups all over London. He was surprised by how many there were.

"There's quite a lot of them," she said, as though reading his mind. "That's because addictions problems in whatever form – drugs, gambling, sex – are very common and all of them are reactions to underlying issues that many people have."

Rachel and Ethan nodded.

"I'll work at helping you to understand what these problems are and how to deal with them. Then we'll be using cognitive based therapy – CBT for short – as the approach to dealing with them."

"How long will this take? I'm not expecting an instant fix, but about how long are we talking about?" asked Ethan.

"That's a difficult question to answer, Ethan," she said, looking directly at him as if there was no one else in the room. "We should see some real progress over three or four months, assuming of course that you fully embrace this treatment and go to support group meetings as often as you can, certainly every day for the first two or three weeks."

"Okay."

After discussing further details and future appointments, they left. Although Rachel seemed apprehensive,

Ethan sensed that she was also encouraged that they were on the right track. He himself was certainly happy that his problems had been shared; it gave him a sense of relief. However, he could not avoid the fact that while he might be able to address his addiction over time, the huge financial mess he had created would be a lot harder to sort out. He certainly did not want a divorce to be added to his list of problems, so he continued to stay quiet about the money issues, hoping to deal with it later.

When they came out it was raining hard. Torrential rain flooded the streets, so they caught a taxi back home. Again, they sat silently side by side on their way back to Onslow Square, as it sped through the glistening streets.

It was the third addiction support meeting that had the most impact on him. It was in a different location to the other two, neither of which had done anything for him. He had walked into the meeting, sat down among the other attendees, closed his eyes and just listened to the stories being told by all the other addicts. Then he heard a voice he recognised. He opened his eyes, looked around. It was Bill Taylor from work, standing there, sharing his misery with everyone. He hadn't seen Ethan, so he just continued about the temptations and how long he had been on the wagon – nine months.

Later at coffee, they talked.

"I never suspected you had a problem," Ethan said.

"I never thought it myself," replied Bill. "But it just started to control my life and eventually I knew I had to do something about it."

"But what about those gambling apps you had on your phone when you were showing me something else a few months ago? How come you didn't get rid of those?"

"I deliberately left them there to remind me every day that I had to be stronger than them."

"I couldn't do that," said Ethan, "Did you ever suspect that I had a problem?"

"Yes, I knew the signs, but I couldn't say anything. I hoped you'd get some help and it looks like you have."

"They can never know at the bank. Otherwise, we'd both be gone."

"I know. Waterman would have us out of there in five minutes to protect his precious bank."

"But they'll never find out."

A new bond grew between them. They had always got on well at work and whenever they attended the same social occasions. But this was different. It was bad, but it was good. Ethan certainly felt that it lightened his load at work – the fact that someone understood his cravings. They agreed to go to different meetings so there would be no pressure on either of them to check up on each other. Each could recover at their own rate.

Full of good intentions, Ethan continued to attend meetings for a while. He also continued the sessions with the counsellor and they helped, to a degree. But deep down he never felt the happiness or sense of satisfaction he had felt at the casino.

Eventually he returned to his old haunts. But now he had to be even more secretive. Neither Rachel nor Bill could find out that he had returned to his old love.

CHAPTER TWENTY-TWO

The Investigation Develops

Monday 27th July, 2015. Kensington Police Station.

11:00

DCI Scott had set the second murder investigation team meeting for Monday at 11:00. He had already arranged with Evelyn Reinhardt, the forensics team lead, to attend via a conference call, to discuss the forensic reports.

Jones and Coulson were already in the meeting room, chatting, when Scott arrived. Foster followed him into the room with the forensic report under his arm, closely followed by Clarke. Scott called Reinhardt in on the conference speakerphone.

"Alright, let's make a start," he said. "What have you got for us Reinhardt?"

"Let me take you through the main findings," she said.

As she spoke, Foster leafed through the report.

"Ballistics first; we've determined that all three bullets were fired from the same gun, a 9mm pistol with a silencer. Based on the bullet analysis we have no record of this gun having been used before at any other crime scene. The killer was approximately six foot one and was left-handed. He shot the unidentified victim first in the hall and then proceeded up the stairs, where he killed Rachel Harris, shooting her twice while she was still on the bed."

She paused for a moment. Foster rustled the pages of the report noisily.

"From the autopsy," continued Reinhardt, "Rachel Harris was most likely killed by the first bullet that entered her right eye, causing massive damage to her brain. The second bullet hit her in the forehead and caused further extensive damage to her skull."

Detective Clarke took a sharp intake of breath.

"The unidentified victim," continued Reinhardt.

"Actually, he's been identified now," said Jones. "The Irish police service were able to identify him as Joseph Morgan, aged 35 years and assumed to have moved to London about three years ago."

"Thanks, Jones. So Joseph Morgan was also hit in the head but it seems he moved just as the bullet was fired. That's what saved him, although he's still in a coma. There are no fingerprints, as gloves were worn, but we have possible fibres from the killer's jacket, caught on the door as he left. As was evident, there was blood from both victims; however, we discovered a third blood sample upstairs in the bedroom close to the door in the form of a cat paw print. The blood was human. We don't have a match for this sample, but from the DNA we can determine that they may have come from north Africa. This is consistent with the fibre dye, of the piece of material caught on the front door, that is only used in Morocco."

"So right now we've no identification unless we have a suspect to match it against," Foster interrupted, cutting to the chase.

"Yes. We've eliminated Ethan Harris's DNA but in any case, and as you know, he was at work at the time when the killing occurred," she replied.

"So it looks like the cat scratched the killer's leg, perhaps in reaction to the gunshot sound."

"That's correct. Moving onto the CCTV camera records, we've identified seven cars recorded during the two-hour period."

"Surely a lot more cars would have passed by during that time," Jones said.

"Yes, but we've determined that the killer was in the house for about two minutes, and that it would have taken them another two minutes to drive between the first camera and Onslow Square and then on from Onslow Square to the second camera. So we narrowed it down to cars that stopped for between two and four minutes between the two cameras."

"We'll check the cars you've identified," said Scott. He looked at Coulson, who nodded.

Reinhardt continued. "Just going back to the blood for a moment, there were two other items of note. She was four weeks pregnant and she may not have known it. Her husband either for that matter."

"He never mentioned it. We'll be talking to him again soon, so we can bring it up with him then," said Scott. "I guess it's not impossible that she was having an affair. That might explain a secret pregnancy and possibly provide a motive for the killing," Scott replied. "You had another item of note?"

"This was most unusual. The blood toxicology results came back as negative. However, we detected traces of steroids in her blood and muscle tissue growth pattern consistent with taking a lot of steroids in her teen years, possibly for athletics. Except that that wouldn't have been normal in this country in the 1980s. In fact, the particular steroid we identified was only ever manufactured in East Germany. Perhaps she grew up there?"

"That's interesting alright," said Scott. "Is that everything?"

"Yes."

Scott stood. "Okay, thanks very much Evelyn, we'll let you go."

"One last thing," she said. "When Zak Turner, our data analyst, examined Rachel's phone, he identified a hidden app sending location information and lots of other data back to a server every sixty minutes. We were unable to determine further information about this tracking activity except to say that it is similar to methods used by the intelligence agencies."

"Thanks very much, Evelyn."

Scott disconnected the call.

"So," he said. "Other investigations?"

Detective Coulson flipped over some pages he had in front of him. "This may be relevant," he said. "Ethan Harris's name seemed familiar to me. Using the report we had on another case dealing with moneylenders and extortion, I checked the list of names we recovered from illegal moneylenders. His name was on it. Perhaps he may have been in a little financial trouble."

"Okay, so we'll need a warrant to get his bank records," said Scott. "I did talk to his manager in the investment bank he works for and managed to persuade him to provide some relevant information. But it's an investment bank – he doesn't have that kind of money. At least, we've confirmation that he had no investments there. But I did get his work phone call records for the last three months. Lucy, perhaps you can analyse that?"

He handed a thumb drive to Clarke. "I think we're starting to see there could be some grounds for having Ethan Harris as a suspect in this investigation," he said. "Maybe he hired the professional killer."

"Yes, that's a definite possibility," Foster replied.

"I'll request a warrant to have his house fully searched. Forensics only looked at the hall and bedroom murder scenes, but I think we need to seize all the computers, phones, hard drives and anything else relevant so that we can get a clearer picture."

"I'll handle the warrant request," Foster said. "Hopefully we can have it by this afternoon. Don't forget we may get some useful information from Joseph Morgan if or when he wakes from the coma. I'll arrange for an officer to wait outside the ICU in the hospital and to report as soon as he is conscious. Effectively, he's under arrest. But this is unofficial; the hospital won't allow that until he has recovered to a certain degree."

"And we need to bring Ethan back in for further questioning," said Scott. "I'll organise that while his house is being searched. Okay, thanks everyone. That's it for now."

Back at his desk, Scott wrote up some notes from the meeting. Ethan Harris was now officially a suspect although he did not know it yet. The unknown contract killer was the chief suspect; however, it might prove more difficult to trace him. There was a possibility that Ethan Harris had a motive to hire someone to kill his wife. Also, if he had hired the killer then they needed to find some connection – a suspicious payment, an email, internet use. They just needed to do more research.

Jones walked up to Scott. "This Harris guy seems to have led a more complex life than we initially thought."

Scott looked up. "Yes, we'll find out more when we interview him again, shortly. I've talked to Waterman at MitaSimi bank and it seems that there was a hacking incident there, directly in the area that Ethan Harris was responsible for. Perhaps there's a connection."

An email appeared on his PC screen. It was from Detective Coulson.

"I've confirmed the moneylender connection from a 'snout'," it read. "It seems like he paid back 25k some months ago. He took a beating at the same time by all accounts. Maybe he had a cocaine habit or possibly gambling. I'll do some more digging."

Scott turned to Jones. "Can you go and talk to Bill Taylor at MitaSimi? I believe he was the closest colleague to Ethan Harris. He may be able to provide more information than that prat Waterman."

On his way home, Jones called Bill Taylor. "Mr Taylor, it's DI Jones here. I need to talk to you about Ethan Harris, can I meet you later today, say three pm?"

"Oh, eh, okay," he said. "I guess so."

Later, Bill Taylor took the stairs to the third floor. He knew well enough to knock on Waterman's door before putting his head around it.

"DI Jones is coming over to interview me later," he said.

Waterman glared at him. "Just tell him what he needs to know and get rid of him as soon as possible. We need to avoid any publicity on this. If Harris is somehow involved in the murder of his wife, we need to get some distance from it. I don't want the bank being implicated in any way in this affair, especially if it gets out to the press. And it always does."

Taylor turned to go.

"Just a minute," said Waterman. "I want you to draw up a list of all the current work items Harris is involved in. You may need to take over on them shortly."

"Really? Right. I mean, of course. Thank you, sir."

15:00

Jones and Bill talked in a small meeting room at MitaSimi Bank.

"What I need to know," said Jones, "is did you notice anything suspicious about Ethan Harris? You worked more closely with him than anyone else here."

Bill paused a moment to think. He knew about Ethan's gambling habit and hoped that would not come up as a topic for discussion, especially since he himself was a recovering gambler. If that came out, then his job might come under threat. Certainly his possible promotion would. But at the same time, he could not deny all knowledge of Ethan's strange behaviour in recent times, because if Ethan's gambling was exposed later, they would know he had been covering for him.

"Well about a year ago, his work level declined a bit. I assumed it was the fact that his young daughter had been so ill. But even after she recovered fully, I had to cover for him occasionally. It was like there was some other agenda in his life."

Jones nodded and continued his notes.

"Do you know if he was involved in anything like drugs, gambling, an affair, or something else?"

"I don't know. Perhaps. He definitely showed less dedication to his work. There were a couple of times where he did ask me to cover for him if his wife called. When she rang, I just said he'd stepped out of the office for a few minutes and then I texted him to let him know that she'd called the office."

"When was that?"

"A few months back, mostly outside of regular working hours. He and I often had to work late but many times it was just me here, trying to get things finished."

"Did he ever give any indication of what was going on?"

"Not really. He was under stress. But then everyone's under stress here. Maybe it was just getting to him."

"Okay, thanks very much Mr Taylor. Let me know if you think of anything else." He handed his card to Bill. Then, just as he was about to leave, he turned back.

"Just one more thing. Did he ever borrow any money from you?"

Bill blushed. "Yes," he blurted, before he had a chance to think things through.

"Well?" Jones waited for him to continue.

"He did borrow some money. I don't know why I didn't think of it when you asked earlier. He borrowed 5k from me about six months ago and promised to pay it back within two weeks. But he never did. I asked him for it several times later and he always promised to have it for me as soon as possible, but he just didn't do it. I was buying an apartment at the time and I needed the money but I never got it back from him. Now I think of it, every time I mentioned it, he got annoyed like there was suddenly extra stress on him. So I let it lie for a while, hoping he'd pay me eventually, when he could."

Bill felt disgusted with himself, as though he had betrayed Ethan. Not that it was intentional.

"Thank you," said Jones again, and he left.

CHAPTER TWENTY-THREE

Police Closing In

29th July, 2015. Onslow Square, Kensington.

On Wednesday morning, the day after Rachel's funeral, Ethan noticed what appeared to be an unmarked police car, directly across the street from his front room window. There was someone sitting in it for hours apparently doing nothing. Normally he would never have noticed this, but today was not a usual day. He was home alone, sitting in his front room thinking about the funeral on the previous day, when he suddenly became aware that the guy had been sitting in the car for hours. Maybe he was just paranoid, but he felt like he was being observed, and once that thought had entered his mind, he could not get rid of it. He paced around the house, peering out occasionally across the street. "That guy is definitely watching the house," he thought. His suspicions were confirmed when Scott and Jones arrived at his door. He was standing just inside, in the hallway, when they arrived, so he opened the door immediately when Scott rang the bell.

"Expecting us, Mr Harris?"

"No. Well, maybe. Is that one of your officers across the street in the car?"

Scott ignored the question and he and Jones walked straight into the hallway, without waiting for an invitation.

"We need to interview you again for further information, Mr Harris," Scott said.

"Okay. Come into the living room," Ethan suggested.

"No, I think it would be better if we had our discussion down at the station," Scott replied. He then ushered Ethan out the door.

"Are you arresting me?" asked Ethan.

"No, not at this time. But we need to ask you some further questions and it's better to do it in the station."

The phrase 'not at this time' filled Ethan with fear and anger. Instinctively, he knew they were planning to arrest him if they could find sufficient evidence to charge him with Rachel's murder. But he knew he was innocent.

"Will I need a solicitor?"

"Not unless you feel you need one."

So if he insisted on his solicitor then they would see it as a sort of sign that he had to defend himself and that might be an indication of some guilt.

Without another word he got into the car and they drove in silence to the station.

In the interview room, Scott sat opposite him and turned on the audio recorder.

"DCI Scott interviewing Ethan Harris on 29th July 2015 at 11:30 am."

Ethan felt both nervous and defensive.

"So, Mr Harris," continued Scott. "I want to ask you about your financial position."

"Yes? What do you need to know?" Ethan's stomach muscles tightened.

"Are you in financial difficulty at the moment?"

"What has my financial position got to do with the murder of my wife?"

"A lot as it seems," said Scott, smiling slightly. "So, can you answer the question?"

"Well if you mean 'am I bankrupt?' then the answer is 'no'. If you mean 'do I have debts?', then yes I do, like most people, but I have a good job and I can pay them."

"I understand that, but most people, especially those living where you do, and with your position at work, do not go to a moneylender when they need a loan. So why did you?"

Ethan was dumbfounded. He had suspected they would probably eventually find out about that, but he was surprised that they had done so already. What else did they know? Was he going to implicate himself by lying? But then he was not just going to roll over and give in, either.

"I needed a loan for some house improvements and I had extended my credit a little too far so my bank wasn't forthcoming."

"Your house looked pretty good to me. And no one in your circumstances would go to a moneylender. Come on Mr Harris, we're not stupid."

"Okay, okay. I had a little gambling debt and I needed the funds urgently. And I needed to hide it from Rachel."

"Would you call 25k a little debt?" Scott asked.

"It didn't start out as 25k; it was 10k to start."

"So you have a little habit then?"

"Yes, I had, but I've dealt with it, that's not a crime is it?"

"No, not at all, what you do with your money is entirely your business, once it isn't anything illegal."

"Thanks," said Ethan sarcastically.

"But," continued Scott. "When your bank accounts are empty, you've got a serious gambling habit, you owe 25k to a loan shark and…"

Scott paused for effect.

"…and your wife has an account with 500k in it, and she has just been murdered, I'd say that was some cause for suspicion, wouldn't you?"

Ethan felt like he'd been punched in the stomach. He gasped for air. Where had Rachel got 500k from? This was beginning to look really bad for him. He summoned what energy he could.

"She didn't have 500k in her accounts, not even 50k. Anyway, since you've been looking at my accounts and

Rachel's too, then I guess you know everything about us. So why the questions if you already know it all?"

"We want to understand your involvement in this affair. We want to know when and how you hired a contract killer to murder your wife. We have a lot of evidence now and it will be much better for you if you cooperate."

"I never hired anyone to kill Rachel, no matter what you think of me."

There was a knock on the door. Scott paused the interview, and Ethan saw him look angrily at Jones as he came in.

Ethan overheard Jones whispering in Scott's ear, "The search warrant has been delayed."

Scott nodded. He turned to Ethan.

"We're going to pause this interview, for now. However, we will be resuming it soon. I'll have you dropped back to your house, but we will be continuing our discussion, possibly tomorrow."

Ethan was relieved; something had bought him some time. He declined the lift, preferring to make his own way back to his home, or, as he tended to think of it these days, his house.

As he walked out of the station, an unseasonal chilly wind blew from the north, whipping up rubbish on the streets and adding to his mood of isolation and impending doom.

He was definitely a suspect now. They had him in their sights. They were going to hang a charge on him, and soon. He knew it.

Who had killed Rachel? Where did she get that £500,000 from? What was she involved in? The moneylenders had threatened him and his family, but he'd paid them off months ago, so it couldn't be them; they would have acted long ago.

One thing seemed for sure – they were going to arrest him soon, for something he did not do.

What to do? Where to go? His mind was spinning as he got back to his house, his empty shell house.

He went to bed. Perhaps he could think more clearly there. Or maybe he could sleep and stop thinking for a while. Even that would be better.

An hour and a half later, he woke, cold and with a crick in his neck. He got up and began searching the house. Perhaps there was something in Rachel's papers that would show how she got that money. But he found nothing unusual, just some business stuff relating to her graphic design work. Sure, she made some money from that, but nothing like £500,000. He found all her bank account statements, except the one that had the big money. Had she been using a different bank for a special hidden account?

He felt cheated; somehow she had been involved in something he knew nothing about. It was a strange dichotomy – somehow it had been okay with him to have a hidden gambling problem and bank accounts, but it was not okay for her to have secrets. He felt conflicted. Then he remembered that the clock was ticking and that the police could call at any moment, charge him and put him on remand. He needed a plan.

The only thing to do was to leave, to go somewhere else, where he could hide and be anonymous, but where? He took down a big travelling backpack from the attic; it was one of a pair that he and Rachel had bought not long after they had got together to go backpacking through Europe and regain some of their memories of their twenties. That had been a good trip. They had never used the backpacks since though.

He packed some computer equipment and some clothes, just barely what he needed for a week or so. He couldn't think what he would do beyond that. Anyway, nothing else in the house mattered, it was alien to him now, a place to kip in but that gave him no sense of belonging.

He booked an Airbnb room for a few nights near Aldgate, close to where Rachel had had her office. And then he was gone, out the door without a backwards glance, backpack on his shoulder, walking to the tube station.

At South Kensington station, he got a text from Bill Taylor at the bank, telling him to read his email. Waterman had suspended him; they did not want him there while he was under investigation by the police. That was Waterman's style alright. "Presumed guilty." Strangely, Ethan was not put out by this. It was as though he had moved into a new dimension, beyond his old life, leaving behind his work, his house, his old life. Escaping, into the unknown.

He did not bother replying to Taylor or Waterman; somehow they did not seem to matter anymore. Then he remembered that he had not packed his portable hard drive with a lot of personal stuff on it. He walked back to the house.

Scott was livid that he had had to let Harris go after only a few minutes' interview, but when Jones had whispered in his ear that the search warrant was not forthcoming, he had no other choice.

"What do we need to do to get a warrant?" he said angrily to Jones. "We have a case where there was almost a confession from Ethan Harris, and now we have to bend over backwards to get the final evidence we need to prove it." He was red in the face.

Although DCI Scott generally did not see eye-to-eye with Superintendent Foster, there were some occasions when he proved useful. Scott called into him about the delay in getting the warrant to search the Harris household and within two hours, Foster had delivered. He had rephrased the warrant statement and managed to persuade Judge Hartford, an old friend of his from his university days, to delay his lunch and sign off on the warrant. Scott was impressed. His team were ready to act.

He decided that they would come for Ethan right away and bring him to the station to continue the interview while, at the same time, using the warrant to search his house. But when they arrived, there was no answer to the doorbell. Scott tried it again; still no answer. He peered through the letterbox but just saw an empty hallway.

He gestured to the officer who had been watching the house to come over.

"It looks like there's no one home. Did you see anything unusual or anyone leave in the past hour?"

"No sir."

"You were here all that time?"

"Yes. Well. I mean. I'm sorry sir, I just had to find a toilet somewhere. I couldn't have been gone more than two minutes."

"I don't believe this." Scott stood on the steps, staring at the house. "Right, we're entering by force."

Ethan was at the corner of Onslow Square, on his way back for the hard drive, when he spotted the police cars and his front door being broken in. He turned and ran, hoping he had not been spotted. Without thinking, he ran into a Starbucks and ordered a coffee. He needed time to think. He was sweating now; it was pouring out of him. His heart was pounding.

Then he turned off his phone to prevent tracing. They were about to arrest him, that much was clear. He could not go back there. But where could he go? If they were searching for him then they might already know he had booked an Airbnb room; if they had access to his bank account, then they would also have access to his credit card details. But wait. He needed to calm down. He took two deep breaths and sipped his coffee. It was unlikely that they had access to the Airbnb account as they would not have thought of that, not yet anyways. And the credit card payment would not show up for at least a day. So he was okay to stay there for one night.

He took a notepad and pen out of his bag and started to make some notes. There were three things he needed to do: change his identity as there were cameras everywhere, get as much cash as possible as his credit cards could be monitored, and get somewhere safe to stay for longer than one night.

His daily limit on his ATM card was £300, which he withdrew immediately. If only Rachel had not insisted the previous limit of £1,000 be reduced after she had learned about the gambling problem. But that could not be helped. Then he went to his bank branch and tried to withdraw some more money but the account was overdrawn. It reminded him of the gambling problems, attempting to get money and trying to hide it. It crossed his mind that a £300 bet could make him perhaps another £600 which would keep him going for a longer while, but what then? And also, maybe it wasn't such a good idea as he could probably more easily lose it than win some more, and then where would he be?

Next the change of identity: he would get his head shaved (he was going a little bald anyway) and start to grow a goatee and get some dark glasses. Or maybe not, the dark glasses might draw attention to him. Scruffy jeans and tee-shirt look and maybe a beanie hat would help him fade into the background. Perhaps a pair of clear glasses, but where would he get those? He settled for a set of the cheap reading glasses available in a bookstore and he went for the lowest magnification, as close to clear glass as possible.

Finally, there was the issue of finding someplace to stay without fear of discovery. He could not think of anywhere. Still, feeling as though he had a plan of sorts with which to buy himself some time, he got on an eastbound District line train, heading for Aldgate East, paid for by cash. Everything would have to be cash now, where possible, to avoid detection. Once he reached Aldgate and got to the Airbnb house share, he ordered a takeaway. Then he settled into his room to plan what to do next.

It took about two hours for the police team to search Ethan's house and locate what they were looking for. In total, they took away about six boxes of documents, a desktop PC, a laptop, a phone and an assortment of portable hard drives. The computer equipment was sent to forensics, while the other boxes were shipped back to the police incident room for investigation.

DCI Scott was concerned at Harris's absence. He may not have enough evidence to charge him yet, but perhaps the computer forensics would yield that.

Forensics went to work on the computer hardware from the Harris household. The found some interesting details. On Ethan's desktop PC they found hundreds of links to online betting sites. He had login accounts for some of the major ones and links and bookmarks for some of the shadier sites. He had also installed a number of gambling apps. As they expected, there was also a trail of links to adult pornography sites and some images and videos downloaded.

Then they moved on to financial sites that showed he had applied for eight credit cards and that he had also looked at some of the loan sites that provided 'payday loans' and 'automatically approved loans', with very high-interest rates.

As well as logging into his own online banking services, he had also logged into Rachel's bank accounts too, including the one that had about £500,000 in it. And, they discovered, he had moved to the dark web, installed the TOR browser and other utilities to access the TOR network and make his online activities anonymous. Unfortunately, none of this left any trace regarding where he had gone once he was in the dark web. It could have been somewhere completely legitimate or it could have been to make contact with a contract killer – there was no way of knowing. The dark web, the seedy underbelly of the internet, the netherworld, was a haven for drug dealers, pornographers, arms dealers and assassins but it was also used legitimately by investigative journalists and other perfectly innocent users who just valued their privacy and anonymity. It was not illegal to be there, though inferences might be drawn.

Further digging threw up a text file with a north African phone number on it but no name. Forensics did not have Ethan's phone so they could not check if he had called this number. However, they did find a trace of a pre-paid phone having been connected.

Rachel's iMac and hard drives were pretty clean, nearly too clean in some ways. Everybody leaves some digital trail behind them and invariably it includes something murky, but her machine was squeaky clean and so were her external hard drives. Even though they were not investigating her, it made the researchers think that perhaps she had another machine somewhere else.

This was all circumstantial evidence, but perhaps enough for DCI Scott to arrest Ethan Harris and hopefully use the weight of evidence to produce a confession or, at least, something further to go on.

30th July, 2015

When Scott read the forensic report on the Harris computer equipment, the most important item for him was the fact that there was evidence that Ethan Harris had seen his wife's bank account containing £500,000. That, combined with his dire financial problems and a reasonable likelihood that he had used the dark web to find and contract a killer, comprised, in his opinion, enough circumstantial evidence to arrest him.

But now Harris was missing – he had not returned to his house. Maybe he saw the police activity there while it was being searched. Scott tried to call him on his mobile but his phone was turned off. He issued a warrant for his arrest. Then he sat staring at his desk for a while to think it through.

Jones came over.

"Looks like Ethan Harris may have spotted us searching his house," Scott said to him.

"Yes, he hasn't been back in the house since yesterday."

"We've circulated his photograph and description to all offices, with an alert to arrest him."

"Perhaps we need to extend it to airports and ports."

"I've done that already."

Jones sat down in the chair opposite Scott's desk.

"What about progress on the contract killer?" asked Scott.

"It's a bit more difficult. Maybe Joe Morgan might help us identify him when he recovers from the coma."

"Yes but that could be a long while, if ever."

"The follow up on the CCTV images of the drivers in Onslow Square has been narrowed down to two possible suspects. One is mixed race African–Caucasian and the other is white Caucasian. Both men look to be in their mid-thirties. I've the enlarged images here." He reached into his laptop bag and pulled out the images.

Scott studied them for a while. "Both are wearing black shirts. That's a possible match with the fibres found on the Onslow Square house door," he said.

"Yes. We haven't been able to trace either car yet, though. One was stolen, and the other was hired."

"Okay. Let's think through what might have happened. A killer is contracted for a hit and payment is made. He most likely does not operate in the country he lives in. So he probably flew in. Or, possibly, he could have been ultra-cautious and come on the Eurostar train from Paris. That would narrow the number of possibilities for us."

"He could have been living in another city in the UK, like Manchester or Birmingham," Jones suggested.

"Yes, but let's just follow my line of thought for a minute. He most likely wants to be here for the minimum amount of time only. So, he flies in, gets a car, drives to Onslow Square, kills the target, returns to the airport and flies out again. All probably within a few hours. We can check Heathrow, Gatwick, Stansted and London City airports' security photos on the day of the murder, against the two images we have here and then possibly car rental and car theft records at the same time."

"I'll get Coulson on it," said Jones.

"I might just call a quick impromptu meeting. Us, Coulson and Clarke," said Scott.

Within minutes, all four of them were gathered in the meeting room.

"So here's a summary of where we're at," began Scott. "Based on information from interviews with Ethan Harris and the digital forensic report, we have issued a warrant for his arrest. However, he is currently missing, and has not been seen since yesterday lunchtime."

"Gone?" said Clarke.

"Yes, gone to ground. We've also narrowed down the contract killer to two possible suspects. They are being followed up at the moment. We need to close in on Harris as soon as possible so let's get his bank accounts frozen, credit cards suspended, phone tracking enabled and alerts sent to transport control to be on the lookout at tube stations and streets using CCTV feeds.

"He last used his debit card yesterday near South Kensington station. He withdrew the maximum – £300," Jones added. "And we also know he withdrew some cash from the bank, thirty minutes later. So he's moving to cash-only transactions to avoid detection."

"What about his phone?" asked Clarke.

"We know his phone is turned off now. However, there are some basic location services that still work, even when the phone is off, so, if he still has it with him, we may be able to get occasional updates on his location."

"The last location recorded was just outside Aldgate East station, when he turned the phone on for a minute, probably to get the address of where he's staying," said Coulson.

"He knows we'll be hunting him," said Scott, "so he may have walked or used a bus. The street cameras might help us."

"I'll follow up on those," said Clarke.

"We're trailing behind him," said Scott, "following where he's been, and that's good but what we really need to do is to gather intelligence and predict what he's likely to do, and where's he's likely to go."

CHAPTER TWENTY-FOUR

On The Run

30th July, 2015. Café, Whitechapel High Street.

Although he was trying to go off-grid to avoid detection, Ethan knew he would not be able to do this all the time; he needed to keep some contact with his former life. "Former life." The phrase made him realise that his life was changing forever; this was not just a problem to be solved before returning to his old life. Maybe he needed to think, not just about his survival from the police hunt, but also what direction his new life was taking.

He thought about getting a solicitor to help prove his innocence, but the police seemed to have enough evidence to arrest him, so if he went that route, he might end up in prison waiting for months for a trial and a chance to make his case. He decided going on the run was better option.

He went into a cafe with Wi-Fi to set up some new contact points, including a new email. It occurred to him that he would need a new name. Not only that but an entirely new identity: a passport, some background history, a job, an address and a life story that was believable. Maybe this was overkill, or maybe not. Who knew how long it might take to prove his innocence? But it would take a lot of time and money to set those up – things he did not have much of. So he settled on a new name and email.

He also knew he would have to check his old email on occasions, just to find out who was contacting him, but he'd have to be careful when doing that, to avoid detection, as he knew they'd be tracing it.

He was not yet satisfied with his new image – shaved head and a goatee beard. People might still recognise him. What else could he do? Maybe use makeup to give himself a port-wine birthmark on his cheek and nose?

After some searching he found a makeup artist's shop. It took a while to get the birthmark to look realistic. But surely it was worth it. People might glance at it, but nobody would study it in detail for fear of causing offence.

Then he had a better idea. An eye patch. He picked one up easily in a Boots pharmacy. This would be much easier to manage on a day-to-day basis, while having the same effect: people would not stare at his face, or if they did then it would be at the patch. It was a method of hiding in plain sight. The eye patch made people look away; they did not notice his other features. So although his face had been published in newspapers and on the internet as a desperate man who had been charged with involvement in the murder of his wife and was now on the run, no one noticed him. He was free to come and go as he pleased.

He knew he would be flying at some stage. Surely airport cameras would be harder to fool. But maybe not – after all, they were not there to find a wanted criminal. They were mostly used to check people at entry and exit points to the airport, and also to check against a list of known terrorists; thankfully he was not on that list. And once his passport photo on his false passport matched his disguise, no one would give him a second look. That made him think about how he was going to get a false passport.

It was strange. Initially, he had assumed that he would need to blend in, in order to become invisible. Yet, somehow, standing out in a very defined way worked just as well.

After a while, he became more comfortable with his new persona. He knew that the disguise was good enough to fool cameras, random police officers and ordinary interested people who sometimes notice everything about a stranger. The more he thought about it, the more he realised that this was not about disguise, but about identity. Once he believed in his new image, and was confident about it, then everyone else would accept it.

So, for now, he had morphed into a mid-forties guy with a shaven head, a goatee beard, and a patch on his eye. He knew it was a bit theatrical, and he wondered how long this image would last. He would need to have a backup plan, a different disguise, one that he could switch to at a moment's notice, if necessary.

He had never really realised before how pervasive security was, with multiple cameras on every street in the city, at ATMs, modern buildings, old buildings, tube stations, in restaurants and pubs, even sometimes in public toilets. Every time he made a call, paid for something, took a train, walked the street, browsed online, everywhere he drew breath it was noted, observed, recorded, stored forever. He was surprised that this weight of intrusion in his life, no, in everyone's life, had gone unnoticed by him for so long. Perhaps it was just that it had crept up slowly over the years, gradually expanding its scope, until every waking moment was being captured. He certainly felt caught, claustrophobic, and contained like never before.

It was a new awakening. Perhaps he did need a new identity, or multiple ones, to live with any degree of privacy in this brave new world.

Knowing that his cash would run low in a short time, he tried to be frugal and only spend when he had to. It was such a change from his old life where he wasted money on every whim. Every purchase was now a considered one, like when he was low on chips at the casino. But he also knew he had to find another source of money to allow him to survive long enough to prove his innocence. How was he going to do that? And how long would it take?

He did not know what exactly the police were going to charge him with but he assumed it was for being complicit in the murder of his wife. From his last police interview, he knew that they seemed to have gathered quite credible evidence that might point the finger at him.

While checking his email, he saw a message from Julia:

"*Ethan,*

I've just had a call and a visit from Inspector Scott, who is investigating Rachel's murder and it turns out that they are looking for you, and they have a warrant out for your arrest. I can't believe it. You're involved in the death of my lovely Rachel. How could you? I always knew there was something suspicious about you and that Rachel had made a mistake in marrying you. I'm glad I took Katy and now I'm applying for custody of her. You're not a fit father, you never were. You'll never see her again and I hope they catch you soon, lock you up and throw away the key.

Don't try to contact me or try anything to see Katy.
Julia."

It was like a bolt out of the blue. He was shocked and trembling and re-read it several times. It felt like his life was crumbling around him. He had felt thankful that Julia was looking after Katy while he was going through this difficult time, but custody? She had always made it clear that she never really liked him, but this was completely unexpected.

His initial thought was to go and get Katy and take her back, but then what? He would be picked up by the police within a day, and now that Julia might soon have legal custody, they'd be throwing another charge at him. Kidnap of his own child. It sounded ridiculous to him and it also incensed him, but he had to let it go. What else could he do? He could not fight this without giving up his freedom – there would be no chance of winning. He was devastated but forced himself to focus. First, he had to deal with this murder charge. Only after that could consider any custody battle.

It brought the whole thing into sharp focus – how important it was that he avoided detection until his name was cleared. His laptop would have to go – it was too risky using it. Who knew what hidden software might be on it? It could be broadcasting his details and location through the wireless and Bluetooth channels?

His time in this café was up already. He would have to leave to avoid detection. He had made a list of 20 cafés with free Wi-Fi in different parts of London that he could use randomly. He drank the dregs of his coffee, packed his kit, and left.

Over the next few days, he wandered around London, trying to keep a low profile and trying to gather what information he could, but he felt aimless. He wasn't sure what to do but he needed to avoid capture by the police while he figured out a plan.

2nd August, 2015

Nearly three days later his money ran out. He had tried to make it last as long as possible, limited as he was to cash. He had been staying in an old style bed and breakfast that took cash, instead of an Airbnb place, which had to be paid by credit card. But now, with no money he had to do what he never thought would happen: sleep on the streets.

He checked out a couple of homeless hostels. Some were clean, some dirty but all of them were dangerous; it only took a moment inside each one to realise he would be a target for the regular residents. It was not the disinfectant they could smell there, it was his fear, they could also see it in his eyes – he did not look homeless, which made those people immediately suspicious. Except that he was homeless. At least for a while. But perhaps that did not count; maybe he needed to earn his homeless badge in some way, before being accepted on the streets? They knew there was something different about him, so he would be a target; they would surely take his belongings when he slept. He could not risk that.

He was tired. He needed a safe place to lay his head and to sleep for a while. Maybe sleeping rough, just for one or two nights, was the best option. After accepting the offer of a sleeping bag from one of the homeless charities, as well as coffee and a sandwich too, for which he was very grateful, he walked around for miles, looking for somewhere suitable, somewhere safe enough.

He found a spot, under a railway bridge. There were no other homeless people around, just him and the constant drone of cars and the rumble of occasional trains overhead. He stuffed his ears with toilet paper to keep down the noise. Then he got a large cardboard box from a skip nearby and flattened it out like a bed; this would keep the sleeping bag dry and warm.

He went around the corner to the 24-hour garage to use the toilet. The girl on the checkout desk had a kind face. She smiled and opened the locked toilet door for him. He guessed he looked homeless to her because on his way out as he thanked her, she gave him an out-of-date sandwich for free. He was so grateful for this little act of kindness; up to that point most people had just ignored him. Earlier, when he'd stopped for a while on the street, a police officer had moved him on. He never thought he would fall so low, to be dependent on the kindness of strangers.

Well at least it meant his new identity must be working. Or perhaps they weren't hunting him at all. He did not know. He would have to find out somehow, maybe on a TV news broadcast in a pub. Not now, but tomorrow, after he had had got some sleep. If that was possible.

His bed was rough and ready, but it was out of the biting cold wind that seem to have blown up in the last few days, lowering the temperature and bringing a little rain too. He got into the sleeping bag and zipped it up to his neck, then wrapped the hood tightly around his head. His makeshift earplugs lessened the noise of the cars and the occasional train thundering over the bridge above him. Although he was sheltered from the rain to a certain extent, larger drops of water occasionally dripped down from the metal mesh overhead, sometimes hitting a puddle nearby and sometimes landing on the sleeping bag that was beginning to show a large damp spot close to his head and shoulder and on the cardboard below.

He closed his eyes and tried to bring his mind to another place and time, to hide the misery and the cold. He thought back to his earliest, happy memories when he was growing up in Norwood South West London. One particular memory came to him. He was standing in a tiny front garden – hardly worthy of the name – surrounded by a three-foot wooden fence, which had been unpainted for several years and was falling down in places. He must have been around ten years old. He was standing at the gate, looking up the small end-of-terrace Victorian house, with its square bay window and the ubiquitous yellow brick frontage topped off by a slightly sagging roof with grey slates mostly covered in a light green moss and occasional spikes of grass on the edges of the gutters. Of course, at ten years old he did not have the vocabulary to describe these architectural features. But strangely, he could remember all the fine detail clearly.

More specifically, he had been looking at the red chimney stack where his kite was trapped. Then James, his older brother, came out of the front door.

"I told you not to fly it too close to the house", he said. "Now, it's stuck there forever."

Ethan had closed one eye and stared intently at the kite as if willing it to be freed. But no such luck. The string was trapped on one of the chimney stacks, and the kite was fluttering in the breeze, like a dog straining at the leash.

James took the roll of nylon string from his grasp and began whipping it back and forth trying to loosen it. Then, suddenly, it was free. Ethan's heart had soared with it as it swirled and dived and came down to earth on the road outside the house. Elizabeth, their mother, came to the door.

"James, can you bring him to the fields where it's safer to fly it?"

James nodded, and they walked off with the kite. Ethan looked back for a moment and gave his mum a little wave. She smiled back, her warm smile. That moment had stuck in Ethan's mind as the happiest day of his childhood. It was a moment where he had not a care in the world and felt safe and loved in his family.

Looking back, he remembered with fondness those summer days, his kite, the freedom, his mother's love, and endless time stretching out in front of him. If only he could find her now and discover what had happened back then, whatever it was that had made her leave. There had to be a reason and now, more than ever, he needed to know why.

That time seemed so far away, like a distant beacon viewed from rough seas. Such darkness surrounded him. He was so cold and lonely compared to then. Shivering, he pulled up the edge of the sleeping bag to shield himself from the cold wind. Then eventually he drifted off into an uneasy sleep, interrupted at regular intervals by the clatter of trains passing on the bridge overhead.

3rd August 2015

Next morning, he was woken with a start by a car horn blaring in his ear. The makeshift earplugs had not been much use; his ears felt tired from the constant noise he had been trying to block out all night. He throat was dry; he was parched. But he stayed a while in the sleeping bag, choosing its warmth over his desire to drink something.

He went to check the time, but his watch was not on his wrist. His arm had been sticking out of the sleeping bag when he slept; someone must have stolen it. He began to grope around at the end of the sleeping bag with his foot, for his backpack, all his worldly goods. And the watch was there. He remembered – he had pushed it inside the sleeping bag for safety.

He got out and stretched. It was slightly warmer now than the previous day. He needed to shower, change his clothes, brush his teeth and of course, an Americano to kick-start his day. But where?

He looked around. Where was he? He had walked so many miles searching for somewhere to sleep that he had did not know exactly where he was. A police car with siren blaring passed by and instinctively he ducked down out of sight before realised how stupid that was; they weren't looking for him, or at least not that crew.

He realised then where he was – he was under the railway bridge on Southwark Park Road, about five minutes' walk from the Bermondsey tube station. That was where he had helped that little old woman off the tube train, about ten days previously, and then had his backpack stolen on the train as it left without him. That was the day Rachel was killed. He tried to block that thought; he did not want to think of that now.

He walked to a nearby greasy spoon, attracted by the smell of fried bacon. There was a betting shop beside it, but he ignored the temptation, driven by hunger. As he walked, he realised that people were giving him a wide berth because of his dishevelled appearance. He caught his reflection in a plate glass window and tried to tidy himself up a bit; it occurred to him the café might not serve hobos. That was when he realised that he had no money for a drink or a bite to eat.

He saw an ATM on the other side of the street and went across to get some money. As he approached it, he pulled a scarf up around his mouth and lower face for the sake of the security camera there, but then he realised that they would know it was him anyway, by using his debit card. After he had put his card into the machine, it sounded some beeps and displayed a message saying that there was a problem with his account, his card was being retained and he should contact his local bank branch to get the card back.

That was it. His accounts had been frozen and his cards cancelled. He would have to get away now, as fast as possible, avoiding the street cameras if he could. The bank's ATM camera was probably not a real-time feed to a monitoring station, but how could he be sure? Although he worked in banking, investment banks did not have retail

ATMs, as their customers are corporations and wealthy individuals, so he did not know if the ATM security video camera was a live feed.

He got on the next bus that came by, not caring where it was going as long as it went away from there. At least his Oyster card was still working, but for how much longer? And perhaps they were checking that too? It would soon be out of funds with no bank account to feed it. Then he would be walking everywhere, or perhaps he could 'borrow' a bike.

It occurred to him that he could go back to his house that night, under cover of darkness. He might be able to get in and salvage something, some money or maybe something he could sell. He was desperate now for some cash, just for survival. Perhaps he could get a shower and a change of clothes there too. They would still be watching his home, though. If they saw any sign of life there, he would be caught. He would allow himself ten minutes in the house at the maximum, no more.

He was starting to feel isolated. The only person he had spoken to in ages was that girl at the garage the night before. He was hiding and he was being hunted. He had no money, no sense of direction. He did not know where to go or what to do. He just needed to survive a while. Then he would try to figure it out and find a way forward.

By luck, he had got on a number eleven bus, which brought him to Victoria Coach station after about thirty minutes. He was much closer to his house; he could walk there in about another thirty minutes. This would conserve funds on his Oyster card. However, it was way too early; it needed to be dark before he could try to enter his house. So he parked himself in a Starbucks, having found the price of a coffee at the bottom of his backpack; there was always loose change down there. There he could think, safely outside the range of the street cameras. He could plan what he was going to do, including maybe a little research on the net.

After a while, he had formed a plan. First, he had to get some cash as his card was gone and access to his bank accounts had been cut off. He could get some of Rachel's jewellery in the house and try to pawn it to get some quick money. Unless the pawnbrokers looked for some ID? Another possibility was to see if he could find Rachel's debit card; her account might still be open, though probably not for much longer. He knew her PIN so he could probably get £500 or even £1,000 out, though he might only be able to use it once before they figured that out and shut the account down. He could call some friends. But then he would be involving them in this mess. Another option was stealing money. But that felt too risky.

He also needed to find out something about Rachel's £500,000. She must have been hiding something pretty big to be able to get that amount of money. Using Google Maps, he zoomed into his house. A property around the corner had a car park. Maybe he could enter his house by climbing that wall into his back garden.

Four hours had passed. The Starbucks staff had clearly noticed his long stay. Ethan made his way to Onslow Square in the dusk. The police crime scene tape had been put up again around the front of the house, and it looked like a police officer was sitting in an unmarked car across the street, keeping a watch on the house in case he returned. He crept back around the corner to where the carpark was, and sure enough, there was a low wall, perhaps four or five feet high, separating that property from his own. If he managed to scale it, he could then walk along the top of the wall and jump into his back garden.

Scaling the wall was easy. Walking along it, a dog began barking madly, and Ethan nearly fell off, but managed to continue to his garden. Just as he jumped, a light went on in the neighbour's house. Ethan heard them call the dog. He waited quietly for a few minutes in the shadows at the back of the garden until everything had settled down and was quiet again. Then he opened the back door and crept in, knowing that he could find his way around the house in nearly total darkness. He used the light from his phone to help him search.

He found Rachel's debit card almost right away, but nothing else turned up for the rest of his search and with a neighbour next door and a police officer at the front, he decided just to change his clothes and skip the shower, even though he badly needed it. He reckoned the sound of the electric pump, fan and the gurgling water would be heard through the walls.

He was back over the wall and into the carpark in a minute. He made his way to Fulham Road where he tried the card. It worked; he was able to take out £800, which would keep him going for a while. But in his hurry to try the card, he forgot to hide his face from the camera over the ATM.

His disguise was blown. He probably had a day at most to change it. But to what? At least he had money for a bed and breakfast. He would worry about the new disguise the next day.

He was never so glad of a shower, a roof over his head and a soft bed.

The following morning, as he was enjoying the luxury of a cooked breakfast and leafing through the Metro, he saw his old face looking back at him. The article was titled, "Police hunt for a man suspected of having his wife killed". He didn't need to read any further. He knew that the next day there would be a similar article with his new mug shot from the ATM camera. He finished his breakfast and left, making his way to the high street to buy two good wigs and two pairs of thick glasses.

But what to do after that? With his new disguise – a grey wig and thick glasses – he looked older, perhaps in his early fifties. His stubble, which was fast becoming a beard, had flecks of grey in it that matched the wig. He ditched the patch; it had not worked as well as had hoped – people treated it as a curiosity, and he had looked like a modern day pirate. How strange, that an idea that seemed so great could turn out to be useless in practice.

He decided to allocate £400 of his cash to buy a new laptop. He knew he could probably get some money for the old one, but he was scared that too much of his former life and identity were on it. On a laneway off the street, with no one around, he picked up a rock and began smashing it, aiming the blows at the hard drive. Doing this felt strangely cathartic – it was both symbolic and satisfying. He was destroying the remnants of his old life, stripping it away. A woman passed on the laneway while he was doing it. He looked up at her, but she quickened her pace, afraid to look at the madman smashing a computer. In five minutes he had finished, and it was in pieces – hunks of metal and plastic. Most importantly, the hard drive was completely flattened, the last remnants of his former life eliminated. He dumped the rubbish unceremoniously into a nearby skip. The past was over now. This was the official start of his new life.

First he made a trip to a café with Wi-Fi and no nearby CCTV – a Costa coffee shop. Using his new laptop, he logged into his old email account. If he had used his phone it would probably be traced, relatively fast, but there was no chance of that with this new laptop.

He looked at the webcam. It seemed to be looking back at him. He asked the waitress for some tape, which he stuck over webcam and the microphone. Then he sighed. Finally, he felt free.

There were lots of emails in his old account, mostly about his former life. Nothing of interest then. He glanced up at a guy who looked a bit like his previous disguise:

shaven head and goatee, about the same age. Strange. But then, thought Ethan, there must be millions of guys who look like that.

*

DCI Scott was concerned that there had been no sign of Ethan for a number of days and that he'd not been back to his house. They had had his accounts cancelled, and they were tracking him by his laptop and phone and occasional images from CCTV, but there was no pattern in his movements, and they were always getting the information too late. He needed some real time tracking if they were going to catch him. Then Jones told him that he had managed to up the priority with the mobile operator, who had agreed to provide almost real-time information on where the phone was located, using data from GPS and cell towers. Jones had just received a message that the phone was located in a Costa coffee shop near Earl's Court.

*

Ethan was just about to leave when he heard police sirens, several of them. But they were so ubiquitous in the city that, for the first time, he did not immediately conclude that they were coming for him. That was until the door burst open and three police officers entered. A woman screamed. Ethan's heart was beating like a drum now. Was this the end? Another two officers came in from the back of the café. They were all armed. He was just about to put up his hands when he realised that he was not the target. It was the guy with the goatee in the corner. The guy protested loudly as they wrestled him to the ground, handcuffed him and bundled him into the police van outside. It was all over in two minutes. Ethan stayed in his seat, stunned by what had happened. It was like he had been watching his own arrest right in front of his eyes.

Slowly, he got up to leave. It dawned on him that it must have been him, Ethan, they were after, not the other man. They knew his appearance from the ATM CCTV, at least his old one. But how did they track him to the café? He had a new laptop. And his phone was off. Surely they couldn't track him on a turned-off phone? Could they?

He sat down again and began searching for information about phone tracking. Yes, they could track it even if it was turned off, somehow; once the battery had some power then it was still active. He would have to get rid of it. Throw it in the bin, or maybe break it up like the old laptop.

Then he thought of a better idea. He would walk down the busy street with his phone sticking out of his pocket until some pickpocket took it. That would throw the police off his trail for quite a while.

It did not take long for the phone bait to work. When it was safely stolen, he felt yet another strand of his old life was gone. He bought a new phone, the lowest tech one he could find. It was like being back in the 1990s.

This new off-grid life was strangely liberating. But how long could he live like this? He had to find more information before they found him or his new money stash ran out.

CHAPTER TWENTY-FIVE

Meeting Amy

1991. Berlin.

The first big story that Amy Knight worked on took place in Berlin in the 1991; it was on East Berliners' attitudes after the fall of the Wall. She interviewed people who had been oppressed by the Stasi before the Wall came down in 1989 and who, in the new Germany after reunification in 1990, still felt that they were being watched, recorded and spied on.

Could this be the outcome of a lifetime of paranoia, which would not just stop because the regime had changed? Perhaps it would take months or years for those people to feel free, and unchained from daily surveillance. Or could it be that western intelligence agencies in Berlin began watching those who came from the East Berlin in case they had secret loyalties to the disintegrating USSR? During this time, she built up a lot of contacts in Berlin, particularly those doing investigative journalism, one of whom was Axel Mueller, who was working on similar stories. Their articles were published in Der Spiegel.

In 2005, Amy worked with Axel again on a major story about the BND – the German intelligence service – spying on journalists. It turned out that they had put a number of columnists, including her and Axel, under surveillance over the previous five years. BND was trying to find out who was leaking their information in connection with Germany's involvement with US's war in Iraq; they targeted investigative journalists to hijack their information.

When that story broke, there was uproar in the German Parliament. A government investigation committee was set up and eventually the BND was ordered by the German Parliament to cease all spying on journalists. It was a coup for the Press.

This gave Amy a much higher profile. She began covering stories on online privacy and cyber-terrorism on the development and rise in the use of TOR, the anonymous network used by many to access the dark web. After the BND story she was always aware that she could be under surveillance, despite what the German Parliament had ordered, so she was very careful regarding what she said, and where she said it. She was also extra mindful of what was stored on her computer and what she emailed. She had developed a type of routine that bordered OCD to keep herself safe. It was a kind of paranoia, but she had a good reason for it. Ever since the BND story, she really understood why those East Germans still felt under surveillance after reunification.

In 2015, she started a new investigation into information leaks from GCHQ that had been going on for a number of years, but which had been ramped up in 2013. A trail of information led to Rachel Harris. Harris was somehow involved, but Amy could not figure out how. Then Rachel Harris was murdered on the 23rd July 2015 and Amy's interest was piqued even further. She started to focus on Rachel's husband, Ethan Harris.

5th August, 2015
The morning after the man in the café was arrested, an email arrived in Ethan's old email account from an unknown person who identified themselves as A. They requested that he install the PGP (Pretty Good Privacy) secure email application so that they could communicate without fear of it being read by police or intelligence agencies.

If this had happened a month earlier, Ethan would probably have considered it to be some type of spam, and would most likely have ignored the email. However, the last two weeks had been a major learning curve for him on security, privacy and surveillance. He had learned all about Snowden and also about PGP secure email. Perhaps it wasn't paranoia, after all, to be concerned about being tracked. He followed the instructions to set up the privacy software, then shared his public key so people could find it and contact him securely. The following day he received a secure email from Amy Knight.

"Hi Ethan,

My name is Amy Knight. I'm a journalist, and I've been following your case for a while. I believe it would be useful if we met and talked. I know you probably find this email conversation highly unusual and possibly suspect. However, I can assure you that I am genuine and that I have no hidden agenda. I believe I can help you, and I think you can help me with a story that includes some of the undercover work in which your late wife, Rachel, was involved. Please Google my name and you will find lots of articles about my background. Once you're happy that I'm genuine, please reply.

Kind Regards,
Amy."

What was all that about Rachel's undercover work? Sceptical but intrigued, he replied.

"Hi Amy,

Although I'm intrigued by your email and have searched and read about your background, how can I be sure that you are who you say you are, and that you're not just someone hijacking Amy Knight's name to get my confidence? I am an innocent man caught up in a murder investigation, and I certainly don't want to be arrested, as I will lose any chance to prove my innocence.

*Regards,
Ethan."*

She replied right away.

"Thanks for your reply; that's the first step. I know you're probably scared at the moment since you're on the run from the police. You can confirm that I am who I say I am, by not replying to this email but instead, by searching for my public secure email key, as I did for your key. There is only one Amy Knight with a published secure email key. When you find it, use it to send me a secure message. Then you'll know it's me."

He still did not feel quite sure. He needed to think about it for a while. Who was this person and why was she interested in him and Rachel? He knew nothing about intelligence agencies, other than what he had read in the newspapers. Why would an investigative journalist want to speak to him and what information could he possibly have that would be of interest to her? He wrestled with it for a while. If she was genuine, this might be his only hope to find the information he needed to prove his innocence. If she was not, then it was a trap.

But Ethan was a gambler in his heart, even if he was a recovering one. He decided it was worth the chance. He Googled her again and found lots of articles and pictures of her.

They arranged to meet in Cafe Nero on Fulham Road. From his seat in the Goat Bar across the street, Ethan had a perfect view of her sitting by the window wearing a red jacket and reading a book. So far the plan was working. He had been sitting there for thirty minutes and felt assured that she had not been followed, and that she was alone.

He walked across the street, into the cafe and sat down opposite her.

She looked up from her book. She was in her early forties, about five foot, seven inches, thin with short brown hair, designer glasses and a winning smile.

"Amy?"

"Hi Ethan." She smiled. "I'm glad you came. I think we'll be able to help each other."

Feeling relieved, he got himself a coffee and sat down again.

"That's a good wig," she said, touching it with her hand, "It looks and feels like real hair. With your beard grown out, I nearly didn't recognise you, compared to the police photos."

He smiled. "It took a while for me to get a good disguise. It was no problem for me to recognise you, as you look exactly like your photos on the net. I was tracking you for a while from the restaurant across the street."

With the niceties over, they got down to business.

"As you know I'm in a hell of a mess," said Ethan. "And I'm not a guy who hires someone to kill his wife."

"I know that," she said. "I've been working on a story for some time now that possibly involves Rachel."

"What's the background?"

"Well, as you know, I'm an investigative journalist. That often involves covering stories on the police, the intelligence agencies, privacy, hacking and all that sort of stuff."

He nodded.

"Before we continue," she said, "I need to know if you have your laptop and smartphone with you."

"It's okay, I smashed up my original laptop and dumped it. Then I let a pickpocket steal my iPhone, so they're tracking him and not me."

She smiled. "You're learning fast," she said. "So you get the fact that it is tough to have a conversation without being monitored in some way."

"I'm paranoid now."

"You ought to be; these guys are worse than the Stasi."

He was taken aback. He thought that he was talking about police tracking his phone, to catch him.

"You mean the police intelligence?" he said.

"Much more than that, it's not just the police involved here, although that's bad enough. It's the intelligence agencies and secret services."

"GCHQ and MI5. But why?

"Yes, and MI6 too. I'm not exactly sure yet, but the story I've been working on involved the leaking of top secret information, similar to the kind of stuff that you'd find on WikiLeaks. It's big and because of that, it's dangerous. These intelligence service guys don't mess around. If you get in the way, they could take you out."

"And how the hell am I and Rachel connected to that? She was a graphic designer; how could she have any link with all that?"

"I don't know yet; all I know is that some of the information I've uncovered leads to her."

He was a little incredulous. "You'd think since I've known and lived with her for the last four years I might know something about her."

"Yes, I'm sure you know a lot about her life, but not everything. Did she know anything about your gambling habit?"

He blushed. "I suppose that's public knowledge now. No, she didn't know, at least not until it became a major problem for us."

"So it is possible that you were living with her and somehow didn't know everything about her?"

"I guess so. But what exactly was she doing?"

"I'm hoping we can find that out together."

"Well, I've nothing here. As you can see, I've been on the run – travelling light too. I've nothing with me that I can show you."

"What about back in your house?"

"The police have been there and taken a lot of computers and phones and other stuff, and I think they're watching it to see if I return."

"I know, but we need to go back in there."

"I tried already. There was an unmarked police car parked out front."

"There's a lot more than that," she said.

He looked at her inquisitively. "What do you mean?"

"There's MI5 surveillance on the house too."

"How do you know?"

"I just do."

"So, surely it can't be safe to go back there?"

"Probably not. However, now that nobody has been there for a week, it probably has a lower priority for them. They will learn that we've been there, but they won't see it in real time. And they won't be contacting the police. The police probably don't even know that they're involved. That's the way that the intelligence guys like it, keep everyone in the dark."

"We could go back there late tonight; there's a neighbour's carpark and a small wall at the back. But – what are you looking for? I couldn't find anything."

"We weren't looking for the same thing. And the police were looking for evidence of your involvement in your wife's murder."

"So what are you looking for?"

"I'm not sure, but I'll know when I see it."

"Okay, we'll do it. But right now I've got other things to sort out. I'm running out of money, I've nowhere to stay and the police are on my tail."

"I have a spare room – you can stay there for a while."

He was surprised at her generosity. "I don't want to impose."

"We're going to need to work together for a while," she said. "If the police catch you then I won't get my story finished and you'll be in prison. We'll go there now, get you set up and then we'll try to get more info on Rachel's secret life."

They took the tube to Chalk Farm and from there walked to the leafy Regents Park Road where she lived, in the top floor flat of a three-storey Georgian house. He got settled into the spare room, had a shower. He was still tired and cold so he took a nap for an hour. When he woke, he felt refreshed and felt back to normal. He was ready to talk.

There was no doubt that he was glad of her help but he could not help feeling a little wary still. Okay, she wanted to progress her story, and he was helping that, but was that enough reason to be so generous? He felt a little on edge. Perhaps she had another agenda. But he needed her help. He was glad to get it, to be off the streets.

Amy did not want to talk in her apartment, so they walked to the nearby Primrose Hill. The sun had come out from behind the clouds now; finally, they were getting some warmth from it, as it shone onto the trees and park. They walked up the hill. The stress of his situation had eased for a while. Finally, he could share with someone the thoughts that had been in his head since Rachel had been killed. For all the ups and downs he and Rachel had had in their marriage, he had always been able to talk to her and vent his frustrations, even if he had not always told her everything. Now, although he had only met her,

Amy appeared to have traits similar to Rachel; she was a good listener, and a good talker too.

"Let me give you a little background to the story I'm working on," she started.

"Yes, that would be useful."

"My investigation started when one of my contacts in the intelligence community mentioned a GCHQ project called 'MindBend', which I had never heard of. As always, any new story was of interest to me, but when I asked for more information, the contact just said that they shouldn't have mentioned it and then they clammed up. I pressured him, but he wouldn't budge and in fact he looked a bit scared. That really piqued my interest – I started digging around. But every time I mentioned it to any of my other contacts, there was always a deafening silence, like they didn't want to discuss it, or were afraid to."

"So you were up against a brick wall?"

"Yes, but then I started to dig into all the documents I'd received over the last few months, and I should tell you that I get quite a lot of documents sent to me, often anonymously. In this way, I was able to get a little more information about it, enough to know that it was a top secret GCHQ project, connected with individual privacy, and that there had been some information leaks. But even in the intelligence circles, there was virtually no communication about it, or who was involved in it. When I asked for names, none was forthcoming. I did eventually get an alias though, called Epsilon, who was apparently running the project."

"Where did you find all this out?"

"I can't reveal the sources but they are reliable, and we communicate securely. They've provided me with lots of information, mostly via the dark web."

Ethan had heard of the dark web, or deep web as he had also heard it called, but he knew little about it.

"I probably should know more about it," he said. "But all I know is that it's been used by drug dealers, like on Silk Road, and arms dealers, pornographers, and all kinds of illegal trading and communication," he said.

"Yes, all that stuff is there, just like there's seedy areas in a city and you know they're there but you don't have to be involved in it. But it's also a place where journalists or any ordinary person can communicate securely and can meet contacts, without surveillance, and can get access to information that would be impossible to get via the conventional internet, without being monitored and possibly compromising the contacts. So yes, you have drug dealers and online pimps living cheek by jowl with ordinary folks, each with their own agenda. The only thing in common between them is that they don't want the intelligence gods snooping on everything they say or do."

He nodded.

"You'll be learning a lot more about it soon. Anyway, I found that there was a leak of information from MindBend, although I haven't seen any of the leaked documents. Apparently it's been going on for a few years. But the information hasn't surfaced anywhere yet, probably because it's being consumed by some other foreign intelligence agency. But by all accounts things got a lot worse for them two years ago."

"So whatever it is that MindBend is doing might never come to light," said Ethan.

"Yes. But if I can crack open this story then it will be in the public domain. There'll be a light shining on those cockroaches – they'll be scurrying into the shadows, to avoid the fallout." She smiled.

"And how is that connected to Rachel?"

"I'm not sure, but I know she was receiving some MindBend information and somehow passing it on, some of which was sourced from GCHQ. So she must have been involved, I just don't know how, yet."

"Was the connection to Rachel at our home or her office? You know she had an office?"

"Yes. It was mostly at her office."

"After Katy was born she didn't use it that much, perhaps for a day or two per month."

"We'll need to check both locations. Let's start with your house. We have to go back there to find something that the police forensics team would have overlooked. They're just police investigators – they know nothing about intelligence activities. In fact, sometimes they are just pawns, moved around and controlled by the intelligence guys when they want someone arrested, or something revealed."

"How can we know if anything is ever the truth then? It could all be just misinformation, propaganda to make us think or believe something."

"That's exactly it. We can't know if something is true or not; we just have to decide on a case by case basis. It's like that quote from some American politician – 'When war comes the first casualty is truth'. And it's a war that the intelligence agencies have been waging for a long time."

After taking in the panoramic view of the London skyline from the top of Primrose Hill, they made their way back through the park, and then through the lovely Georgian streets back to Amy's apartment. Ethan wanted to know more, particularly about how Amy had been following information about Rachel. But they had arrived back to her apartment, and she would not talk there. She just did not believe that the conversation would be private, she explained to him. It was just a way of life for her.

CHAPTER TWENTY-SIX

Ethan Investigates

6th August, 2015. Amy's flat, Regents Park Road.

Back in the flat, Ethan returned to his bed for a second nap. While he slept, Amy sat at her window seat for a long time, gazing at the street below. Who was this Rachel Harris? What was her deal? These were not new questions. When Amy first came across Rachel online she had known straight away that her interests extended beyond graphic design. She had read some online articles about privacy and activism, for instance, that had been posted by an anonymous source on a blog. More significantly, some rather blurred images of buildings and of people posted in these articles contained hidden, embedded location information, which she had had tracked to Rachel's office. At first, that seemed a surprising lapse by Rachel, especially as she was writing about privacy. But even the most private people can let their guard down for a moment. Maybe, thought Amy, Rachel did a lot of this kind of thing. That's when she started to track her.

Then, while researching a separate story about a leak from a department in GCHQ, Amy analysed some data on the IP addresses – the digital locations – and the routes that the secret files had taken on their journey across the internet. Reading through a list of such locations, one stood out and triggered something in her memory. She had seen it somewhere before, but where? She searched through her files, only to find that it matched the digital address of Rachel's office. Bingo.

She knew she was on to something. Further analysis led to the discovery that some secret files had ended up at Rachel's computer. Not just once, but approximately every two weeks.

Earlier, Ethan had mentioned that Rachel had only used her office approximately every two weeks. That must have been when she received the secret files. But Amy still had no idea what Rachel did with them. It was like a dead end. What was her involvement with them and why?

That evening, on their way to Ethan's house, she asked him if he remembered any specific dates when Rachel worked in her office. Ethan thought a while and then was able to give three dates he was sure of because they were days after public holidays and he remembered them.

It was dark as they walked towards Onslow Square. When they arrived, the first thing they did was check to see if the police officer in the unmarked car was still there. He was. So they took the back route through the car park, up onto the wall and down into the back garden. Fortunately, the dog did not start to bark this time and they gained entry to the house without any problems.

Ethan showed Amy all the places where Rachel had stored files but, of course, her phone and computer were no longer there as the police forensics team had taken them. They searched everywhere and were just about to leave when Amy opened the drawers in Rachel's desk pedestal and put her hand underneath each open drawer. It was a pretty obvious hiding place, a bit like hiding something under a potted plant outside a door. But on the last drawer, she felt a key stuck to its underside. She pulled it out, stepping back excitedly. As she did so, she knocked over a large floor lamp. It hit the ground with a huge crash.

They stood motionless. Then voices started up from the other side of the wall. "That's the neighbour's bedroom," whispered Ethan. As he spoke, the neighbour's security flood lights came on at the back of their house. There was no doubt but that they would call the police. Ethan and Amy ran down the stairs and out the back, just as the front door creaked open. Without pausing to look behind them, they jumped up on the wall, now fully lit by the floodlight from next door. Ethan scaled it easily, but Amy fell back onto the ground. The dog from next door was barking madly now from on the other side of the wall and the neighbour had opened a window and was shouting at them. The police officer appeared then at the back door, just as Amy was scrambling back onto the wall. Ethan put his hand down to help her as the police officer grabbed her foot. If he had been one second earlier, he would have had a firmer grip but Amy managed to pull away from him. She and Ethan ran along the wall to freedom, with the sound of police sirens in the distance.

By the time they reached in the car park, the police car had arrived at the front of it. They had just enough time to run around the corner and through the gate into the park where there was lots of cover under the trees. They stood still for a while to catch their breaths. Should they wait until it quietened down or would that give the police time to trap them in the park? They were acting on instinct now, and fear, pumped up with adrenaline.

But there was no time to think. Ethan led the way to the gate on the other side of the park and then they were out onto the street and down an alleyway, out of breath and out of sight and safe for a while. As they hunkered down behind a small wall, Amy started laughing. Ethan began laughing too. Then they heard footsteps in the alley. He shushed her, putting his hand over her mouth. They watched in silence as a man with a dog walked past. The dog sniffed the ground close to them and gave a short bark before its owner jerked its lead away and they continued out of sight. Amy and Ethan were safe again, for now. But had they been caught on the street CCTV? It was possible.

Back at police HQ, DCI Scott was both pleased and disappointed. Ethan had surfaced again, which was good, but he had escaped, which was not so good. And it looked like he had some help. He flicked through the street CCTV cameras for images. Two showed potential. But it was dark. He zoomed in to see if he could identify either person. He was reasonably sure one was Ethan, but it was not impossible that it had just been a random burglar. Scott needed some real evidence. It was a black and white image, and was not very clear; when he zoomed in it became pretty grainy, and the two figures were not that recognisable. Maybe Detective Clarke, who was the local photographic expert in the station, could enhance the images enough to be identifiable? But she was on a day off. It would have to wait until morning. With a little luck, they would get an enhanced image showing Ethan and his accomplice.

Back at Amy's flat, Amy and Ethan went down to the end of the communal back garden so they could talk in private. She took out the key and looked at it.

"Do you know what it's for?" she asked.

"No, I've never seen it before. I'm pretty sure it's not for anything in the house."

"So her office then?"

"Possibly. I haven't been there for quite a while. Or maybe it's for a bank security box."

"They could be watching the office too."

"Most likely. And now that they've seen us at the house there will be extra security at the office."

"Okay. We know we need to check there, but not just right away. Why don't we search the internet to see what kind of key it is, what it could open? A lockbox? A safe? At least then we'll know where we have to look."

Amy opened her laptop and searched anonymously. They found two possibilities for the key and their assumptions had been correct: a bank security deposit box and a business security lockbox.

"So did you and Rachel have joint bank accounts or separate ones?" she asked.

"Separate ones, and at different banks."

"Then she would never have thought there would be any reason for you to be at her bank. That's good. It means there is a possibility that the safety deposit box is at her bank. Or maybe she used one of the specialist deposit box companies. Let's think. If I wanted to keep something hidden and safe, I'd probably use something unconnected to my life, so a specialist company is a better bet. But it would also have to be reasonably accessible. Let's find all the safety deposit businesses that are relatively close to her office at Aldgate – there can't be that many of them."

Ethan was already searching. "Just five, one in Chancery Lane, and one at Hatton Garden, both of them only a few tube stops away from Aldgate and three others, a little further away. But how do we do it? We can't just walk in there with the key; we'll have to produce some ID."

"You have Rachel's details, and I have a contact who can make up a fake ID with my photo on it," said Amy.

"But if we arrive at the company that doesn't have the box, then they'll get suspicious and maybe call the police."

"Okay. So what if you ring each of them, give them your name and tell them you want to get something from your wife's deposit box? You could say she's ill or something. Then they'll either say that they're sorry, there's no deposit box under her name, or they'll say that only she can access the box."

"That could work," said Ethan.

"I'll arrange that fake ID." She reached for her phone and called a number. Then she put it on speakerphone so Ethan could hear.

"Gino? It's Amy, I need an urgent favour."

"Good to hear from you, Amy. What can I do for you?"

"I need a fake driver's licence."

"No problem, I'll need your photo and details. I can have it ready in a few hours."

"Thanks, Gino, much appreciated. I'll drop the photo over to you later." She hung up.

"Wow, I'm very impressed," said Ethan. "You've got great contacts."

"You need to, in my business. Gino owes me big time – I helped him get his brother and mother into the UK, which was proving difficult for him, given his prison record. But he's basically a sound guy, just in the wrong business."

Ethan nodded, then wrote down Rachel's details on a piece paper and gave it to her.

"I'm going out now to get a passport photo for Gino. You can call the safety deposit companies tomorrow morning to find out which one we need to go to, assuming, of course, we are on the right track."

7th August, 2015
The following morning, Ethan had bad news. None of the security companies had a box for Rachel.

"Perhaps she used a different name, or maybe she did use her bank's safety deposit facility. Or maybe the key was for a safe at her office."

But the bank did not have a safe box for Rachel either. It was beginning to look like they would have to go to her office to see if it was there.

They waited until it was dark. Her office was on Osborn Street, just around the corner from the Whitechapel Gallery. It was on the second floor, over a café and facing a derelict lot. When they arrived they could see that the café was closed, and the street was pretty deserted, but just to be safe they watched a while before walking around the nearby streets. To their surprise, no one seemed to be watching the office. And there was only one CCTV camera at the end of the street, too far away for them to be recognisable should they be caught on it.

Fortunately, Ethan had Rachel's spare office key on his key-ring and he remembered the alarm code. It was simply a matter of walking inside and deactivating the alarm.

Inside they left the lights off so that they would not attract attention. It was just a single office, with a desk, some computer equipment and some storage presses. While Amy kept an eye on the street outside, just in case anyone was coming, Ethan found a safe at the end of the storage press. The key fit. He called Amy over, then opened it. Inside were a number of items: a small MacBook laptop, two passports and a large, bulging envelope. He opened the envelope to find three packets inside it, each stuffed with cash: one in pounds sterling, one in US dollars and one in Euro.

They were so absorbed by their discovery that they never heard the security man come into to the office and turn on the lights. He was a small, obese man in his mid-fifties.

"What the hell is going on here?"

They looked up and then at each other. Ethan stuffed the money packets into his backpack. Amy had the MacBook in her hands, and she grabbed the passports. Without a word they both ran in opposite directions. The security man didn't know where to turn.

"I don't want any trouble," he said. He backed out of the office and out of their way, letting them escape. He seemed more concerned for himself than for what they were taking.

As they were running down the stairs, he called after them. "Run you bastards, the cops are on their way."

But they were down the stairs and out the door in a few seconds, running on to Whitechapel Road, past the Gallery and heading towards Aldgate East Tube station. No one pursued them. Neither of them spoke until they were back in their little spot at the end of the garden.

"There's 5k in each packet," said Ethan "So she had an emergency escape plan." He looked at the passports. "Whatever about me, she would never have left Katy. Would she?"

Amy did not know about how Ethan's mother had left when he was a child. But she could see he seemed particularly disturbed by the idea. "Perhaps she made this plan before Katy was born. I'm sure after Katy came along, she could never have considered leaving her."

"No, you're right." He looked at the cash. "Although she didn't intend it, this will keep us going for quite a while."

"And the passports might come in useful if we need to get out of here for a while. I'll get Gino to change them, so we both have new identities."

"What about the MacBook? Hopefully, we'll find what she was up to."

"We can do that back in the apartment."

But they found nothing on the MacBook. It was such a let-down.

"Maybe there's stuff hidden here that we just can't see." she said.

Ethan thought for a moment. "A friend of mine from work, Bill, has a background in digital forensics. It's what he did before he joined the bank, and when we were hacked he used those skills to uncover a hidden trail the hackers left behind. Perhaps he can help with this. I don't want to get him involved in all this mess, but we really need to know what's on this Mac."

"You'll have to be careful; the police have probably interviewed him, given that he worked with you."

"I think I can trust him. He's a good guy, and he knows I'm not a killer. I'll try to talk to him tomorrow morning. He likes to get into work early, when there's no one around, so perhaps I can arrange to meet him and give him the Mac."

8th August, 2015

The next morning, Ethan was up at 06:00, trawling again through the contents of Rachel's MacBook, but to no avail. At seven, he called Bill. He knew he would be in by then.

"Bill, it's Ethan."

There was a long silence.

"Ethan," said Bill finally. "I heard the police were looking for you. But I know you didn't do it."

"Thanks, Bill. They think I'm involved because of the gambling and the debts, you know what it's like. It feels a bit like I've been set up. Actually, I'm trying to work on a few leads to prove my innocence."

"Let me know if I can help."

"That's what I was hoping you'd say. I appreciate it. I don't want you to get involved in this mess, but I just need a little favour. I need your help in an area of your expertise – digital forensics."

"Okay," said Bill, hesitantly. "What do you want me to look at?"

"It's a MacBook that Rachel owned. She was using it for some work on the dark side."

"What do you mean?"

"She seems to have been leading a double life and was involved in some intelligence agency spying activity. I know it sounds unbelievable, but I've already got some proof. The thing is, this MacBook was a secret laptop she used for that undercover work."

"So, what's on it?"

"I was hoping you could help there. It looks pretty clean on the surface, but I know that there is bound to be a lot of stuff hidden on it. And you're the guy who can find it."

"Okay, make an image backup of the main hard drive and put it on one of those small portable drives. I'll have a look at it when I can."

"Great, I'll get that over to you later."

Ethan went out to buy a portable hard drive for the backup. When he came back, Amy was up.

"Bill has agreed to do some deep scanning on the MacBook hard drive, so I'm making a backup for him."

"Are you going to see him later?"

"Yes, at lunchtime. Hopefully he'll have some update by the end of the day."

At lunchtime, it was a quick matter of passing the portable hard drive to Bill in the café they usually went to. Later that evening, Ethan got a text from him.

"Ethan, I've analysed that drive and found lots of interesting stuff. I'm sending you a secure email with the details."

Ethan's hands shook as he pointed the cursor to the secure email. He read without pausing.

"Ethan,

I've recovered a cache of hidden files from the backup drive you gave me, which I've attached to this email.

There was a hidden folder containing hundreds of encrypted files, but the source of them is unknown as they were routed around the world anonymously. Each file has very strong encryption, which would indicate that they are top secret, but there is no indication of their content. Without the encryption key, even the best encryption-breaking applications could take months to process each one. I searched for the encryption key that she used and found it eventually, hidden on the drive, but I didn't decrypt any of the files as I don't want to know what's in them. Once that Pandora's box is open, you can never close it.

I'll leave that up to you, but my advice is only to look at one or two of them to confirm their content and leave the rest as they are. You don't want to be burdened with this dangerous knowledge, which could get you killed. It's best you just don't know it so it can't be tortured out of you (I know that sounds awful, but that's what could happen if you come in contact with the people involved in this).

Rachel appears to have been merging the encrypted files into ordinary JPEG image files and posting them along with her text on her blog site. In this way, no one would know they were there except the people who were expecting them, and they obviously have the encryption key so they can decrypt and view them. She was hiding the files in plain sight where no one would ever expect to find them.

There was also an accounting log of sorts, which detailed payments made on a monthly basis, approximately 20k per month for about the last two years and about 5k per month for the previous five years. In all, slightly more than 500k.

It's fairly clear from this that she was part of a spying ring. And based on the money she was paid, it must have been highly valuable information. One last thing of note is: for some reason the amount of work she was doing increased four-fold from about mid-2013."

Ethan was stunned. How could that have been happening without him knowing anything about it? Suddenly he felt different about her, like she had been betraying him all the time they had known each other. He felt cheated, disgusted. But despite that, he still needed to know the full story. Who had she been working for? What was in those files that was so important? Why was Rachel doing this?

And who had arranged to have her killed? It seemed like the more this investigation went on, more questions were being raised than were being answered.

He and Amy went for a chat in the garden.

"I know this is difficult for you Ethan," she said.

"I'm so angry at her. I feel cheated."

"You were. But we still don't have the full story yet. You need to decrypt some of those files."

"Let's leave it for tonight. We can take it up again in the morning when we're fresher."

"How could someone do that? Deliberately lead a completely hidden life. My life with her has been a complete lie. She probably never loved me. I was just a handy cover for her. Perhaps even Katy was a mistake?"

"It may not have been like that. Maybe she started out in that direction and then was unable to change. Hopefully, we'll find out more about her motivations. It's late now; let's sleep on it and discuss it further in the morning."

The following morning, Amy and Ethan looked at the rest of the details that Bill had uncovered from the MacBook. They noticed that two names had shown up in a number of documents: Petra Meyer and Nadine Richter. Bill had also managed to access the website administration area of Rachel's blog and so he had been able to analyse the location of users who had viewed her blog articles. Although he didn't know who the users were, he was able to determine that they were located in Berlin using their IP addresses, or digital locations. All of the images containing encrypted files had been accessed from Berlin on the same day that they were posted by Rachel. This seemed to indicate she had somehow been communicating to someone the fact that new encrypted information had been uploaded.

It was a fairly strong indication that the person who was receiving the top secret encrypted GCHQ files was located in Berlin.

"These names sound German," said Amy. "Perhaps Nadine Richter and Petra Meyer were the people in Berlin receiving the secret files."

"Can we investigate them from here in London?" asked Ethan.

"Yes we can, but we may have to go to Berlin; it's likely we'll need to talk to some people there, to get more information."

"Unfortunately, I don't speak German," he said.

"That's ok; they mostly speak perfect English there. The research will definitely require German, but luckily, I'm fluent as I've spent quite a bit of time there in the past; some of my articles were published in Der Spiegel."

"That's great, but the police are looking for me. I may have a disguise that seems to be working but my passport has my real identification on it; they could arrest me at the airport."

"Perhaps I should call Gino again and see if he can change the two passports we found in Rachel's safe box."

"Good idea."

Amy called Gino, who agreed to help modify the passports to create fake identities. But it was going to take two days at least.

"We can do some research and planning in the next two days before the passports are ready," said Ethan.

"Okay, let's go and grab some coffee and breakfast now and discuss it."

They walked up Camden Town to Café Rouge, which was close to the train bridge on Chalk Farm Road. As Ethan was getting the food, Amy began reading a newspaper that had been left on the next table. She never bought papers now as she got all the news she needed on the net. Well, perhaps not all the news – there was an article on the inside pages titled, "Police hunt for Ethan Harris". The piece noted that he was being helped by a journalist, Amy Knight, as they had both been caught on CCTV camera leaving the house in Onslow Square two nights previously.

She called Ethan over.

"Look, they caught us on one of the CCTVs when we went to your house the night before last."

"They'll have a search warrant for your apartment, by now."

"No they won't, because it's not my apartment. I've just borrowed it from a friend who's travelling for a few months. They have no way of finding me unless, of course, we're being followed."

"We better leave now, separately. We'll meet back at the apartment, but check if you are being followed. If you are, try to lose them by going through the crowds in Camden Market."

They met back at the apartment. Neither thought they had been followed.

"Perhaps we should go to Berlin right away to investigate the story and to escape the heat of the police hunt," said Ethan.

"In a week, this will have all died down – no one will remember, except the police of course. But the press and publicity will be gone. Anyway, we have to wait for the passports for two days. Why don't we just keep our heads down and stay in the apartment as much as possible? Fortunately, no one knows me here, so there's little chance of a neighbour recognising us."

"I think we should pack though. Just in case we have to leave at a moment's notice."

"You're right. And we need to buy some prepaid debit cards." She paused. "We can't book our flights until we have the cards and the passports, and then I think we should fly from different airports. You fly from Gatwick, and I'll fly from Heathrow."

"That makes sense."

With his identity blown again, Ethan had to change something, so he shaved off his beard, which was quite thick and bushy, and left his moustache. It felt so strange; he never had a moustache before. Amy laughed when she saw it.

CHAPTER TWENTY-SEVEN

Going to Berlin

9th August, 2015. Amy's flat, Regents Park Road.

The following evening, Gino emailed Amy to let her know the "products" were ready to be picked up. Once they had them, they booked their flights for the following day. Amy's flight was in the morning, from Heathrow, while Ethan's flight was at lunchtime from Gatwick. They arranged to meet up at the Alexa Centre near Alexanderplatz in Berlin later in the afternoon. Now they were using false passports and credit cards, they could book Airbnb, so Ethan booked an apartment for a week near the trendy Prenzlauer Berg area, which was relatively central.

Amy's disguise was simple. She'd dyed her hair dark red and wore a hat that came down over her forehead, shading some of her face. She was wearing tight black yoga pants and a sporty top and looked like she was in her mid-thirties. Her journey went smoothly – she had no problem with security and her passport was accepted. Perhaps it was because of her confident nature and the fact that she had been in similar situations in the past. Her heart was beating fast but on the surface, she looked cool, calm and collected.

Ethan had fared worse. He had forgotten that in his false passport, the photo of him had a full bushy beard, while now he just had a moustache. He was nervous too and sweating profusely. At baggage security, they pulled him into a side room to be interviewed.

"Just come this way, sir," said the woman at baggage security, pointing to a small room. "We need you to bring your bags, ticket and passport over here."

"Is there a problem?"

"No, we just need to talk to you for a moment, sir." The words were spoken politely but the there was a certain underlying tone that made him more nervous. Was he caught? Was this the end of the line? Maybe the start of a prison term? He felt guilty even though he had not done anything wrong. Perhaps it was all those years of Catholic guilt drummed into him as a kid when he was growing up; he always felt guilty in situations where his innocence was questioned.

He tried to steady himself. What was he guilty of? He hadn't killed anyone or even stolen anything. Then he remembered that he was using a false passport, and blushed at the thought of it. Luckily he was alone in the room.

After ten minutes, an airport official came in. He didn't know if this guy was airport police or some other airport official.

"Sit down, Mr Copley, I just want to talk to you for a minute."

He was about to say "but I'm not Mr Copley, you've got the wrong person," when he realised that that was his false name – Kevin Copley.

He sat down.

There was a knock on the door: it was a police officer with a drug-sniffing dog. The other officer waved him in. First, the dog sniffed Ethan front and back and then his luggage. Finally, he sat back beside his master looking disappointed. They left. The remaining officer continued.

"We noticed that when you were coming through security you seemed very nervous."

Ethan did not reply.

"So you're flying to Berlin, is that your final destination?"

"Yes." He could barely speak. His heart was thumping.

"Is that business or leisure?"

He thought a moment. If he said business, then they'd want to know more. "Leisure," he said.

"We've checked your bags and passport, sir, and they seem in order, but – " He paused for a moment and then studied the passport photo. He looked at Ethan and then back at the photo again.

"You shaved your beard? And left a moustache?"

"Yes, it's very hot in Berlin at the moment."

"You appear to be extremely nervous. Is there something wrong?"

"N-no, no, I'm just scared of flying," he lied. He was surprised how easy and believable it sounded.

"Okay, Mr Copley, no problem. Are you flying with someone else, perhaps they can help?"

"N-no, it's just that I was already nervous coming here, and this interview has increased the stress even more."

"No problem sir, we'll let you back to your departure gate right away."

The man stood and opened the door. Ethan rushed out, grabbing the tickets and passport from his hand as he left. He was only able to relax after he had strapped himself into his seat and the plane had taken off. Then he slept a while, glad to be free.

A few hours later, having landed at Berlin's Schönefeld airport, he was stopped again, this time by passport control. There seemed to be an issue with his passport. There was a queue building up behind him, so they moved him over to a small side room.

"We're having a little problem with your passport, Mr Copley. Where was it issued?" the officer asked him.

He should have paid more attention to it before he left. "I'm not sure."

"But it's your passport."

He was tempted to say, "I'll bet you don't remember the fine details of your passport." But he bit his lip.

"Is there a problem with it?"

"Maybe, we're not sure, we're have trouble finding your details on our database."

He needed something now to prevent further investigation. "My passport was lost, and they had to issue a replacement one at short notice, perhaps they changed the number."

"Perhaps," said the officer but he did not seem satisfied. "Okay, Mr Copley, we're going to let you through. But we'll need to photocopy your passport so we can verify it."

He copied the passport front page on the photocopier behind them and then handed it back to him.

"Thanks."

The officer nodded and opened the door.

At this stage, Ethan was sweating profusely again. He needed a drink. A large one. He ordered a brandy at the airport bar and sat back in a comfortable high-backed leather chair. He had arrived, finally.

Kensington Police Station
DCI Scott had lost the trail again. Even with a published article and some photographs of Ethan and Amy they had not found them. There had been a few calls from the public but none of them had turned up anything of interest.

"Let's just sum up what we know," he said to Jones. "Our main suspect, the contract killer, appears to have vanished. They probably left the country, and we have no clear identification for them. We know they used a stolen car. It was found burnt out near Dagenham. So the killer's gone. We can continue to try and find out more about them, but it won't move this case forward. Harris is our best shot, no pun intended."

Jones smiled.

"So Harris has that investigative journalist, Amy Knight, helping him for some reason," continued Scott. "She must have another agenda. The CCTV image was a bit blurry even with photo enhancement, but there was enough detail to identify them both. The ports and airports have been notified to watch for them, but nothing has turned up so far."

There was a knock on the door. Detective Coulson came in.

"Sir, I thought you'd want to know – I arrested Gino Corelli on a counterfeit documents charge this morning. In his office we found evidence of recent activity in forging two passports. When we looked at his PC, his last email was a message to Amy Knight letting her know that the "products" were ready. So I think we can assume that he made false passports for Knight and Harris."

"Good work, Coulson, that's excellent news. Can we get the false passport names and check against the airport passenger lists for yesterday and today?"

"I've done that already, sir. Amy Knight flew to Berlin this morning from Heathrow using her false passport and Ethan Harris flew to Berlin at lunchtime from Gatwick using his false passport."

"Excellent work, Coulson. I'll notify the Berlin police with their details. Hopefully they can be picked up there."

Coulson left.

"Thank God for that," said Scott. Foster had been putting him under pressure to get some results and up to that point, he and Jones had had very little to show for their efforts. Now there was progress. Even better, it was out of his hands for a while, until the Berlin police caught up with Harris and Knight.

Perhaps he could celebrate with a trip to an art auction? Or maybe he should wait until they were actually arrested. He decided the latter was probably best.

Alexanderplatz, Berlin

Amy was worried that something had happened to Ethan. Maybe he had been arrested. She recapped. They had arranged to meet in the Alexa Shopping Mall, which was close to Alexanderplatz, at around 14:00. His flight had landed at 12:00, giving him plenty of time to get from Schönefeld airport by 14:00. But it was now 15:30. She sent a few texts using a new smartphone she had bought under her fake name, but there was no reply.

And then, eventually, he arrived.

"Have you been drinking?" she said.

"Just a couple of brandies," he said, slurring slightly. "To calm myself."

"What?"

He described his airport ordeals.

"I see. That does sound pretty bad." She was surprised by herself; even though she had only known him a short time, she was starting to feel a certain closeness to him. Perhaps it was just the intensity of the situation they had found themselves sharing over the last week. Anyway, she was glad he had arrived and was safe.

They decided to go straight to Prenzlauer Berg, to the apartment they had rented for the week, so they could rest a while and talk freely.

It was a studio apartment that comprised one large room with two single beds pushed together at one end and a large living area at the other end, with French doors out to a balcony overlooking a small park. There was also a separate kitchen. Though basic and sparsely furnished, it was perfectly satisfactory for their needs. They separated the beds and lay down on them for a while.

Then Amy put together a list of places and people to contact. Firstly, they needed to find more information about the two people who had been identified on Rachel's MacBook: Petra Meyer and Nadine Richter.

Amy had quite a number of contacts in Berlin, as she had worked there for a few years. Her closest contact was Axel Mueller, who she had already contacted before they left, in order to bring him up to date on the story and possibly get him involved in researching some of it.

She went into the little kitchen and closed the door so as not to disturb Ethan, who was still resting. Then she called Axel.

"Axel, we're here in Berlin, how are you?"

"Amy, it's so good to hear from you. Since you emailed, I've done a little research on the information you're looking for."

"Great, can we meet tomorrow morning to discuss?"

"Sounds good, see you later."

11th August, 2015

The following morning, Amy and Ethan took the U-Bahn together to Potsdamer Platz. They went to the Sony Centre where she had arranged to meet Axel. It had been more than nine years since Amy had talked to Axel and she almost did not recognise him in the café – he looked a lot older and heavier. His hair was grey and balding, although his eyes still had that bright sparkle she remembered from almost a decade before.

They embraced and she was reminded of a deeper connection from the past. Then she introduced Ethan.

"Axel, this is Ethan who I've been working with since his wife, Rachel, was murdered."

"Good to meet you, Ethan." They shook hands.

"So, I've seen your articles online and in print from time to time," she said.

Axel smiled. "Yes, still in the same sea of betrayal, corruption and murder, but there's always something new."

"I don't know if you've seen the story of the murder of Rachel Harris in London? It may not have had much visibility here."

"Yes, I know all about it. I – " He paused. "You go first."

"Well, this story has links to intelligence agencies both in the UK and here."

He leaned closer. "Go on."

"I've been following a trail of leaked information from GCHQ that leads to Berlin. I've got some names of the people who might be involved. However, a lot has changed since I was here. I was hoping that you might be interested in working on the story with me. You could help us get the information we need."

"Sure Amy, I'm happy to help. And I'd like to know more about your investigation and what DCI Scott thinks happened."

She was surprised that he knew that DCI Scott was investigating.

"So you know a bit about the case?"

"Yes, maybe more than you're aware. As you know, I usually track what the police and intelligence agencies are following as it gives me good leads into new stories. I think you should know that the Berlin police have been notified this morning, by DCI Scott, about you and Ethan's arrival here."

"They're tracking us already?" She was surprised.

"Yes, they have your alias names and passport photos, and there is a warrant out for your arrest."

This was a blow. She had not expected them to be on their trail so fast. She had hoped for some time in Berlin to investigate, without the pressure of a police hunt.

Ethan was taken aback too.

"Do you know anything more about the Berlin police involvement?" he asked.

"No, there was no further information available," said Axel.

"But there are higher profile cases here at the moment, so it may have a lower priority for a while."

"Thanks, Axel. We could have walked right into their arms, completely unaware that we were being tracked. This makes things a bit more urgent."

Axel nodded.

"Obviously, the BND are not going to just talk to us," she continued. "Especially since our last encounter with them led to their severe embarrassment back in 2005. In fact, they'd be delighted to find Ethan and me and hand us over to the Berlin police, for payback. But I need some way to leverage information, which they have."

"I've been thinking about that since you contacted me a few days ago," said Axel. "This could be a bit dangerous and it could backfire. But if it works you might get what you want."

"Go on."

"Well as you know, a certain number of people in the BND came from the old Stasi, after reunification. Many of those guys went into hiding; however, some key people in the Stasi were of interest to the BND. They had the right skill set and a lot of knowledge. I was researching a story on three BND officials who had been in the Stasi, guys with a bad reputation. I felt there might be a story in it, by searching the Stasi archive. But I've never had enough time to finish it. You know the way it is, there's always something new coming along. So I just put this story on the back burner for a while, until I had time."

"Okay," said Amy.

"I know these guys have a dirty past, and they'd like to keep it in the past, but the information is there, in the public domain, in the Stasi archive, which, as you know is open to the public. It's just that it will take a bit of time and perseverance to dig out the incriminating information. If you and Ethan can do it, then you'll have the leverage to force them to tell you what you need to know."

"They'll hardly roll over that easy."

"No, they'll certainly put up a fight, and it might even be seriously dangerous for both of you."

Amy was worried.

"The minimum retaliation they'll do is to turn you over to the Berlin police and have them deport you. But depending on how bad the story is, they might consider taking you out."

"It's always a worry with those guys. You have to have something to bargain with in order to stay alive," she said.

"Yes, so when you find the incriminating information, copy it to me and I'll put in in a secure location. I will also set it up so that it will be automatically emailed to a number of journalists and made public after a week, unless we stop it. In this way, if they harm you the information will get exposed. That way, they won't risk it."

She nodded. "Great idea, Axel."

"So when we make contact with them to trade information, show them a bit of what you have found. Then we'll let them know that their dirty little secret is set to go public unless they cooperate. They'll want to trade then, but they won't be happy."

"Yes."

"One other thing," said Axel. "You mentioned the code name Epsilon as the person running the MindBend programme. I've managed to find out that his name is David Powell. Does that name mean anything to you?"

"No, I've never heard of him." Said Amy.

Ethan was surprised.

"Are you sure it's David Powell?"

"Yes, do you know him?"

"David Powell is Rachel's father. They never got on and hadn't spoken in years. But I saw him at Rachel's funeral. I wasn't talking to him because I was never introduced to him, but Rachel had showed me a picture of him a long time ago; that's the only reason I recognised him. He didn't seem to talk to anyone."

"So, the director of MindBend attends his daughter's funeral anonymously," said Amy. "Was he involved in her killing? Surely not."

"Well, someone contracted the hit-man," said Ethan. "So it's possible."

"We know Rachel was involved in handling leaked information from GCHQ, possibly MindBend. We know she was estranged from her father who is the director of

MindBend. Someone ordered a hit on her, so it is possible that he was involved," he said.

"How could we ever prove it?" said Amy.

"I don't know. It's not what we're here to find out, but there may be much more to this story than we think."

"I've got to go guys," said Axel. "But I'll arrange some new IDs as soon as I can. I'll call you again tomorrow, and then you can start your research on the Stasi archive."

"Thanks, Axel, without your help we'd have had no chance."

"You're welcome, but be careful."

He hugged Amy again, shook Ethan's hand and left.

For a while after Axel had left, Ethan and Amy sat in silence. Then Ethan spoke.

"So we're on the run again," he said.

"It never really stopped, did it? It was just delayed for a while. I was hoping for a bit longer – time to find out who was handling the GCHQ files. But at least we have a plan now."

"What about the Berlin police being after us?"

"Well, we better only use cash from now on; they might be tracking our credit cards. Just as well we have Rachel's stash. We need to move to new accommodation. But we'll have to wait until we get the new IDs."

Later, back at apartment, Amy turned on the TV to get the local news. At the very end of the broadcast, there was a small segment about a police investigation and hunt for Ethan Harris and Amy Knight, "two fugitives from the

UK wanted as part of a murder investigation". Amy translated for Ethan. Then a photo of the two of them appeared on the screen.

"We need to be ready to get out of here at a moment's notice," she said. "As soon as Axel has the new IDs for us, we'll go."

"At least the photos didn't show us in our current disguise. And they didn't use our aliases."

"Yes, but the police know them. We'll still need to change apartment."

12th August, 2015

The following day was busy. First, after Axel had called, Amy met up with him to get the new IDs and the names of three BND agents to research. Then she and Ethan found a new apartment available on a short-term lease close to the S-Bahn station at Tiergarten. Once they had done that, their first destination was the Stasi Records Agency (BStU), which was open to the public and which holds all the Stasi records.

They made their way to the BStU offices on Karl Liebknecht Strasse, close to Alexanderplatz. Axel had given them press cards as their form of ID, so they pretended they were doing research for a magazine article. This gave them wider access to the records held there. The three people they were searching for were Werner Huber, Andreas Keller and Max Schreiber. Axel had also given Amy some basic information about each of them to help with the search. There was a recent photo of each of them, their dates of birth, and what part of Germany they were from.

Ethan suggested that it might also be useful to search for Petra Meyer and Nadine Richter as well while they were there. He worked on that; the information in the filing cabinets was organised alphabetically, so his lack of German was not a problem.

After a few hours of searching, he had located files for both women. He brought them over to Amy so she could read them. The file on Petra Meyer was small and only contained information up to 1987. There was nothing of interest in it except only mundane life events recorded on a monthly basis, up to 1987, which was odd. Perhaps she had died or escaped or moved somewhere else, but the reason the records stopped at that time had not been recorded.

The file on Nadine Richter was much more detailed. It showed some connection to Petra – the two girls had gone to school together, and there was only a year between them in age. In this case, copious details about Nadine's daily life were recorded, as they were for her sister Helga and their parents. No doubt their house had been bugged. In 1986 both parents were charged with offences against the state and were sent to prison. The testimony of two neighbours was recorded showing that they had noticed unusual behaviour by the Richter family, that the father was anti-Stasi, and that they seemed to be in regular contact with some English-speaking people because they heard phone conversations through the adjoining apartment walls. After their parents had been taken into custody, Nadine and her younger sister Helga were sent to live with an 'approved' family in another part of the city.

The file also contained letters written by Petra to Nadine, but none of them had ever been delivered. She had sent her letters via their old school, who she had asked to forward them on to Nadine if possible. But nothing was ever delivered. The letters had simply ended up in the Stasi file.

The close monitoring of the sisters continued after their placement with the new family, right up to 1989. But there were no further records in the file about their parents. It was if they had just disappeared. Perhaps they had.

It was a poignant story; possibly one of thousands of similar stories. But it did not bring them any closer to identifying how they were connected to Rachel Harris. There were some phone numbers and addresses in the files but the chances of anyone still being contactable after so many years seemed slim. Perhaps the information on the three Stasi officers would bring more useful information.

Unfortunately, it was a lot more difficult for Amy to gather the information she needed on the three officers. That was because all the information recorded by the Stasi Records Agency was organised by each individual that had been monitored. She ended up looking through about one hundred files before she could start building up a picture of the activity of these guys.

By the end of the second day, however, she had assembled enough information to discuss the issue with Ethan.

"I'm starting to see a pattern for these Stasi officers, well for two of them anyway; I can't find anything on Andreas Keller."

"So what have you found?"

"It looks like Werner Huber and Max Schreiber worked together in the same Stasi unit. They were tasked with identifying and spying on those who were on the fringes of society, anyone who didn't fit the social norm: gypsies, members of some religious sects, gay and transsexual people, foreigners, non-whites, and some disabled people. Most of the cases they dealt with seem to disappear. The information in the files just stops after the individual is arrested and interviewed. There's no further record of them doing anything and no record of them being sent to prison, or being transferred somewhere else. Hundreds of them simply disappeared at the hands of these two Stasi officers."

"God."

"My guess is these guys may have been operating their own agenda, above and beyond their normal surveillance duties. We've no direct proof but it seems like they sometimes killed the people they arrested, because they did not fit in with the norm."

"That sounds a bit like ethnic cleansing," replied Ethan. "More like something out of Nazi Germany than Stasi East Germany."

"Well, back in the 1950s some of the original Stasi officers had also been Nazis in the war years, not that many people knew about it. So perhaps there's a link further back to the Nazis. But that would be much more difficult to find, without a lot more research and time."

"And if it's true, as well as helping us, this could be a big story."

"True, but for our immediate purposes, we just need to get enough information to enable us to force these BND guys into helping us. The bigger story can be handled by Axel. We can pass on what we've found to him, in return for him helping us."

"That makes sense," said Ethan.

"Now we've some idea of the kind of activity they were involved in, we might need to find some hard evidence that proves individual cases. To get the in-depth detail in a few cases may take a while. And I'll have to search other parts of the archive."

"Well," said Ethan, "every day we're here, we run the risk of being caught. So why don't we just use what we've got so far, and decide how we're going to approach these guys?"

"Okay, that's a better idea. Though as soon as we contact them, they will immediately start to use all their intelligence agency resources to find us and shut us down."

"With the BND and the police on our tail, we'll be under serious pressure," said Ethan.

"I know. We need an escape plan as well. Well, for now, let's collect what we've got into files and scan them, so we have an electronic copy of the data. Then we can put it somewhere safe, encrypted, in the dark web, beyond their reach. And then we can get Axel to set up that automatic email plan to publicise the information in a week unless we stop it."

"That might be the only thing between us and prison."

"It might be the only thing between us and death."

CHAPTER TWENTY-EIGHT

BND Information

14th August, 2015. Café Krone, Prenzlauer Berg.

"Now we have the leverage, how are we going to play this?" asked Ethan.

Amy thought a while. "Well, we have the BND details Axel gave us, the email addresses and photos, and also all the info we've dug up on them from the Stasi Archive, but we can't just call them. So, how do we make contact, given they are high-ranking BND officials, and it could be hard to get to them directly?"

"Perhaps an anonymous email, showing a little of what we've got, and that we want to trade information," suggested Ethan.

"Good idea, but we have to be firm that we will only deal with Huber and Schreiber."

Ethan nodded. Then he drafted the email and Amy sent it.

A day passed before they got a one-line reply saying that it was not their policy to operate on that basis. They were expecting that kind of response, so they decided to up the ante. Amy replied, describing some more of the information she had found and indicating that there was a lot more where that came from, and that it would all be released unless they made contact immediately, using an anonymous messaging service on the dark web.

A reply came through almost immediately. It was from Schreiber.

"*I am interested in meeting you. Schreiber.*"

That was all it said.

Amy replied.

"*Schreiber,*

We have a lot of information of interest to you and we want to exchange it for details that are of interest to us. From our research at the Stasi Archive, we have proof of your involvement with Huber in many cases where you arrested people who simply disappeared. We know you killed them and we have proof.

We need the following information:

– Details of payments made to Rachel Harris.

– Rachel Harris's contact in Berlin.

– Who in GCHQ ordered Rachel Harris's killing.

– Details on the MindBend project.

If you provide these details, then we will not publish our research findings.

Our information is already in a secure location and is set to be automatically released into the public domain in two days' time, on 17st August 2015, unless we stop it.

Amy Knight."

The last two demands were a long shot but given the BND had been sucking information from GCHQ for quite a while, she knew that they would know.

A reply came back from Schreiber. He needed to know the full information they had, so they agreed to send the USB memory stick to him. Ethan put it in an empty cigarette box and stuck it in a waste bin on Alexanderplatz. Once it was in place, Amy sent another email with instructions on how to find it. Then she and Ethan watched from a safe distance, across the crowded square, as a tall, thin man wearing a dark coat picked it up. It looked like Huber.

Within an hour, they got another email.

"We are willing to trade but we will not send the information via the dark net. It will be on paper and you will have to pick it up."

Amy knew if they had to pick up a letter, Schreiber and Huber would be lying in wait to arrest them or worse. That was clear. And there was another problem: how could Schreiber and Huber ever be sure that the secret information about them would never be revealed? They could not – they could only plant other information in the Stasi Archive that would contradict it.

So it was a very dangerous game that Amy and Ethan were playing. These guys were not really on the BND team; they were ensuring their own survival.

Time was running out for both sides. Amy and Ethan would have to leave soon; already they had seen more police reports in the news, this time showing their fake ID names and photos of them in disguise. It was becoming increasingly dangerous to go out during the day, so they began staying indoors during daylight, only going out at night time, and even then they tried to cover themselves up. Every time they saw the police on the streets or police cars passing by they felt the pressure and knew they were looking for them. If the police stopped them for any reason and checked them out, there was no doubt that they would be arrested.

But then it occurred to Ethan that maybe some of this pressure could be used to force Schreiber and Huber to act. If the police arrested them, then the timed release of the Stasi information would happen automatically, and there would be no one there to prevent it.

Amy sent a message to Schreiber:

"Time is running out and if we are arrested by the police we will not be able to stop the automatic release of your information into the public domain."

16th August, 2015

Eventually, Huber and Schreiber agreed to drop the information in a letter at a location to be decided by Amy. In this way, she could switch the drop location at the last moment and avoid an ambush. There was only one day left for them to act before the automatic release was triggered. Once that happened, they would have nothing to bargain with, and they would face eventual capture and imprisonment. That was the lose–lose situation that they wanted to avoid at all costs.

And then it happened. Ethan had just gone out to the shop to get some milk. It was late in the evening so the sun was down and it was getting dark. While queuing to pay, two police officers came in. Immediately he turned away. That knee-jerk reaction was probably what gave him away. He should have just remained calm. Then they passed by him on one of the aisles. Ethan breathed a sigh of relief. But the relief was short-lived; a moment later, just as he was about to pay, they returned. There was one on each side of him.

One of them said something to him in German. He replied in English that he did not understand.

"Ethan Harris, we have a warrant for your arrest."

Ethan simply nodded. Then they handcuffed him with his hands behind his back, took him outside and radioed for a police car to come and pick him up.

By the time the police car arrived, a small crowd had gathered around the outside of the shop, where the policemen waited with Ethan. Then he was whisked off to the police station where he was checked in and then put into a holding cell.

It was completely windowless with a bench bed on one side and a toilet opposite it. The white–grey walls were mostly clear except for some initials scratched into the paintwork and bits of sentences scrawled in German over the bench. The thought crossed his mind that this could be how his life was going to be – cooped up in an eight-by-ten cell like a dog – for months to come. Possibly years.

Would he be shipped back to the UK to face murder charges? What would happen to Amy? If he was going to be extradited back to the UK that could take weeks or months before the legal work was sorted out. Did that mean he would be transferred to a German prison on remand?

The eye-level flap in the cell door opened, and a cup of tea and a sandwich were placed on the shelf. The officer said something in German, which he did not understand. But he was delighted with the food. Only when he saw it did he realise how hungry he was.

When half an hour had passed without Ethan's return, Amy knew something was up. But how to find out? How could she even be sure he had been arrested? Perhaps there had been an accident? Or maybe he had been attacked and robbed?

No. She knew it in her heart – he had been arrested. Soon there was a report on a local news bulletin that a man had been arrested, possibly Ethan Harris, who was wanted for murder in the UK.

It was all down to her now. She alone had to get the information from Huber. Hopefully that would eventually lead to Ethan's release. Unless – could she could force Huber to help?

She sent him a message.

"Ethan Harris has been arrested. I need you to go to the police as a BND officer and demand that he is released into your custody, stating that it was an intelligence case he was involved in and that no information about this should be released by them to the press. Unless you do this I will trigger the publication of the information immediately, as I have nothing to lose. Once you have secured Ethan's release from the police, then give him the letter with the information we requested and set him free."

It felt a bit ridiculous, this new demand. But who knew? Maybe it would work.

Huber replied.

"Why should we do this? Our arrangement is to trade the information you have, for the information we have. That has nothing to do with Ethan Harris's arrest. That's his problem. We don't want to get involved."

She replied.

"It's your problem now. This arrangement can't work without both of us being free. Do what I've asked or this will be the end of your life in the BND."

Half an hour later, his reply came.

"Okay, we'll do it. But remember if you break your side of the bargain and reveal anything about us, Werner and I will make it our life's goal to hunt you down and kill you. We have a lot of resources, and if you cross us, we will take you out."

The warning struck fear into her core; she felt both relieved and shocked at the same time. They were reaching the end game now. She needed to plan their escape from Berlin once Ethan had been freed and had the information they needed.

Online, she reset the deadline for the automatic release of the Stasi information, pushing it back by a week.

Later that day Huber and Schreiber arrived at the police station where Ethan was held. After showing their BND identification to the senior officer at the station, they were ushered into a meeting room where the Polizeihauptkommissar, or chief inspector, who was dealing with the case, came to meet them. They said they were from the BND and were dealing with a case that involved national security. They needed to take Ethan Harris into their custody.

The Polizeihauptkommissar was surprised at the request; this had never happened before and he did not like this interference in his work, even if it was from an agency that somehow had precedence over the police. He refused to release Ethan, a position that Huber accepted before respectfully requesting to see his superior, the Polizeirat – police superintendent – Andreas Neumann.

A while later, they were directed upstairs to the Polizeirat's office. Neumann was a tall, slim man in his mid-fifties, with greying hair and a certain toughness in his face that spoke volumes about his authority.

Huber and Schreiber greeted him with respect before outlining their request again. He was also surprised at the demand, but he usually complied with BND requests as he had some contacts there and liked to keep on good terms with them. Huber was an expert in getting what he wanted. Noticing straightaway that Neumann's weakness was his ego, he began by praising the work Neumann's command had done, particularly in capturing Ethan Harris. Neumann took the bait; he was like a purring cat having his belly stroked. He offered them some drinks and enquired on how some of his contacts in BND were doing. Then, with the niceties over, they got down to business. Neumann explained that although he would be happy to release Harris into their custody, he needed to get some recognition for his capture, at a higher level. Huber assured him that his boss would draft a memo to the

Polizeidirektor – Police Director – thanking him for his cooperation. Then he added that, for security reasons, this arrangement needed to be kept private. Neumann agreed. Within half an hour, the arrangements were made.

Ethan's cell door was thrown open, waking him from a fitful sleep. Two officers stood over him.

"Mr Harris," said one of them. "Please come with us. You're being transferred."

"Where am I being transferred to?"

They shrugged their shoulders, then directed him out of the cell and into an interview room where Schreiber and Huber were waiting with the Polizeirat, Neumann. He signalled to the police officers to leave, and he turned to Ethan.

"Mr Harris, these are two officials from the intelligence service, BND, Max Schreiber and Werner Huber."

Ethan was momentarily speechless at being confronted by the BND officials. He nodded, and they smiled, coldly. He assumed that they were going to interview him.

"As your case is part of an intelligence investigation, we are transferring you to their custody."

Ethan backed away.

"No, no, these guys want to kill me."

Neumann raised his eyebrows in surprise.

"Kill you? What do you mean Mr Harris? You've never met these gentlemen before so how do you know they want to kill you?"

If Ethan revealed what he knew about them, then his bargaining power to get the information he needed would be gone. But at the same time, he was afraid that they would harm him.

"Well, Mr Harris, what's your issue with these officials?"

He decided to say nothing.

"Well?" Neumann continued.

"Nothing, I've nothing to say."

"Okay, then you need to sign here." He handed him a document and pen and pointed to the signature line.

After signing the document, Ethan was led out of the police office with Schreiber and Huber on either side of him. They said nothing as they put him in the back of their car and locked the doors. Then they drove off at high speed.

"Where are you taking me?"

Schreiber was driving and Huber was in the front passenger seat. Neither answered.

"Where am I being taken?" he shouted.

Huber turned around and punched him in the face, which knocked him back and bloodied his nose.

"You bastards."

He grabbed at the doors, but they were locked, and so were the windows. Schreiber and Huber were talking in German. Then Huber turned around in his seat and smiled at Ethan.

The car turned off the Kopenicker Strasse onto a small laneway where there were some old warehouses at the side of the Spree river. They stopped at one. Huber got out and pulled up the shuttered door. After Schreiber had driven in, Huber pulled it down again. It was dark in there. Ethan was starting to feel like this could be the end for him.

"Let me out of here, you bastards."

Schreiber then opened the boot and took out two baseball bats. Huber open the back door.

"You wanted to get out, Mr Harris," he said.

Ethan crouched, but Schreiber reached in and pulled him out. Then he threw him to the ground. Huber hit him on the legs as he tried to stand. He fell back in agony. Then they started to beat him on the back of the legs and on the head. He cowered, covering his head to avoid further blows there. They stopped for a moment.

"We're not going to kill you, Mr Harris. If we wanted to, we could have."

"So what do you want?" he managed to get out, wiping the blood from his nose and mouth.

"We just want you and your bitch whore, Knight, to know we mean business. We're giving you some information, and you are going to forget you ever heard of us."

He threw down a small packet on the ground beside Ethan.

"This is it, no more investigation, no more contact, nothing. If we hear anything more about you or anyone else investigating this matter, you're dead."

He lifted Ethan up from the ground by his coat lapels and pulled his bloodied face close to his. Ethan could smell his fetid cigarette breath.

"Got it?"

"Yes."

He threw him back on the ground before taking up the bat again to swing one last blow at him. Ethan flinched as it cut into his back. And then they were gone. Schreiber had pulled up the shutter while Huber was talking. They got into the car and drove off.

It was a while before he felt able to sit up. He was bruised everywhere. His nose and ear were bleeding, and his hair was matted with half-congealed blood. He looked over at the small packet on the ground and reached over to open it. There was a bundle of pages inside, all in German. He put them back in the packet to protect it from his dripping blood. Then he tidied himself up as much as he could and limped out of the warehouse with the package under his arm.

He passed some kids; they just stood and stared at him for a while as if he was some wounded monster coming out of his lair. Eventually, he reached a street with bars and restaurants on it. He ran into the disabled toilet of a busy bar to clean himself up as much as possible. He stayed there for quite a while and only left when people began banging on the door and shouting. Then he was back on the street walking until he eventually came to the Warschauer Strasse U-Bahn station. With no wallet, money or phone he got onto the next train ticketless, hoping that he would not be stopped by an inspector on the train.

When Amy opened the door of the apartment, he fell into her arms, exhausted. She helped him upstairs to the shower and then to bed where he fell asleep straight away.

While Ethan slept, Amy looked through the bundle of papers that he had brought back. There were about ten pages, but only a few were really of interest. Most were in German, alongside a few scans of English documents. The German ones confirmed that Rachel Harris had been working for a branch of BND, and that they had recruited her in 2010 through another agent, Nadine Richter. They had an unnamed contact operating in the GCHQ project MindBend, filtering information out, and they needed someone to process the files and move them on to Berlin. That was what Rachel had been doing using her graphic design company as a cover.

There was also a list of payments made to a bank account. The money was transferred once or twice a month and corresponded with the payments made to Rachel's bank account. But there was nothing about the contents of the encrypted files. They still did not know any more about the MindBend project.

There was a hypertext link typed on a page pointing to an encrypted file on the dark web, but there were no details about the encryption key. Perhaps this was the information about MindBend? But without the key it would be impossible to access.

In another document, David Powell's name appeared in a partially redacted email from him to another person in MI5, expressing his anger at the continued leak of information from the project. He urged them to "use any force necessary" to close down the leak, but noted that they must ensure they had proof first.

So he may have been partially responsible for Rachel's death. However, there was no evidence he knew she was the spy, and MI5 would certainly not have known they were related, especially as her married surname was Harris. He had just requested "any force necessary" to be used on an unknown spy.

It was most of what they needed, but there was still some items unknown. They still did not know who Petra Meyer was and how she was involved.

A few hours later, Ethan came into the living room.

"How are you feeling?"

"Wretched. My body aches all over."

"Do you need a doctor? Or the hospital?" She could see he was in a lot of pain.

"Probably, but we can't go there, can we? Although – the police may have arrested me but then they handed me over to BND. So they're no longer looking for me."

"Perhaps, but they're still looking for me," she replied. "I don't know what the situation is. There could still be a warrant out for our arrest, or it could be stood down, we just don't know. We can't take the risk – we have to assume the worst – that they are still looking for us."

"Okay."

"We need to plan our exit strategy as soon as possible."

"Did you look at the papers I brought back?"

"Yes, I've pulled out the important stuff and translated the German documents."

"So it's all on your computer?"

"Yes. I've also encrypted a copy and put it in the secure location on the dark web, along with the information we got on the BND guys."

"Good. So? Did they give us what we were looking for?"

She told him what she had found in the papers. It was most of what they needed and possibly enough to get the murder charges dropped.

"I still can't believe that Rachel was a spy. I never knew anything about it. It changes everything about the life we had."

"I know. I guess it's like finding out about an affair."

"Worse, because it was going on all the time we knew each other. Anyway, we need to go back to the UK soon."

"I was thinking about that when you were gone. But I need to meet Axel before we go. And we probably need to travel separately to minimise being caught. We can meet up when we get there."

"Let's arrange it for the day after tomorrow. That will allow us time to see if we're still being hunted."

She arranged to meet Axel, alone, the following day in a small café on a side street in Ku'Damm.

It was busy when she got to the café and outside the streets were thronged.

"We're planning to leave Berlin tomorrow."

"So you found what you were looking for?"

"A lot of it. Thanks, Axel. We would never have managed without your help. We got most of what we needed. But also the makings of a good story, for you."

"For me?"

"Yes, it's something I can't tell you about until we've left Berlin; Ethan and I are under threat from the two BND officials and we're wanted by the Berlin police. So here."

She handed him the USB memory stick.

"This is the research Ethan and I have done. It reveals a lot about BND and GCHQ activities. Can you keep it, possibly publish it, if Ethan and I are arrested here or in the UK? I'll contact you if we need you to do it."

He nodded. "Okay."

"Also, publish it if we are killed," she added.

"You're in that amount of danger?"

"Possibly. If Rachel Harris could be taken out so easily, then they could do it to us too."

"Is any story worth your life?" he asked.

"I guess not, but it didn't start out like this. The danger grew the more we learned. Now I suppose we have to see it through. It's the only way to prove Ethan's innocence and to reveal what's going on in the UK."

"I've got one last piece of information for you," said Axel, as he handed her a sheet of paper with a name and number on it. "It's Nadine Richter's number."

"How did you get it?"

"One of my contacts in the intelligence community. If she agrees to talk to you, she might be able to fill in the missing pieces of information."

"Thanks, Axel, we'll try to meet her before we go."

"So how are you going back to the UK?"

"We're going to go separately. I'm going via Copenhagen, and he's going by train to Szczecin in Poland and will fly back via Prague. We'll meet up when we're over there and try and get the story published."

"But what about the police hunt for you there?"

"They're hunting for us here too. But we have to go back there sometime to clear our names. I know it's dangerous though."

"Have you arranged anything about publication?"

"I'm talking to some guys in the Guardian and Der Spiegel, but nothing's agreed yet. There's still a lot to work out, and I haven't got all the information I need. I've enough to focus my research though."

"Let me know if I can help."

"Thanks, but you already have, a lot." She put her hand on his. "And I'm very grateful."

They looked straight at each other for a moment. Then Amy looked away.

"Anyway, you'll be working on the other story, the one about these BND officials. Now you can finish it. That's dangerous too."

He nodded.

"I've got to go now," she said. "I'll be in contact when we're safely home."

Then they hugged. It was a long hug that brought back memories from the past. Then she left.

When she got back to the apartment, she told Ethan about getting Nadine's number. He was excited; meeting Nadine would probably be their best chance of getting background information on the MindBend programme.

Amy made the call.

"Yes?" came a soft voice.

"Nadine," said Amy. "My name in Amy Knight and I'm here in Berlin with Ethan Harris, Rachel's husband."

"How did you get my number?"

"Through a contact who knows many people in the intelligence community."

"What do you want from me?"

"Just to meet and talk for a short while. Ethan has some questions about Rachel. Now she's dead he needs some background. He needs closure."

"Okay. I suppose we can talk for a while."

They arranged to meet at the Victory Column in the centre of the park in Tiergarten; they would walk and talk in the park. Nadine was as paranoid as Amy about being overheard.

She was waiting for them when they arrived.

"Nadine, I'm Ethan," he said, "and this is Amy."

They shook hands.

"I'm so sorry to hear about Petra, I mean Rachel." said Nadine.

"Did you say Petra?"

"Yes, that was Rachel's name originally. Petra Mayer."

Ethan was stunned and the blood drained from his face leaving him pale. "Rachel was Petra," he said to himself a few times, trying to believe it. "Yes," said Nadine, "Her father worked for the Stasi and the whole family defected to the West while they were at a conference in London."

"So that's why the Stasi file stopped at 1987," he said. He was trembling now. All his memories of Rachel were suddenly changed. She'd lived a lie, or at least she'd kept yet another vital secret from him. A complete hidden life. It felt like he'd never really known her and it hurt. Amy put her arm around him.

"Perhaps she really wanted to tell you, but was afraid it would drive you away or put you and Katy in danger. Like the spying work, she just couldn't tell you, but that doesn't mean she deliberately set out to deceive you."

Ethan nodded, but the words fell on deaf ears. He felt Rachel was dead to him now, more so than when he had looked down on her lifeless body lying in the open casket in the funeral home. He felt sick and weak and sat down on the ground.

Nadine turned to Amy. "Is he okay?"

"No, but he will be. Just give us a few minutes."

She sat down beside him and put her arm around him again.

Nadine walked off and had a smoke. She came back after about five minutes.

"Are you okay?"

He nodded.

"Before we talk any further," said Nadine, "I have to get your assurance that nothing I say will ever be linked back to me."

"I can promise you, as a journalist, I always keep the identity of my sources confidential," said Amy. "Nothing I write about will ever be traced back to you."

"Alright," said Nadine. "Let's begin."

And the three of them began walking along on a gravel path surrounded by trees in the park, where it was private, and they could talk freely.

She told them everything – her friendship with Petra, how they were split apart when she had been forced to live with another family after her parents were imprisoned by the Stasi and, many years later, her meeting with Petra, who was by then Rachel. She told them about Rachel's desire for revenge on her father, who she had hated since a child, and how Nadine had used that as a means of recruiting her into the spy ring for the BND.

Rachel may have never told anyone else that story, explained Nadine, but she had wanted to tell Ethan. The only thing that stopped her was her fear that she would lose him if she revealed it, and as time when on, the idea of telling him became more and more difficult. When she became pregnant with Katy, she had wanted to give it up, but that was not an option for spies. Her life would have been in danger.

"Spies never retire, they just die in service. In fact," continued Nadine, "around the time Katy was born, the amount of information that was leaked from GCHQ increased enormously because the Snowden story had motivated two more disillusioned people in GCHQ to leak information. Those contacts were high up in the organisation; it was better for them to stay in place rather than to try and leave with a cache of files. So Rachel's workload grew from that time."

Ethan could kind of understand Rachel's motives. Perhaps she had not set out to deceive him. But she had, and everything between seemed like a lie.

They moved on to MindBend. Amy had lots of questions. She had to remember all Nadine's answers because she could not take notes as they walked, and Nadine revealed critical information about the project.

When they had all the information they needed, they thanked Nadine and assured her again that she would not be identified when the story was published.

"You know, I'm glad I've told you everything. It feels – cathartic. Before now, I had never spoken about any of this to anyone else except Rachel."

They were back at the Victory Column, having come full circle. Nadine hugged them both and they said goodbye.

CHAPTER TWENTY-NINE

Returning Home

18th August, 2015. Prenzlauer Berg.

The following morning, their tickets were bought and they were packed and ready to leave. Ethan's journey was relatively straightforward: a two-hour train journey to Szczecin in Poland, then a four-hour wait before his flight to Prague, from where he would catch a flight to Birmingham, UK. Amy was to fly to Copenhagen and then to Birmingham where they would meet up. From there, it was a simple matter of getting the train to London. They hoped that by using false passports and a circuitous route they could avoid arrest by the UK police.

Even though the pressure seemed to be off Ethan ever since the Berlin police had arrested him and presumably assumed that he remained in the custody of the BND officials, he still felt hunted and exposed. When he reached HauptBahnhof – Berlin's central station – it was as busy as usual. He enjoyed his anonymity in the crowd until he arrived at his platform, where a group of policemen were talking and laughing close to where he stood. He turned his back on them, fearing that he might be recognised. But they seemed to have no interest in him. And when the train arrived, he slipped through the doors with no incident. In less than two hours he had crossed the border into Poland and had arrived at Szczecin Central station. He felt free for a while, at least until he transferred planes at Prague en route to Birmingham, when that sense of fear and impending doom returned. He was returning to the UK, where he was wanted for murder; after all, it would not be long before the UK police would be wondering why the German police had not put him on a plane home.

When he arrived at passport control at Birmingham airport, his heart thumped as the passport officer stared at his passport. But eventually, he was waved on through and he was through the first hurdle. The only problem with that was that it returned him to the most heavily monitored country in the world. Cameras were everywhere, and while that did not necessarily mean that every one of them was looking right at him, the fact was they could be doing just that. It was enough to keep him constantly on edge.

He had a two-hour wait for Amy's flight to arrive. He grabbed a couple of newspapers and went to the airport bar, where he scanned the papers from cover to cover. There was no mention of him or Amy. In today's world, he thought, a story was lucky if it lasted a day. Everyone had forgotten about him and Amy, except of course the police. But maybe they had other priorities.

After two and a half hours he began to feel restless. He looked at the arrivals screen and saw that her plane had landed thirty minutes earlier. She should be here, so where was she?

An hour later and she still had not arrived. He began to feel really nervous. Had she been caught? Were they looking for him now?

A group of police officers walked through the lounge, looking around as though they were trying to find someone; immediately Ethan raised his newspaper. Once they passed by, he decided he had better go somewhere else. He had been sitting there for a long time, after all. Perhaps he was being observed. He looked at the news bulletins, but there was no report of her capture. Should he run in panic and risk drawing attention to himself? Or should he patiently wait, assuming that there was some good reason for her delay? Why did he always think the worst was going to happen? Perhaps there was a perfectly normal reason for her delay. But he could not wait any longer – the suspense was killing him. Where was she?

He got up, gathered his bags and walked out.

*

When Amy left for the airport, she was confident that all would be well, just as it had been travelling to Berlin over a week earlier. She knew that the Berlin Police were still looking for her, but she was fairly confident that her disguise and false passport would get her to Copenhagen, and it would be straightforward from there. She was flying from Schönefeld, Berlin's smaller airport and one used by low-cost airlines such as Ryanair or EasyJet. Security was much more relaxed there, so she expected little trouble. And she was right – she flew without incident to Copenhagen and on to Birmingham.

However, when she arrived in Birmingham, for some reason the security seemed much tighter, with long queues at passport control. Something must have triggered a security alert. Everyone's identity was being closely examined.

After queuing for about twenty minutes, the passport officer signalled her to come forward to the office window. She handed him the passport, which he examined in detail, looking at the photo, then at her, and then back at the photo again. Then he seemed to be running searches on his computer, followed by two calls. Amy began to sweat, from the heat and the stress. Was there a problem with the passport?

A male and a female officer arrived.

"Come with us please," said the female officer.

"Is there an issue?" asked Amy.

But they did not reply, as they walked her towards an empty room.

Once inside the room, they left her alone. She heard the door being locked. She looked around her. It was probably an airport security room, used for holding people suspected of smuggling drugs. There was a desk, some chairs, a changing cubicle and a shower and toilet. They had taken her suitcase and backpack to another room.

She sat down. Did they know who she was? If they did, then using a false passport would be added to any other likely charges, like 'aiding and abetting a murder suspect'. She needed to keep her cool. She repeated this over and over to herself, like a mantra. But it wasn't working. She knew she was visibly stressed and she was sweating profusely, with large damp patches under her armpits.

She could see that there was a lot of activity, with officers coming and going. Her bags were brought in and she looked on as they took every single item out. She stood up and a drug-sniffing dog was brought up close to sniff her and then her luggage. But they found nothing. She felt relieved after they left.

Then the female police officer led her to a cubicle.

"Strip off completely, please," she said in a cold voice, before stepping outside the cubicle.

Once Amy had taken off all her clothes, the police officer returned, this time wearing a pair of surgical gloves. Amy knew what that meant: it was to be a full body search, including an 'intimate personal search'. She felt invaded but she had to succumb to it.

"Why are you doing this?" she asked. "Am I under arrest? What are you looking for?" But the officer did not answer her and just continued with her search. Afterwards

Amy felt violated and disgusted. They found nothing but they had left her with no dignity. It was routine to them, but de-humanising to her.

Then she was allowed to shower and dress, after which they brought her to another room, with a desk and a couple of chairs. They asked her to sit down. Across the desk sat a male officer.

"Ms Amanda Baxter?" he asked, looking at her passport.

"Yes?"

"What was the purpose of your visit to Berlin?"

"Just a personal trip."

"And do you normally bring a laptop and other computer equipment on a personal trip?"

"I'm a journalist, so I always do some writing on my trips."

"So you travel a lot?"

"Yes," she answered without thinking.

"But you've no visas or travel stamps on your passport."

"It was a replacement for a lost one," she said quickly.

"Well, we seem to have a problem with it. We'll be detaining you until we can sort it out."

"But I'll miss my appointments," she complained.

"Yes, I'm sorry, you will."

Another officer came into the room and whispered in the interviewing officer's ear, but Amy could hear it too. "The biometrics have identified this person as Amy Knight."

The officer who had been interviewing turned to her and stood.

"Amy Knight, also known as Amanda Baxter, I'm arresting you on suspicion of using a false passport. Anything you say or do may be used at a later stage in evidence."

"Fuck," she said under her breath.

"We are moving you to a police station for questioning."

Suddenly she felt extremely tired. She nodded her head. They handcuffed her and led her out, through some back corridors, down a flight of stairs and into a waiting police car.

CHAPTER THIRTY

Arrest

18th August, 2015. Kensington Police Station.

Scott and Jones observed her for a minute from the room adjacent to the interview room, via the security camera. Jones zoomed into her face, enlarging it on the monitor. She was flushed, tired and very stressed looking. She looked like she needed a strong coffee, a shower and a lie-down.

"This is the best time to talk to her – she's at her weakest," said Jones.

"Let's do it."

They entered the interview room. Scott switched on the audio recorder and spoke into the mic on the table.

"DCI Scott and DI Jones present, starting interview of Amy Knight."

Then he sat down opposite her while Jones remained standing in the corner.

Scott smiled faintly at her. But she did not meet his gaze, continuing to stare dejectedly at the table.

"Amy, or should I call you Amanda Baxter?"

She said nothing.

"Well?"

"Okay yes, I am Amy," she looked up defiantly.

"Good, now let's start from when you left London with Ethan Harris."

"I need a solicitor."

"Do you? Well, we can stop this interview right away, and you can arrange one. And I have to let you know that we will be charging you with a number of offences, immediately, if you take that approach. Or, if you like, we can continue without a solicitor, and perhaps you can explain your story and then there may or may not be a different outcome. You choose."

"I want to have a solicitor present."

Scott was disappointed that his gamble had not paid off.

"Okay, we'll stop the interview now and get one."

They allowed her make a few calls and then brought her back to a holding cell to wait for the solicitor. Two hours later he arrived and she had a brief meeting alone with him in the cell. He advised her to only say the minimum. Scott brought them into the interview room, and restarted the interview.

"Interview with Amy Knight with solicitor present on 18th August 2015."

She sat with the solicitor on one side of the table and Scott and Jones faced them on the other side.

He glanced at Jones for a moment and then started.

"So, from our brief discussion earlier, you were going to tell me everything that happened after you left London with Ethan Harris."

"What exactly do you want to know?"

The solicitor stopped her and whispered in her ear and then said "My client is under no obligation to answer general open questions like that. You can ask specific questions, which she may or may not answer."

Scott glared at him and then turned back to Amy.

"What was the purpose of your trip to Berlin?"

"I can talk about that in a moment. But first, as I understand it, I have been arrested for helping a murder suspect escape, which I did to help prove his innocence. So, once I can prove that he is innocent then you have no case against him or me. Is that correct?"

Scott appraised the thin woman across the table from him. She might be tired, but she was certainly still strong enough to put up a fight.

"Well, that may or may not be true, it depends on what you tell us and whether we believe it. And if you have proof. There are lots of possibilities. Perhaps you can tell us your story and answer our questions, and we'll take it from there."

She looked at the solicitor for approval and he nodded.

"Okay." She took a deep breath. "Before I contacted Ethan Harris I had been following a case involving a leak of top secret information from GCHQ. A leak that seemed to point to Rachel Harris. I needed to talk with Ethan Harris to move this story along; however, before I made contact with him, he went on the run, obviously for fear of being arrested by you. Anyway, I managed to make contact with him, and we met. Then together we found some information and a MacBook belonging to Rachel, which gave us some connections to Berlin. "

Scott stopped her.

"Information? A MacBook? Where is the MacBook now?"

"It doesn't matter," she said.

"It does to us."

"Okay. We destroyed it after we found what we needed."

"You destroyed evidence?"

"No we destroyed a MacBook, you have no proof it was evidence and we still have a copy of the information that was on the hard drive. Now let me continue."

"Okay."

"When your hunt for us was getting close, we decided to go to Berlin to investigate. I have a lot of contacts from many stories I've covered over there."

"What were you investigating?" he asked.

"We managed to uncover proof that Rachel Harris was passing top secret information from GCHQ to the BND – the German intelligence service – over a number of years.

And that she was very well paid for it. We also discovered some information about GCHQ's secret operation, including the fact that they hired a contract killer to murder Rachel."

Scott raised his eyebrows, looked at Jones.

"So, where it this proof then?" he said.

"It's hidden in a secure location, which I don't have access to at the moment."

"How very convenient," said Scott, laughing. "I put it to you that you and Harris were having an affair and that you may have assisted him in procuring a contract killer to murder his wife so he could inherit her considerable savings to pay off his gambling debts."

Amy was taken aback. "That's completely ridiculous," she said, starting to laugh.

"Oh really?" said Scott. He was intensely annoyed, embarrassed by her laughter, but he also believed that he had got as much as he needed from this first interview.

"I'm terminating this interview," he said. "You may laugh. However, I'm having you remanded in custody pending further investigation and our gathering of evidence."

"You can't do that." She turned to her solicitor. "Can he?"

"As this is a murder investigation, I'm afraid so. But I'll work at getting you out on bail as soon as possible."

Scott smiled.

"We'll be formally charging you. But you can rest up for tonight, in police central luxury hotel."

"You bastard. I have proof of Ethan's innocence."

"Then show me."

She did not reply. How could she, with the proof hidden online in a dark web location? But there was some hope – even if she could not access it, Axel would eventually retrieve it and publish it. Then everyone would know the truth. But when would he do it? It could be weeks. And she had no way to contact him securely, and she didn't trust the solicitor enough to give him Axel's details.

She awoke early the following morning feeling her whole body stiff from the restless sleep. An officer came in at 07:00 and gave her a mug of tea and some toast.

"How long am I going to be kept here?"

"I don't know. You can call your solicitor again if you like."

She arranged for the solicitor to come back to the station.

She wondered where Ethan was. Had he been arrested too? Was he still on the run? Where would he go now?

She lay back on the bench and closed her eyes.

*

After Ethan left the airport in Birmingham, he was at a loss about what to do. He could only assume that Amy had been arrested somewhere along the way – Berlin, Copenhagen or most likely when she landed in Birmingham.

That meant the police would definitely be looking for him.

On the train to London, he thought through his options. Amy's documents, which were stored secretly, were crucial to proving his innocence. The problem was he had no access to them. And if she was in custody there would be no easy way to contact her. He had enough cash to survive for a while using the remainder of Rachel's money. But after that, what then? If he was caught and both of them were in custody, then it could be a long while before he could prove his innocence and get free.

It was a ninety minute train journey. By the time he reached Euston station in London, he had a plan. However, as soon as he got to the station he realised that the police hunt for him was more intense than he had thought. Although it was in a crowded station, he was still strongly aware of the security cameras and three or four polices officers who were weaving their way through the crowds looking at everyone in their path. He managed to avoid them without looking suspicious; however just as he was entering the underground, he turned a corner and nearly walked directly into a police woman.

She stared at him, then reached out to grab him. But he was off. On through the streets he ran, pursued by her, people turning to watch as two other officers joined the chase.

Ahead he spotted a bus stop, an approaching bus. He turned for a moment, threw his suitcase at the police, buying himself enough time to just make the bus before the doors shut. Through the windows he could see the three officers. One of them was radioing his position while another banged on the door, but the bus was halfway into traffic now so the driver ignored them and continued on his way.

Ethan got off at the next stop – Euston Square. Soon he was in University College London, his old college. The familiar sight brought back a few memories as he let himself blend in with the crowds of students hanging around, safe for a while.

But he needed to get online soon, to search for the files that Amy had stored. He had written down the online location information on a piece of paper, which was in his backpack. But he needed a machine with TOR on it and the other tools to get into the dark web anonymously. His laptop had been in the suitcase, the one he had thrown at the police; no doubt they were examining it now. But at least all his money, or Rachel's money – about £4,000 and €5,000 – was in a money belt around his waist, inside his clothes. This and his backpack were everything he had.

He bought a pack of disposable razors and some shaving foam and went into a toilet. There, he took off his jacket, shaved his beard, put on a second wig he had in his bag and some glasses. Immediately he felt more relaxed. Weird, he thought, how second nature all this disguise changing had become. It was like being a chameleon, constantly trying to blend into the background.

After picking up a new laptop, he went to the library where he could get free Wi-Fi. There, he began downloading the software he needed. His plan was to find the secret files and print out some of them as proof, in case he was caught. He was so intent on doing this that he did not notice two officers approaching him. He was typing furiously when he heard his name called.

"Ethan Harris." He looked up. Before he could move out of their reach, they were on him, and in seconds had him pinned, face down, to the floor. A crowd gathered almost instantly.

"I'll bet it's a drugs hit," someone said as his hands were being handcuffed behind his back. He had stopped struggling – what was the point? Two big beefy police officers were virtually sitting on top of him. One of them radioed for support and then they grabbed an arm each and lifted him up and walked him out of the library. He had been so close to getting what he wanted. His downloading activity must have triggered an alert on the library servers, he figured. He watched as one of the officers folded his laptop and returned it to his backpack.

*

Ethan had been sitting alone in the interview room for a few minutes, when the door opened and DCI Scott entered, a faint smile on his face.

"Mr Harris, welcome back to London. I hope your Berlin trip was successful," he said in a cheery voice. "We've been expecting you, by the way."

DI Jones followed Scott into the room. Scott sat down opposite Ethan and cut to the chase.

"Mr Harris, we have all the evidence we need to charge you and Ms Knight with murder, as well as with travelling with false documents, perverting the course of justice, and a number of other charges. But first I'd like to get some information from you. Your cooperation at this stage could result in a shorter sentence."

"Where is my solicitor?"

"He'll be here in a while but I thought we could have a little chat before the formal interview."

Ethan looked at him intently. "I'm innocent, so soon I'll be walking free."

"Are you, Mr Harris? Well, let's see." He reached into a folder and drew out some documents. "You have large gambling debts, your employer has confirmed that your behaviour in the last few months has been erratic, the computer forensic reports show that your account on your desktop computer from your home was used to access your wife's bank accounts, including her special savings account containing over 500k."

"I never knew about that account or money. I had no access to her accounts," he replied.

"Really, Mr Harris? Well, I guess the courts will have to decide who to believe." Scott continued. "We also have proof that you were using the TOR browser to access the dark web, most likely to hire a contract killer anonymously, to murder your wife. And we can show that you transferred a payment of £10,000 two days later to a numbered Swiss bank account."

"I never moved any money. I never had TOR on my computer at home or knew anything about it," said Ethan.

Scott threw a scan of Ethan's bank statement in front of him and pointed to the highlighted transfer on the statement. There it was, in black and white, but Ethan could not explain it.

"Earlier you threw a suitcase at my officers when they were pursuing you. It contained a laptop. Already our analysis has shown that the TOR browser has been installed on it. So, Mr Harris, it seems you were very familiar with the dark web."

Ethan shifted in his seat.

"We have your motives and a record of your actions connecting you to the murder," continued Scott. "Now perhaps you'd like to answer some questions."

Ethan was shocked. He knew he was innocent, but the weight of evidence, including that 10k transfer, was pretty damning. Where did it come from though? He hadn't transferred any money. Someone must have accessed his accounts. But how, and when?

"I need to know what your connection is with Amy Knight."

"Well, I met her," said Ethan. "I mean, she contacted me for the first time after I went on the run, when it looked like I was going to be arrested by you."

"Really, Mr Harris? We have video footage of your wife's funeral and guess what? Ms Knight was there, among the crowd. We were there too as you know. Now, why would she be there if you had never met her before?"

"I don't know, but I hadn't met her at that stage," he replied.

"Perhaps you were having an affair with Ms Knight, and you needed your wife out of the way, and her money to clear your debts?"

"No that's not true."

"You can't deny, Mr Harris, that your wife's murder was very convenient for you financially. And within a week of her death you go on a trip to Berlin with a younger, more attractive woman."

"She was investigating a story that involved Rachel," said Ethan. "Rachel had been spying – passing top secret information from GCHQ to the BND. Amy was helping me find out the truth about Rachel's hidden life. That's all."

"So why have you got no evidence of this? And why was none found by my officers and forensics experts' investigation?"

"I don't know; I guess you weren't looking for that."

"Are you sure this isn't a complete fabrication, a lie, just to try and hide the truth."

Scott looked at Jones, who had been standing in the corner of the room the whole time. Then he stood.

"It's obvious that you and Ms Knight have concocted a story, but it won't hold up in court. Your solicitor will be here in a while and we'll have talk further then. But I'm holding you on remand for now."

Ethan said nothing. They brought him back to his cell.

Later, Scott met Foster on the stairs.

"We have enough proof to have them both charged, arraigned and held in prison on remand while we build the book of evidence," he said.

"Then do it," Foster replied. "We've had a lot of negative publicity in recent times. I need a result here, and fast."

Scott nodded.

CHAPTER THIRTY-ONE

Prison

20th August, 2015. Kensington Police Station.

The following day, at Kensington Police Station, both Ethan and Amy were formally charged. Ethan was charged with procuring the murder of his wife Rachel, alongside the other charges, while Amy was charged with aiding and abetting Ethan in the murder of his wife, as well as travelling with a false passport. Later, at the court arraignment, both of their solicitors requested bail but the police made a strong case against it, given that they had previously left the country while fleeing from the police investigation. The judge agreed, remanding them both in custody until the trial date, which was expected to be in about two months' time.

After the arraignment, Ethan was taken down to the holding area by the police and handed over to prison officers to be transferred to Wormwood Scrubs. Three other prisoners were being transferred at the same time. It was raining heavily as the prison van drove through the London traffic, eventually making its way to the prison gates. As those gates loomed above the van, casting a shadow over it and blocking out the light inside, he suddenly became acutely aware of the awful reality of his situation. He thought of James, his brother, whom he had always seen as the black sheep of the family, serving four years for armed robbery. And now here he was himself, on remand for a murder charge, perhaps only a few weeks away from a murder conviction and a lifetime's imprisonment.

He dreaded everything about prison – it was his worst fear come true. Knowing he was innocent made it even harder to accept. Yet here he was, being stripped of his clothes, showered, searched, lectured and issued his prison clothing.

Then he was moved to a cell already occupied by two prisoners. The third bed looked like it had been squeezed in; it took up all the space left beside the bunk. It was hot in there; the air smelled stale. The nightmare had just begun.

But it wasn't the rancid smell in the room, or even the thinly veiled aggression that he sensed from his cell mates that affected him the most. No, it was the barely concealed drug paraphernalia – the burnt silver paper – and that vacant look of heroin on the faces of his cell mates that scared him the most. He was in a cold sweat, almost shaking, like them, and afraid that one misinterpreted glance or an ill-considered word could result in a needle stick attack, starting him on the downward opiate spiral and possibly a HIV infection.

This was one of the worst days of Ethan's life, on a par with his memory of the day his mother left, all those years ago. And the night was even worse, when the lights were switched off at 23:00 so the darkness enveloped him and he was left with only his thoughts. He hardly slept that first night, tossing and turning, listening to the snoring of his inmates. He was overcome by an intense feeling of abandonment, something he thought he had left behind in childhood. That cloud that had settled over his life when he was twelve had come back to haunt him through the night.

But he got through it. Early next morning, at 07:00, it was wake-up time and the start of the prison regime. Everything was grey and drab; the only real colour in the cell was in the pinup posters that his inmates had stuck on the walls, reminders of the world outside they had left behind for months or years. Ethan was quite sure that these fantasies helped get them through the endless days and nights. After a week, the routines of opening and locking doors, of being counted, being told where to go, what to do, when to eat, when to wash and an extreme sense of claustrophobia all started to get to him. He began to understand how any possible escape might be embraced – in most cases it was drugs that provided that release; it lessened the pain and made the prospect of interminable imprisonment just a tiny bit more bearable. He hoped he would never resort to that.

He had decided not to use the first solicitor because he was unhappy with not getting bail. But he could not understand why he had to wait six days for an appointment with his new solicitor to discuss his case. It was the longest week of his life, living with the stench of fear and depression for every waking moment. But by keeping his head down and saying nothing to anyone, somehow he made it through. At the end of the week, a prison officer brought him to an interview, where his new solicitor was waiting.

The solicitor shook Ethan's hand – he had a firm grip, full of confidence. Ethan was encouraged.

"Hello Ethan, I'm Michael Howard and your case has been assigned to me."

Ethan nodded, barely making eye contact and saying nothing – his new modus operandi in prison.

"I've looked at your case file. We need to plan your defence for the trial."

"When is the trial?" he asked.

"With luck we might get a cancellation slot in the courts' schedule in three or four weeks' time. Otherwise it could be a few months."

It was a blow and his hopes were dashed. How could he survive that long in prison? Even if Amy got the hidden files – proof of his innocence – who knew how long the trial would take? And what would be the outcome? He would be here for months, maybe years.

"I know you hear this all the time," he said, "but I'm innocent. I did not arrange the murder of my wife."

Howard looked at him. "I believe you and from reading your case file, it looks like they are relying on a lot of circumstantial evidence. But I need you to take me through what happened, from the day your wife was murdered until now."

About an hour later and feeling much better, Ethan made his way back to his cell. It had felt cathartic to let it all out, explaining everything to someone who was sympathetic. It was the first time he had spoken for more than a minute in the last week. He hoped that Amy was faring better in her prison and that she had somehow managed to get one of her contacts to retrieve the files on the dark web. But even if she did manage to get them, would they be enough to prove the case?

*

When Amy was taken down to the holding area under the courts, she was immediately handcuffed to a female prison officer, a large woman, who seemed to be almost bursting out of her uniform. The officer was calm and pleasant, totally the opposite to what Amy had imagined. She told her what to expect in the prison, and that they would be driven there by another officer. As she was the only prisoner being transported that day, they would go by car rather than van. Somehow, that made Amy feel a little better. Her destination was Holloway Prison in Islington, an old nineteenth century building that had been refurbished and extended many times.

Once inside the prison, she was hit by the smell of disinfectant, which continued all the way down the hall and into her single cell – a tiny, ten-by-five foot room. But at least, it was one she had all to herself. Although she felt down, she hoped that it would only be a matter of time before she was freed. It all depended on getting someone to access the encrypted files on the dark net. She asked for some paper and a pen so she could start writing the articles about the MindBend project and the murder of Rachel Harris. She was confident that once the articles were published, Ethan's innocence would be proved and they would both be freed.

As soon as she was allowed make a phone call, she called Joel Hartman, a journalist she knew and trusted, who sometimes wrote articles for the Guardian.

A few days later he came to the prison.

"Good to see you Joel," she said, shaking his hand.

He smiled. "You too. I know from our phone conversation roughly what happened, but I need the details and a little background on Ethan Harris and your contact in Berlin, Axel."

She was prepared for him as she had all the time in the world.

"I've written it all out for you, but I think it would be good to discuss it too," she said, handing him a set of hand-written pages.

They talked for about an hour and when he was leaving she handed him another few pages. "Can you send these on to Axel too?" she said.

"Sure."

"It's ongoing work on the article I'm going to publish with him. And just one last thing." She handed him yet another page. "It's the secret code for decrypting the files hidden on the dark web. Make sure he gets this as soon as possible."

Joel nodded and took the page.

"I'll get all of this to Axel as soon as I can, and hopefully he'll be able to progress it fast, to help get you out of here."

She smiled. "I'm learning to be patient. Things go very slowly in here. You just have to wait a long time for even the smallest thing. Can you come back again soon?"

"Of course."

She could not call Axel directly herself because foreign phone numbers could not be cleared by the prison officers. But Joel was happy to act as a relay for her.

She was only allowed a few visits with Joel over the following weeks. But when he came back, he brought a ream of paper, envelopes and stamps: this would be her lifeline, her primary contact with the external world. It was such a shock to go from the instant communication tools out there – phone, email, social media – to the occasional phone call and handwritten letters. It felt like travelling at one hundred miles per hour, before suddenly slowing down to one mile per hour. Everything in prison felt slow and challenging, but she just accepted it. She had to. And she knew that the right attitude would help her get through the weeks ahead.

She wondered how Ethan was getting on in prison. She had no way of contacting him because she had no idea where he was detained. For now, she decided that she would try to focus on getting her story written and published.

In the meantime, Joel began to talk to Axel on a regular basis, passing information between him and Amy. She was glad when Axel began his investigative work. Again, she wished she could talk or write to Ethan but how? Joel said he would find out where he was.

It took two weeks for Amy to finish her articles, which the Guardian and Der Spiegel had tentatively agreed to publish. However, Joel's first email to the editor of the Guardian was not sent securely, and his email accounts were being monitored by GCHQ. They began to focus on his activities. That was how they discovered that an article was being written on the MindBend programme. They got the Home Office to send the Guardian a DA-Notice – a formal notice to suppress press publication for reasons of national security. That meant involving lawyers, but the Guardian was not going to roll over that easy. They pushed back, well aware that the DA-Notice, although a serious request, was not legally binding. They could publish the articles if they really wanted to, though that would come with a price – there would be hell to pay and a lot of senior feathers ruffled.

But then they knew that Der Spiegel was going to publish anyway, and soon it would all be in the public domain. So they decided to print the articles on the same day as they were being published in Der Spiegel.

CHAPTER THIRTY-TWO

Evidence

2nd September, 2015. Berlin.

When Axel managed to retrieve the secret information that Amy had stored on the dark web, he finalised the articles that were co-written by him and Amy and sent them to editors in both Der Spiegel and the Guardian. Then he requested a video conference to discuss them.

The following day, 3rd September, they had the video conference, at which both newspapers agreed to publish the articles simultaneously on 5th September, 2015.

There was also the evidence that Amy and Ethan had got from BND. That was what was going to secure their release; it showed beyond doubt that Rachel Harris had been involved in spying, and that the intelligence agencies and secret service had possibly orchestrated her murder. Of course, there was no way that they would be charged for this, but at least Amy and Ethan would be freed.

Axel couriered the evidence letters to their solicitors, hoping that their release would be secured before the publication of the articles so they would be able to give press interviews. Their release would be significant news in itself.

The solicitors acted right away, contacting the police and the court service and requesting that both prisoners be released immediately. It took a while for the relevant authorities to review the evidence but eventually they agreed. It would not happen immediately though; the legal process meant that it could be several days before they would actually be released. But finally, with a little pressure, the courts agreed to their release on 5th September.

CHAPTER THIRTY-THREE

Publication

5th September, 2015. Guardian Offices, London.

The article was published in the Guardian Newspaper and Der Spiegel and syndicated to other news publications around the world.

Inside Mindbend
By Amy Knight and Axel Mueller.

It all started in Berlin in the 1980s, when the EinzelGeist (Single Mind) project was set up by Gerhard Meyer, as part of a broader, experimental field of research. Funded by the HVA and Stasi (East German foreign and internal intelligence services, before reunification), it was a top secret project, largely for one main reason: its heritage was partly rooted in Nazi ideals. Specifically, it was focused on methods of mass population control, the natural step beyond mass surveillance. Although Meyer was intensely involved in the project, he also became increasingly disillusioned and frustrated with the East German Communist system.

Stasi files from the open Stasi archive in the Stasi Records Agency in Berlin show that in 1987, Meyer defected to the UK while attending a university conference. It was a trip he had been planning for some time (he had arranged to have his family with him on the trip). This was a massive coup by the West. After months of debriefing, he was assigned to GCHQ. The project he had been working on in East Germany was considered too radical when he started in GCHQ; however, they did use his skills and expertise on intelligence gathering and surveillance.

As part of their protection, Meyer and his family had their names changed and entered into an intensive programme of integration. This included elocution lessons to change their accents and memorising false information about their family histories, schools attended, work histories. Even old photographs were fabricated. Everything was changed and then ingrained into them on a daily basis for perhaps six months.

David Powell used some of the techniques he developed during his time with the Stasi to virtually brainwash his family, moulding them into a new shape, bending their minds to assume their new identities as a British family. Eventually, their former lives were distant memories. Powell himself remained as he always was, a scientist who had worked for the Stasi and who now had a new master – GCHQ – even if the elocution lessons had changed his accent to an English one.

By the late 1990s, when Powell had been in the UK for about ten years, the internet started to get some traction in the general population, and he was given the opportunity to set up a programme based on his work on the EinzelGeist project he had created for the Stasi. However, after two years it was deemed a failure, and the programme was 'put on ice', to be revived at some later stage.

It was nearly another ten years, in 2009, before the project was revived in GCHQ under new, tech-savvy management and of course in the increasingly relevant context of the rise of the internet, the smartphone and growing widespread addiction to social media.

As the UK government became increasingly concerned about the increase in immigration figures, the effects of multiculturalism, and the rise of powerful groups whose agenda was often at variance with the ideals of the more conservative politicians, they lent their support to fund the new top-secret project, codenamed MindBend.

Powell's new department, which drew on colleagues from GCHQ, MI5 and MI6, was an unholy trinity of intelligence, surveillance and control that targeted both the UK and foreign populations.

The aim of MindBend, which Powell had developed over his life's work, was to take all the information gathered through surveillance activities on a population and build a social model for each person in the country. A 'social norm model' was then created based on the information gathered specifically from white, middle-class, middle-aged, conservative people. This was then used as a kind of baseline, against which to measure the 'social norm' of every individual.

They then used any recorded variations from this norm to inform the development of plans for targeted individuals, the aim of which was to covertly influence the individual's behaviour, attitudes, beliefs and actions. This was achieved by tailoring and filtering what that individual saw, heard and experienced – slowly, they reinforced and rewarded certain characteristics, while discouraging other traits, to mould them towards the norm.

This individual-based population conditioning exercise only became possible when the majority of the population began using the internet to a significant degree. That was what gave MindBend its real capacity to secretly control targeted individuals' perception of reality, methods of communication, views, the news they heard, the social attitudes expressed, the training they took, the items they were encouraged to buy, what they considered good and bad – every major aspect of their lives.

In essence, these individuals were unknowingly living a programmed life –they appeared to be free but in reality they were being controlled by the government. Initially, this was planned as a long-term programme, perhaps five to ten years, after having been secretly piloted on a small target population in English midlands. The initial results after four years were encouraging, according to Powell's internal reports.

On the morning of 5th September, following their release from prison, both Amy and Ethan were driven to the offices of the Guardian for a press conference. When they arrived, the place was buzzing. The press conference was organised for 11:00, by which time a huge media circus had gathered, including international TV crews and representatives of various radio stations and newspapers.

There were five people on the panel: Ethan Harris, Amy Knight, Axel Mueller, one editor from the Guardian and one from Der Spiegel. After the introductions the questions started.

"Amy and Axel, there has been a huge reaction to your articles, at the highest levels of the government – questions are surely going to be asked at the House of Commons. How did you uncover such earth-shattering, top-secret information?"

Amy took that one. "I was working on this story for about six months. Through a number of sources, I found that information that was being leaked from GCHQ seemed to be in some way connected to Rachel Harris. I had no further leads until she was murdered, at which point Ethan Harris became a prime suspect as the procurer of the contract killing. His innocence is what sustained us and drove us forward to uncover the truth."

"How did the police react when you told them your story?"

Ethan took that one. "From the very start they seemed to have come to the conclusion that I was guilty – once that idea was locked in, they wouldn't consider anything else. They refused to help me show them where the proof of our innocence was. Instead, they opted to have us locked up for several weeks."

"What are you going to do next?"

"Apart from enjoying my freedom again, I'm going to court to get back custody of my daughter Katy," said Ethan.

"I'm already working with Axel on the next story," said Amy.

After the press conference, Axel had to fly back to Berlin right away. Amy and Ethan went back to her apartment.

*

Superintendent Foster stared at his computer screen in fury as he watched the televised press conference. He picked up the phone.

"Are you watching this, Scott?"

"Yes."

"I want you and Jones in my office as soon as it's finished." He slammed down the phone.

Two floors below, Scott looked at the phone and then at Jones, who had heard it across the desk.

"I guess we're going to get a beating," Jones said, smiling wryly.

"You could say we're his whipping boys," Scott replied, "ever since someone in the office gave him 'Fifty Shades of Grey' as a Kris Kindle present at the Christmas party."

They laughed.

CHAPTER THIRTY-FOUR

Winning Bid

7th September, 2015. Scott's house, Ealing.

DCI Scott looked through his modest art collection and picked out a 1920s print by a German artist. He had bought it two years previously, at an auction in France for about €2,500. It was just the type of work his nemesis dealer – that attractive art dealer who was always bidding successfully against him – would like to bid on. Then he called an auctioneer in Christies and told him that he had a rather special limited edition print he would like to sell.

The following day, he was at the weekly art auction, as was she, as he knew she would be, sitting in the middle row in a red dress, perusing the catalogue. She saw him glancing over at her, and she smiled. He nodded in acceptance of the challenge ahead.

"The next item is lot number 34, a delicate 1920s limited edition print by the Berlin artist, George Grosz. Who'll start me at £1,000?" the auctioneer announced.

The room was quiet. Scott's heart sunk. If it sold for less than he had paid for it and his dealer adversary did not bid on it, his plan would come crashing down.

"Perhaps £800?" the auctioneer continued.

An elderly German woman at the back raised her paddle.

"£800 from the lady at the back."

"£850 from the gentleman at the front."

"£900, £1,000, £1,200, £1,400, £1,600, £2,000." The auctioneer rattled off the prices as the auction frenzy took off.

At £3,500, Scott's nemesis joined the battle. There were just two bidders left. She had waited until the melee was over to join in.

"£3,600." She raised her paddle.

Scott glanced over at her, and she caught his eye.

"£3,700 anyone?" the auctioneer continued

Scott raised his paddle.

"£3,800."

She raised hers again. The bidding was just between the two of them. Before long it had reached £4,600. Scott decided to stop.

"Sold to the lady in red for £4,600." The auctioneer brought his gavel down with a sharp tap.

She had won again. She glanced over at Scott with a triumphant little smile. Scott nodded, feigning his disappointment.

On the way out, she introduced herself.

"Amanda Joyce."

He shook her hand.

"Matthew Scott."

"Perhaps you'd like to join me for a coffee or a drink?"

"Oh. Sure. That would be nice." He had not expected it and he was delighted. But if this was the start of something between them, how would he ever tell her about the print that she so proudly clasped under her arm?

CHAPTER THIRTY-FIVE

The New Frontier

10th September, 2015. House of Commons, London.

There was uproar in the House of Commons. All week, all parties had been expressing their consternation regarding the uncemonious removal of the veil of secrecy around GCHQ's MindBend project.

The leader of the Opposition – the Labour Party – stood and faced the recently reaffirmed Conservative prime minister, for question time.

The uproar continued in the house.

"Order, Orrrderrrrr, Order I say," barked the Speaker of the House.

Things quietened a little. The opposition leader cleared her throat.

"Does the Prime Minister condone the covert actions of GCHQ and their MindBend programme, which the press has described as little more than systemised racism?

Have we as a nation decided that we can no longer tolerate any difference of opinion, difference in races and differences in religion among our population and that we must now control them and mould them into a so-called 'British norm', with everyone speaking, thinking and acting the same? Is that not the ultimate denial of freedom?" she asked.

Rapturous applause followed.

"Order," barked the Speaker again as the Prime Minister stood up to answer.

The Prime Minister smiled.

"Obviously from the Right Honourable Member's question and the amount of opposition in this house, the MindBend programme has not yet managed to brainwash members of this parliament."

There was a titter of laughter from his side of the house.

He saw the opposition leader smile at his comment, and he glanced for a moment at the Home Secretary, sitting stony-faced beside him, before continuing.

"We have discussed the activities of GCHQ and other intelligence agencies involved in this project," he continued. "Although our nation's security, both home and abroad, are of paramount importance, we have decided to halt this project in advance of a full review."

There was a cheer from the opposition benches. The opposition leader, clearly delighted with the response, continued.

"Will the Prime Minister comment on whether the officials responsible for the GCHQ MindBend programme will face any disciplinary action, given their gross overstepping of their authority and, dare I say it, the way in which they threatened the very core of democracy itself?"

"Here, here." The opposition members voiced their support in unison.

The Prime Minister stood again. "I have today accepted the resignation of David Powell, the director of the MindBend programme. He has given me his assurances that the programme's activities have been put on hold until further notice. Now, we must continue with the order of business for today."

The Speaker tapped his gavel, giving a short, sharp rap to terminate further discussion on the topic.

The following day, the story was in all the newspapers, with headlines varying on the theme of, "Government shuts down out-of-control security programme," though one of the tabloid press newspapers put it much more succinctly with: "Democracy 1, MindBend 0."

It was over. Reason had prevailed, it seemed. The most radical security programme, which had come to light in recent times, had been shut down. MindBend had been put back in its box.

Back at Amy's flat, she and Ethan discussed the events.

"Even though I knew I was innocent and we had found the evidence in Berlin, I still thought I'd be a long time in prison," he said.

"Well, the truth had to come out eventually and we had the proof," she said.

"You know, back when I was gambling I was always aware that the house always wins, but this time, I think it's us who have won for a change."

Amy smiled. "What will you do next?"

"I'm not sure, although the first thing I'll do is to get back custody of Katy."

"All the charges against us have been dropped so they've no reason not to give you custody."

"It's not as simple as that – it still might take a few months and Julia is determined to keep her. So I'll have a fight on my hands. Anyway, what about that new story you're working on with Axel?"

"While I was on remand, I was putting my thoughts on paper, an outline for a follow-on investigation, some of it based in Berlin again," she said.

"I can't go back to my old life or my old house," Ethan said. "I'll have to find something new to do, and somewhere new to live."

*

In the suburbs of Cheltenham, on the edge of the Cotswolds in South West England, in a giant building they call

The Doughnut, otherwise known as the GCHQ headquarters, life continued as normal following the public disapproval of MindBend and the government's curtailment of their activities. They had always been somewhat removed from and insulated against the public and the press.

MindBend may have been shut down and David Powell forced to resign, but it was not long before a new programme, OneCom (One Community) had been set up, with Gordon Turner as the new director. He stood at the top of the conference room where his new five senior managers and David Powell were gathered. He cleared his throat.

"I'd like to welcome you all to the OneCom programme. As all of you already know each other from MindBend, we can dispense with introductions."

There were a couple of faint smiles.

"You are also aware that David Powell resigned after the fallout from MindBend. This was expected, and I'd like to personally thank him for all his work on that project and to let you know that he had planned to retire after the successful implementation of the project. I can now confirm that it has been successful, very successful."

There was a surprised flurry of whispers, followed by an expectant silence. No one present besides Turner had thought of MindBend as a success.

"Perhaps it might be better to let David explain," said Turner, and he sat down.

David Powell stood up and cleared his throat.

"You may remember that we ran a pilot project for MindBend in a community in Leicester for several years, where about 30% of the population are from minority cultures and religions. The goal of this was to monitor how effective our approach was at moulding a mixed race community. We targeted every single individual, via their smartphones, websites, email and TVs, by individually filtering the news they received, advertising, interaction in their jobs, funding for local projects, their education – in essence, all of their communication. The results have been excellent. By comparing attitudes, crime rates, voting patterns and all other social indicators, we can now say, with a high degree of confidence, that within that four-year period these people were moulded into a more 'British norm' city. This has been done without a single person suspecting it – a battle won in silence and secrecy, without a drop of blood spilt. It has been dramatically more successful than anything else we have tried in the past in relation to multi-cultural integration."

He looked around at the faces. "The press called it 'systemised racism', but it's not. We don't care about culture, ethnicity or religion – we're just focused on control. Now we're working on subtler ways to control the press."

He paused again to let them absorb what he had said. And then he continued. "You also may not have known that we ran an earlier pilot in more volatile communities in Tottenham, Wood Green, Hackney and other areas in London. This was back in 2011. This, however, was a failure, resulting in the London riots that year. We created the agitation in the communities and hoped to be able to control it, but it exploded into an orgy of violence and looting. Thankfully, as we all know, that eventually burnt itself out. Despite that setback, we gained vital information from that earlier test run. We had to know how the whole country would feel and react when they found out about the MindBend programme, as they eventually would, and we needed to be able to control that reaction. Our friends at the NSA and other intelligence agencies in the US had, in 2013, leveraged Edward Snowden's revelations about their security programmes, and very successfully weathered the ensuing public and media storm."

A couple of heads nodded.

"Globally," continued Powell, "it's assumed that Snowden, the whistle-blower, was able to extract a huge cache of information about the NSA's programmes and activities and publish it before the NSA realised the data had been taken. Actually, they did know about it and decided not to arrest him before publication. That was because they wanted to gauge the world's reaction to their programmes; that information alone was worth the fallout for several months afterwards. After that, they were able to continue as before, and now that the public already know about them, any further revelations will be easy to handle. It was a high-risk strategy, but it worked out well for them, and in many ways they have a lot of support from the American public whom they continue to spy on. It's surprising – the power of patriotism."

He smiled for a moment.

"By learning from their success, we decided not to capture Ethan Harris and Amy Knight, when we had the chance. Do you think that two private individuals, one with a little knowledge of our operations, could manage to stay undetected while being hunted by the London Metropolitan police force and our intelligence agencies in London and then travel to Berlin and back?

No, we pursued them and could have caught them at any time, but we let them continue their way without capture. We had to get the police to arrest them eventually to give credence to their story and generate a public outcry when it was published. We knew GCHQ would face public criticism and that I would be forced to resign. However, I had planned to retire anyway. And now the storm has blown over, and we got to control public reaction to MindBend. In effect, we have successfully tested the MindBend methodology on the whole country. We monitored, filtered and controlled every message, every comment, every email and article about the story, for every individual in the country, dampening them down when necessary. Think of it like a controlled explosion. We shaped it and contained it."

He glanced around him again. "We can change the programme name, but the approach is still largely the same. Ethan Harris, Amy Knight, the press, the police, the government departments and the British public all think that they have won and that we have been shut down, reprimanded and put back in our box. They think that justice has prevailed, which is exactly what we want them to think. However, they should have known better; they should have known that we could never be shut down because they are the punters but we are the House and – The House Always Wins. Welcome to the new order, gentlemen. Gordon, you and your team are now in total control of the country. You could call it a coup d'état, followed by a benign dictatorship. I am happy to act as an advisor, whenever required."

He sat down. A hush followed.

Then everyone in the room stood and spontaneously burst into applause.

Then they began chanting.

"The House Always Wins. The House Always Wins".

A new era had begun. They were masters of the New Frontier.

ABOUT THE AUTHOR

Frank Daly is a Business Intelligence Consultant. He lives and works in Dublin, Ireland and likes to write and travel. This is his first novel in a crime / spy trilogy featuring murder suspect, Ethan Harris and investigative journalist, Amy Knight.

Printed in Great Britain
by Amazon